Living Inside
Your Love

Living Inside Your Love

Gigi Gunn

Urban
soul

URBAN BOOKS

www.urbanbooks.net

This is a work of fiction. Any references or similarities to actual events, real people, living or dead, or to real locales are intended to give the novel a sense of reality. Any similarity in other names, characters, places, and incidents is entirely coincidental.

URBAN SOUL is published by

Urban Books
10 Brennan Place
Deer Park, NY 11729

Copyright © 2009 by Gigi Gunn

ISBN-13: 978-1-59983-099-5
ISBN-10: 1-59983-099-X

First Printing: September 2009
10 9 8 7 6 5 4 3 2 1

Printed in the United States of America

To my mother, Evelyn Gunn-Horad,
inside whose love I've always lived
. . . and she in mine.

*"A person who stands for nothing
will fall for anything. . . ."*

Malcolm X

Or

"Never sleep where you earn your meat. . . ."

Big Brody Mac

Chapter I

"I don't understand what the problem is," Georgia snapped, folding her arms across the pin-striped suit, causing it to wrinkle.

"The 'problem' is we are prosecutors for the state of Pennsylvania, not social workers," he mustered as calmly as he could.

"It's a breach of contract," she challenged, and leaned across the conference table again.

"Where's the written, notarized contract?"

"The doctors promised him a slot in the cancer control group and then reneged."

"No proof. A doctor makes an offhanded remark—"

"Representing the hospital—"

"—and later indicates he made a mistake. No contract. Therefore, no breach of contract."

"Verbal," she interjected stubbornly.

"A casual comment in a hospital hallway? Unethical? Yes. Criminal? No."

The antique clock on his bookcase began to quietly chime twelve times.

"No contract. No crime," he restated. "It's a 'he says/she says' situation. Let some downtown law firm take it on pro bono." He went to his desk chair to get his suit jacket and glanced out at Philadelphia laid out before him. "Doesn't belong here," he said evenly in his classic, Jared Jaymes dismissive tone.

Jared pulled on his tailor-made suit jacket and yanked his monogrammed cuffs down so that his embroidered initials showed. He glanced up at her again and watched her attempt to control her anger and asked, "Why is this case so important to you? Any other time you'd see its black/white dynamics and quash it. Is this personal?"

Their eyes locked. His bottomless black eyes assaulted hers. Neither of them blinked.

For the first time in her five years in the DA's office, Georgia MacKenzie was speechless. For the first time in five years, she was glaring into her boss's eyes: espresso-colored eyes, so dark she could see her reflection in them. Her heart stalled, her breath caught, and she felt unsettled— something was happening, something beyond her control. She didn't know what, but she didn't like it.

Although taken aback by his brazen, questioning stare, she gathered her reserve enough to reply, "It seems to me if a doctor makes a promise of better treatment and recovery—to prolong a patient's life—it should be honored." She stopped, realizing that she was babbling. Georgia MacKenzie didn't babble. Looking into his dark eyes, she knew she was losing control, losing her ability to communicate. She was angry at herself for not being able to convince him. She was angry at him for being so cavalier about a broken promise—about a man's life. She felt her ears get hot and her nose begin to burn and she knew her temper was about to blow. As a defensive mechanism, she gritted her teeth. She would not lose her cool in the workplace—in front of her boss. She would not lose either the professional edge she had honed in law school, or the reputation she'd built in these courts. She watched him break their gaze and walk back to his desk to check his calendar. When the antique clock stopped chiming he glanced at his watch and proceeded to walk past her to go to lunch.

She refused to be dismissed and piped up, "If the defendant weren't black, we'd prosecute." She knew it was a lie as soon as it left her lips, but the comment served its purpose—it stopped Jared Jaymes dead in his tracks.

He paused at the door and slowly turned to her. "The race card, MacKenzie?"

She watched disappointment claim his eyes.

"I thought better of you than that," he said. "It took you over five years to play it."

He glared at her and Georgia witnessed his cold, bottomless black eyes warm into that fake, political-plastic obsidian he used to disarm dissenters during his bid for mayor.

"Don't let it happen again," he warned, and opened the door for her to leave. As she walked toward him he thought that perhaps his response had been too harsh. He offhandedly added, "Let's finish this over lunch. I've got a two o'clock with the mayor, but we can—"

"What!" Georgia felt her face flush as if she'd been slapped. In all these years Jared Jaymes had never once suggested lunch. Did he think the nonlogical, hysterical woman lawyer needed to be placated and soothed by a lunch with him? What arrogance!

"If you're this upset, apparently you aren't finished with it," he explained. "I'm on a tight schedule and lunch is the only free time I have."

Georgia stared at him unbelievingly, as if he'd just asked her what color panties she was wearing.

"It's not like I'm asking you on a 'date,'" he added with a charming chuckle.

She narrowed her eyes and sniped, "Is the thought of a 'date' with me so offensive?"

Damn! She immediately chastised herself for that remark, but noted that now it was his turn to look like he'd been slapped.

His eyebrows knitted together in question and he stared at her without saying anything.

It was the first time she'd known Jared Jaymes to ever be speechless.

"Just forget it." She dismissed him, walked through the open door and across the hall to her office.

She closed her door without slamming it and went to her desk chair, swiveled it around to face the window so she couldn't see him or his dazed, confused expression. *Damn! Damn! Damn!* she mentally scolded herself. How uncharacteristically unprofessional. Once in five years, she'd had an outburst. Wasn't she entitled?

"No!" she answered herself.

What in the world made him ask her to lunch

after all this time? Did he see something in her that made him invite her out? Did the dreams she was having about him somehow show? Did her unconscious nocturnal images pierce her polished demeanor and create a chink in her seamless professional armor? Something he recognized as opportunity?

I cannot lose my edge, she thought. She was trying and intended to win the high-profile Rocco Cusamano case, which would not only keep her name a household word in the North Atlantic region, but introduce her to legions of interested firms, nationally. Besides the long-standing offer from the prestigious Felton, Mayfield and Dasher in L.A., she would be courted with enviable positions from coast to coast. She didn't want any editorials attached to her victory, like "Georgia MacKenzie is good but a little emotional." She was known as, and would always be, the epitome of professional terror and grace—no one wanted to be opposing counsel and face her in a courtroom. She would not blow her career over some unconscious dream crap over which she had no control.

The dream. That daggone dream, she thought, *a nightmare, actually.* She'd gone over the dream ad nauseam, analyzing it and letting it go, hoping each time it visited her at night was its last; it had reoccurred four times. The same dream . . . with Jared Jaymes as the unlikely object of her attraction. "Simply absurd," she scoffed aloud.

Without prompting, right now it appeared as a daydream superimposed on the Philadelphia skyline. . . .

It was summertime. A hot sticky afternoon that only Evelyn, Tennessee, knew how to host. Sweat clogged, then rained from every pore of Georgia's body like liquid humidity as she rocked on the side porch swing trying to hydrate herself with her grandmother's sweet tea. The ice cubes felt like menthol against her lips. She fanned an insect and listened to the beckoning cool of the crystal waters from the swimming hole. From her grandmother's stereo Jerry Butler crooned "Moon River" as Georgia walked the dusty dirt path toward the welcoming wet. Once she arrived, she stuck her manicured big toe into the water, then lowered her brown body slowly into the chilly liquid, submerging herself to the neck, allowing the water full access to her body, mind, and spirit. Her drenched clothes clung to her curves. She was both exhilarated and soothed by the lake's embrace. She closed her eyes and the aroma of summer-ripened peaches swirled around her. She felt the presence of a man behind her. She wasn't afraid as he neared her and encircled her gently with his body, buoying her in the water. As she listened to the harmonica refrain of "Moon River," he supported her tenderly and Georgia felt nurtured, comforted, and protected in his strong arms.

She leaned against his bare muscled torso and nuzzled playfully as he caressed her and rocked their bodies. She smiled and his breath felt like a breeze on her ear. It was a man she knew and trusted and, as she turned toward him, he covered her lips with his . . . a long, languid, satisfying kiss. In the stirring sensations of her body pressed against his, she opened her eyes.

It was Jared!

Georgia jerked at the ludicrousness of it and the image poofed, leaving her to look at the traffic through her office window. With her head against the high-backed leather chair, her thumbnail absently found a resting place between her two bottom teeth as she recalled her reactions to the steamy dream in an effort to "get behind me, Satan." The first time she'd screamed herself awake at the audacity of her and Jared. The second time she systematically analyzed her way through the shock of it, and concluded that, in her trying to get over Tony, Jared was a natural candidate. Besides Neal, Jared was the only other man with whom she was in constant contact. The third and fourth times dream-Jared came to her, she leaned against his glistening bare chest, and he said simply, "I've been waiting for you." Within the dream state, she longed to ask him, when was this crazy stuff going to stop? But she could not direct her dream, and Jared proceeded to hold her affectionately . . . and kiss her.

If only the kiss didn't seem so real—so satisfying, she thought. So full of promise and passion. If only she couldn't taste him—his ripe and luscious—

"Mac?" A male voice pierced Georgia's reminiscing. "Mac!"

Georgia turned from the window into the face of her old friend.

"Where were you?" Neal Preston asked.

"Not here," Georgia said, clearing her throat and tucking her hair behind her ear.

"Obviously."

"What's up?"

"How about some lunch?"

"Brenda didn't fix you any?" She tried to recoup from the interruption by shuffling through files.

"Morning sickness has taken a hold of my woman. I try to eat my biggest meal at lunch since the smell of food triggers her 'evening sickness' too."

"Who woulda thunk you'd make such a sensitive husband?"

"Let's go. Got to be back by two or your 'boyfriend' will have my hide."

"Judge Conway is not my 'boyfriend.'" Georgia removed her raincoat from the rack.

"Yeah, but you knew who I was talking about, didn't you?" Neal teased, opening her door. "He's been after you since you got here."

"You know I don't play that."

"Pygmies in equatorial Africa know 'you don't play that,' Mac," Neal said wearily. "'Don't sleep where you earn your meat.'" He recited her daddy's mantra for success in the workplace.

"Got that right," Georgia said, and shot him a backward glance as they walked toward the elevator. "Served me well. No work romances. Easy in—messy out. So not worth it."

"Or as my wife says—you are the Queen of Compartmentalization."

"See, a psychologist knows the proper terms. You either believe in something or you don't. It's like either you are pregnant or you're not. There are no situational ethics on the matter. You don't just let go of your convictions 'just this once' 'cause the guy is cute, or smart or rich . . . and then, after the deed, try to justify it on the back end. Nothing worse than a wishy-washy woman."

"Oh, I can think of a couple of things worse."

"Yes, we know you've taken advantage of

women's breaches in their personal ethics from
time to time."

"Timing is everything."

"Women make bad choices, and then wonder
why they have bad consequences. They do it over
and over and over again, like they never learn
from their mistakes."

"I say you're just a 'my way or the highway'
woman," Neal said as he pushed the elevator
button.

"You and your wife are both right." She positioned her shoulder bag. "Besides, I've come to
accept that I will never find what I had before."

"True. You'll decide when you're ready to try
love again, and pick a 'proper' husband before
your eggs turn to dust."

"Which means I have at least ten years. I am
not pressed."

As Jared Jaymes walked to the restaurant his
thoughts were consumed with the exchange
he'd just had with Georgia MacKenzie. He didn't
believe for one minute that he could determine
what triggered her aberrant response, but it had
been a strange encounter. First, her issue with
the breach-of-contract scenario was odd, then
the race card accusation outrageous, but the
entire idea of him being offended by a date with
her was plain bizarre. A date with any of his prosecutors would be highly improper and professional suicide, but certainly not offensive.

Georgia MacKenzie had proven to be one of
the best assistant DAs he'd hired over the last

seven years. Jared never regretted hiring her or Neal Preston straight from Georgetown University Law Center to round out his diverse team. Both, in the top ten percent of their class, were impressive. His perception about Neal had been on target and, initially, he'd been intrigued by MacKenzie's résumé; the transcripts, her credentials, her clerking choices, and her reputation, which he'd checked with some of his buddies in D.C. Based on such an accomplished application package, he had not expected the pretty, poised, and articulate woman who entered his office for the first interview. He was pleasantly surprised and equally concerned about his office's dynamics. How would someone so attractive and accomplished fit in with his existing team? He didn't hold her looks against her, hired her, and decided that, if necessary, he'd just have to give her the conversation on professional office etiquette and deportment as he often did with new male and female ADAs. Again, Jared was pleased that the conversation was never required. In short order, MacKenzie established that she was there to work, not play, as many of the judges who asked about her found out. Jared enjoyed watching her verbally spar and expertly fend off advances as she gained professional respect and showed all the courthouse cats that a woman can be good looking, smart, and not interested. Jared relaxed when he realized that he and Georgia shared an unspoken philosophy on office romances. He would never expect his ADAs to do anything he would not. Jared Jaymes would never compromise his current position or his road on the fast track to the mayor's office by succumbing to an office dalliance, and he would not tolerate it in his ranks. Georgia MacKenzie's sharing his values and beliefs made his job, on so many levels, easier.

Now Georgia's proven research preparation on cases was exceptional, her closing arguments legendary, and her jury selections skills—stellar. Her colleagues sought her expertise for their jury selections as, in one sweep of the eye, Georgia could spot a bleeding-heart liberal or a racist bigot. She had a keen, analytical mind and a rock-solid reputation as a hard-nosed, no-nonsense prosecutor despite her stunning figure, smooth mocha complexion, and chestnut-colored hair. He thought he was going to lose her once to matrimony and the suburban motherhood scene, but luckily for the city of Philadelphia, that didn't happen.

Jared entered the restaurant and spotted his racquetball buddies at a back table.

"Nice of you to grace us with your presence," one teased. "You know, squeeze us in between your high-powered job and your weeklies with the mayor."

"Hey, man," Jared greeted them all, and ordered a Philly cheesesteak platter. "And the mayor isn't until two," he counter-teased with a grin.

Jared settled in at the table. His eyes swept the restaurant patrons and he saw Georgia and Neal come through the doors.

"Crowded," Georgia remarked as she entered the restaurant and looked around perfunctorily for an open table. She spotted Jared in the far corner.

Neal noticed Georgia flinch at the sight of Jared and suggested, "We can sit at the bar."

"That's fine." Georgia slipped off her coat and slid onto a bar stool. "Let me guess," she said to Neal. "A Reuben?"

"Is there anything else? All four food groups in one sandwich."

Georgia ordered jambalaya and a cup of hot green tea and took Neal's menu, noticing how his round bald head made him look like a chocolate jack-o'-lantern.

"So," Neal said. "You and the boss feuding?"

"What?" Georgia asked evenly, flashing a smile most folks at work never got to see.

"Don't dump water on my shoes and tell me it's rain. I saw you jump when you spotted him."

"I expected to see Courtney."

"Psst. She's all wrong for him."

"That's not for you to say."

"I don't have to. Jared knows." Neal redirected the conversation. "So, you all feuding?"

"We had a discussion about a case this morning that got a little heated. He reminded me that we were prosecutors, not social workers."

"Hmm. He's good at that." Neal sat back so the waiter could serve the sandwich. "Guess that's why he's the boss." He took a french fry and grabbed the bottle of ketchup.

"So why haven't he and Courtney married? It only took you and Brenda two years."

"A year and a half. Brenda and I are in love.

Jared and Courtney aren't. Well, Courtney was—
Jared wasn't."

"I beg to differ."

"On what grounds, Counselor?" He tasted another french fry. "Everybody knew the deal but
her. At their age and economics, it doesn't take
four years to get hitched if the relationship is
solid. Neither of them are spring chickens."

"You keep using the past tense." Georgia spun
a forkful of pasta and placed it in her mouth.

"They broke up."

"When was this?"

"About a month back."

"Psst—that all? It takes four weeks to miss somebody and realize you can't live without them.
They'll get back together."

"Not this time."

"They're perfect for each other. She's a PR/
fund-raiser for nonprofits, and has the bucks,
contacts, and connections he needs—and she
wants to be a mayor's wife. Perfect."

"The PR/fund-raiser job she has is thanks to
her parents' money, and their Philly-society
status and position."

"Hey, who knows where we'd be if our folks had
connections?" Georgia said. "I ain't mad at her."

"We *earned* ours. She got hers through no credentials of her own except DNA. Born into the
right family. The only thing that is truly Courtney
is that she wants to become the wife of, not only
the most charismatic, sought-after bachelor in
Philly, but on the entire eastern seaboard. And
Jared can get to mayor without Courtney. He's

his own man in his own right; she's just hitched her designer butt to his shooting star."

"Don't sell Courtney cheap. She's intelligent, articulate, attractive, and can work a crowd—"

"Wears too much makeup."

"Is that the best you can do?" Georgia asked, and thought of Courtney's flawless chocolate skin and how her hair was always coiffed. "Attack her looks?"

"I'm just saying—at the end of the day some men want more than a good-looking woman in good-looking clothes. I wanted more, so does Jared. The upkeep on that superficial stuff can get old and real shallow after a couple of years. You don't want her to be mother of your children, cute but dumb kids you can only hope will marry well. That's no legacy. Besides, he didn't love her."

"Four years?"

"They weren't ready for 'the home' yet. You know how it is when you're comfortable in a relationship and your partner doesn't do enough to really piss you off, so you just go along with it until it limps to its inevitable end."

"No, I don't. And she doesn't strike me as the kind of woman who'd go quietly into that 'goodbye' after a four-year investment with such a high-profile man. You can count her gone but not out. She'll be back."

"To what? For what? I hope she has some pride."

"I didn't know marriage made you so calloused."

"I prefer smart. Perceptive." He offered her a fry. "If Jared were to find a woman he loved? He'd marry her in a New York minute—not four years. Has he ever seemed like a man confused? A man who would wait on something he truly wanted? It may take a while but when a man decides on a woman . . . you got no chance."

"*I* got no chance?"

"Not you per se . . . *women* have no chance." Neal looked at her. "Want me to put in a good word for you?" He chomped down on another fry and grinned.

"With who? Who do you know that I would possibly consider as a mate?"

Neal inclined his head playfully toward Jared.

"You know I don't play that." She rolled her eyes at him. "But I have girlfriends who'd be thrilled." Neal liked to tease, so she didn't totally believe his story about the Jared/Courtney breakup and she certainly wasn't going to ask Jared a private question regarding his personal life. She wasn't going there. Not after today with Neal, and not ever with Jared.

"Please don't unleash your girlfriends on Jared. He's a good man." Neal threw his napkin into his plate. "But you . . . you'd be just his shot. If you could get around that old-fashioned little boss-dating rule."

"It's not a 'rule,' it's a 'thou shalt not' family commandment. Besides, there's something sadly incestuous and predatory about it."

"Nowadays the workplace is the only place folks can meet."

"You didn't meet Brenda at work. And what are you trying to say about my friends?" She cut her eyes playfully, not taking Neal's bait. "Frankly, I don't care who Jared Jaymes ends up with."

"Oh, really?"

"I ain't got a nickel in that quarter," Georgia answered, unable to look her old friend in the eye. "Just so 'whoever' makes him happy. I don't want to work for a grumpy, horny boss."

Despite his best attempts, Jared's eyes kept returning to the bar and Georgia. While his buddies discussed sports and women, Jared feigned interest, ate, and tried to remember what, if anything, he'd heard about Georgia MacKenzie and her personal life. He didn't care about any ADA privately as long as they did their job and did it well, and with her ninety-five percent conviction rate, Georgia never disappointed him—until today. The race card between two black DAs was patently absurd.

Jared remembered only seeing Georgia twice in an out-of-the office context. She'd been engaged to a "pretty boy" black detective with a Spanish name who'd died in the line of duty. She'd asked for a leave of absence and, after disappearing down South somewhere for three weeks, returned to work full of fire and grit. That was about two years ago. After their Monday case review last week, someone remarked that Georgia had removed her engagement ring. Jared hadn't noticed until today when he thought she was on the verge of giving him the finger. Did that mean that after all this time she was finally moving on? Had this decision made her surly, sensitive, and tense, ergo the office tirade an hour ago? Or was it PMS, bad timing, or the death of summer and the onset of fall? He glanced over at the bar and saw that she was laughing with Neal. Had he ever seen her laugh like that? he wondered absently.

One time in particular answered his mental query. One Saturday, he and Courtney were cutting through the park on their way to the Mayor's Breakfast and ran into Georgia and her boyfriend. Georgia was suited up in a hot-pink jogging outfit, her hair caught in a ponytail and no makeup; he remembered because Courtney had made such a big deal out of him noticing that Georgia had freckles. Jared recalled that Georgia'd just bought a restored brownstone and her boyfriend was helping her paint. Jared remembered Georgia laughing like she was now at the bar with Neal. He also remembered back then that he would have given anything to be spending his Saturday morning playing racquetball with his buddies, walking in the park with a pretty girl, or washing his truck; doing anything else but going to the stiff-neck-tie mayor's function.

"Hey, man. How about this weekend?" one of Jared's racquetball buddies asked, interrupting his recollections.

"We'll see. Right now I got to jet. The mayor and commissioner await," Jared said, not knowing when he'd finished his platter.

Jared left the money to cover his meal and tip, bid good-bye to his buddies, and passed Neal and Georgia at the bar; Neal acknowledged him with an upward jerk of his chin—Georgia did not.

As Jared walked in the crisp autumn air to his meeting, he mused how he loved this town, its people, and the change of seasons. Time seemed to be speeding by and before he knew it the holidays would be here. He thought about varying the menu for the upcoming Christmas party that he hosted at his home for his staff and colleagues every year. Suddenly, he recalled that Georgia hadn't come her first two years after being hired. Surely part of her creed of not mixing business with pleasure, but on the third year, she'd come on the arm of Tony Machado. Jared remembered how Courtney thought he'd spent too much time with the couple.

During that next year, Jared met Tony on the basketball court when the DAs and detectives played their annual basketball game, which rivaled the Army/Navy match. Georgia was there at the games cheering Tony on, and the more she cheered, the harder Jared played, realizing that he wouldn't be outdone by this Tony guy with his slam dunks and all-net three-pointers. On the last play of the final game, Tony failed to block Jared's three-pointer and the DA's office won. The crowd's cheering and congratulatory slaps from his teammates was heady, until Jared looked back. Tony had slung his arm around Georgia's neck and they were walking out of the gym like high school teenagers. Jared had the winning shot, but Tony got the girl. Jared was irritated because Courtney wasn't there, but he'd discounted the entire episode as juvenile and ridiculous, and blamed it on raging adult male testosterone. Funny, he should recall it all now, he thought.

As Jared climbed the steps of City Hall, he remembered having to sit out the next championship game because he'd hurt his ankle in a handball accident. He had wanted a rematch with Tony Machado as much as the fans who wanted to see the duo ball again. But by the third year, Tony was gone.

Jared paused at the top of the steps. "Umph," he said aloud.

For the first time in his conscious mind he wondered if he had some nonprofessional interest in Georgia MacKenzie as Courtney had twice accused, and he'd summarily dismissed. Clearly something had happened between him and Georgia today. Exactly what, he didn't know. There was some exchange of personal emotional energy between them in his office. An undefinable connection that might or might not happen again. Had they crossed the line with a look? Was he the only one who felt it? Or did she feel something too? He was an expert at reading women, which was how he'd managed to stay single and maintain the label of "decent guy," but Georgia MacKenzie had thrown up something this morning that Stevie Wonder's sixth sense couldn't have deciphered.

"Hmm," he uttered, and looked out over the Commons and up at the crystal-clear sky. He was familiar with her sharp mind, her unflappable convictions, and her love of the law. He'd never thought about her *personally* before. Never really thought about the way her thick, heavy chestnut hair fell midneck, and was shot with gold in the summer months. The way the August humidity played in her silky locks and made her hair curl. The way her chocolate freckles were expertly concealed beneath a thin coating of makeup. The way her dark amber, intelligent eyes could stop any argument with a look. The way she tilted her head when she didn't buy what was being said. The way a crooked, smile-smirk would claim her face when she was cold-busted. The way she'd sweat on her nose when she was agitated, or swoop her hair behind her ear when she wanted to clarify a point. The way her razor-sharp tongue hid beneath perfect lips. The few times he saw her laugh—really laugh—how her eyes would be reduced to slits. The way her laughing, dark amber eyes sparkled with pleasure when she nailed a conviction.

"Hmph," he said aloud. *I didn't know I knew so much about ADA MacKenzie,* he thought.

With his too-busy eighteen-hour days and dead-to-the-world nights, he'd never considered the prospect of it. He wouldn't. Not only did she work with him, not only was he her boss, but she was attached. She was in love and engaged to be married. She was inaccessible. Had he subconsciously wanted to be the man she was in love with? The prospect was too complicated to entertain then—until now. Now she was free. Now she had stopped wearing her engagement ring and was moving on. Only now did his unconscious bring the possibility of her to his consciousness to ponder. Would she even be interested? Since neither one of them believed in work romances, would she be willing to conduct a surreptitious relationship? Was now the time? Was it *his* time? His opportunity? The fact that he was even entertaining these questions gave him pause. Then stabbed him with surprise. Jared Jaymes was considering dating a woman he worked with? A woman he actually supervised.

Had the world stopped rotating? But Georgia MacKenzie wasn't just any woman.

I'll have to think long and hard on this one, he thought, and then smiled at the uncanny realization.

"I'll be damned. Never say never."

From an open window of a passing car, The Spinners asked, "Could It Be I'm Falling in Love?"

In answer, Jared broke into a wide schoolboy grin.

With breakfast and exercising out of the way and a load of clothes in the washer, Georgia watered the plants in her den and gazed out of the French doors to her waning backyard garden. She noticed how the sun's slant signaled the departure of one season and the advent of another. She'd weeded and mulched, preparing her perennials for whatever winter Philly had in store. She passed her kitchen and dining room to water the plants basking in the solar rays from the oversize, arched living room window—that unique feature and the turret were the reasons she'd bought this house. This elegant, slender, three-story structure was so unlike the robust frame house with the wraparound porch and sprawling acreage she'd grown up in. But there was something really appealing to her about the urban, brick row house with its long, narrow rooms, formidable plaster walls, ten-foot ceilings, and gleaming hardwood floors. In the summer, she did long for the fresh vegetables that her postage-stamp-size yard couldn't yield. *That's what farmers' markets are for,* she thought, chuckling, as she pinched off a dead leaf.

She glanced out at the quiet, tree-lined street where the well-kept row houses stood sentry. She was glad Jared hadn't returned to the office on Friday. She hoped this weekend would dull the memory of that awkward moment in his office and everything would get back to normal on Monday. Surely with all his usual political and social obligations, he would forget about their peculiar encounter by Monday.

As Luther Vandross crooned "A House Is Not a Home," she passed Tony's picture smiling from the fireplace mantel. She let her fingers outline his features and eyed the dish that held her engagement ring. He was proof positive that death did not put an end to love. It was getting better. Not easier but better, she thought as the phone rang. She cut down the volume of Luther's voice and answered, "Hello." She listened to the familiar voice and replied, "No. Not today."

"Why?" Neal challenged. "What you got going on?"

"Housework, then going to dinner and the movies with 'the girls.'"

"You mean the 'barracudas.'"

"That's right. You would know. You dated all three of them, didn't you? I should call them 'Neal's Harem.'"

"C'mon, we need a fourth for doubles and our nice autumn days are numbered. Brenda'll cook."

"No, I won't!" Brenda yelled into the phone.

Georgia chuckled as her doorbell rang. "Gotta go."

"Seriously, next week, Mac. Tennis," Neal decreed. "You got to get out of that house."

"We'll see. Somebody's at my door. Check you later." Georgia hung up.

Georgia opened the door for the mailman, spoke to and smiled at him and the package with the familiar writing and the Evelyn, Tennessee, return address.

"Thanks." She closed the door, put down the letter mail, and tore into the box. "Grandma Mac's elderberry jam." She identified the neat rows of Mason jars. "Now I know it's officially fall." She popped one jar open with a whoosh, plunged two of her fingers into the sticky, garnet-colored substance, and stuck them in her mouth. "Umph, umph, umph. That is good."

Georgia looked at the card, which read:

Dear Willow, it's about that time. Made with no preservatives and all love. Enjoy. Love, Grandma Mac.

Georgia went to the kitchen, sliced two pieces of thick challah bread, placed them in the toaster, and chuckled at her nickname, Willow. She recalled how she was to be the stately tree in a preschool play and couldn't get with the concept. Her mother and father had tried to help her, but it was Grandma Mac who told her to *become* the willow—*Be* one with the willow as she and her grandmother had flitted all over the house becoming the graceful tree. Then, taking her commitment one step further, Georgia declared that she *was* Willow and wouldn't answer to anything else. She was the best weeping willow tree Ross Preschool had ever seen. After the play, Grandma Mac continued to call her that . . . it was her special name for the preschooler, which had lasted all these years.

The toaster oven dinged. Georgia spread the butter over the golden brown surface and watched it disappear before she smoothed on Grand's Jam. "Umph! Take me home." She devoured one slice, then the other, rinsed her hands, picked up the phone, and hit the speed-dial number 2.

When her grandmother answered the phone, Georgia said, "Thank you!"

"You got it already?"

"I don't live in east g-blip."

"Really? As often as you visit I thought you did."

Georgia listened to her grandmother's chuckle rock and soothe her lovingly. "Point taken."

"How's my favorite granddaughter doing?"

"I'm fine. How about you?"

"Not so fast. Are you *really* fine?"

"You know—I really am. For the first time in a long while." She sighed. "I took off Tony's engagement ring last week," she admitted quietly. "I was working in the garden and it got caked with dirt, so I took it off when I came inside and cleaned it. I just decided not to put it back on."

"Good for you, Willow," Grandma Mac said with a genuine mixture of love and pride. "That's progress. You know life is short and he wouldn't want you to waste all this time mourning him. He wasn't that kind of man."

"I know." Involuntary tears brimmed Georgia's eyes but didn't fall.

"Just let me know when I can arrange for you to meet my friend's boy, Pernell. If you haven't met him already. He's a lawyer up there in Philly too."

"Pernell? No, Grand. I'd remember a Pernell." She chuckled and added, "And do you know how many black male lawyers there are in Philly?"

"Named Pernell?"

"Pernell, cheez . . . that's the dorkiest name I've ever heard." She laughed. "The only Pernell I know is Pernell Roberts."

"That's not his last name."

"That's the actor who played Adam Cartwright on *Bonanza*. I'm not ready for either of them, okay? But I'll let you know."

"He played the harmonica. He was gifted on the old mouth harp—"

"Harmonica, Grand? Cheez!"

"I have a picture of the two of you when you were a little girl and he was holding you."

"Ah! And he's old to boot?"

"Not that old. I'll show you when you come home. And just when will that be?"

"Hopefully, for Christmas. I got Mom's postcard from Aruba."

"She's having a high ole time. You need to take a page from her book."

"You don't want me to take up with any old man, do you?'

"You know better than that. You can do bad all by yourself. You don't need a man to help drag you down further. Men are supposed to make things better, not worse. It takes a mighty good man to beat having no man at all. This Pernell is a good man. Course I haven't seen or spoke to him in years, but his people speak highly of him."

"Well, that's a ringing endorsement. So what are you going to do today?"

An hour later, Georgia hung up the telephone. She put the opened jam in the refrigerator and the unopened jars in the pantry under the kitchen's back stairs to her second floor.

"Pernell. That old lawyer dude will be alone a long time with a name like that. A black man named Pernell." Tony didn't clear her for a Pernell.

She smiled remembering how Tony had teased her a few years back after they'd run into Jared and Courtney in the park; her boss and his girlfriend were going to some mayoral breakfast . . . on a Saturday morning. The four had stopped politely to chat and Jared noticed, "You have freckles."

The personal remark had stopped the conversation cold. "All my life," Georgia had said. After the well-dressed couple proceeded on their way, Tony had jokingly mimicked, "You got freckles" and run away from Georgia. She'd caught up with him at the ice cream vendor and told Tony it was a simple observation since Jared had never seen her without makeup, but Tony disagreed.

"He's got the hots for you big time. He looked like he coulda just licked those freckles off your face. His girlfriend was none too pleased with the observation either," Tony'd teased, his mischievous eyes dancing before telling her, "It's okay, babe." He took a quick lick of her ice cream as well. "Somethin' happens to me, you can date Jared Jaymes. He's the next best thing to me. The man can ball."

Georgia now laughed remembering her crazy, funny fiancé. His characteristic jovial playfulness in the face of a gunman was what got him killed. Usually, he could talk his way out of anything—except a gun in the hand of a scared, cornered thief. He died doing a job he loved. He may have loved that job more than her; she was pleased it was never put to the test. He was an adrenaline junkie who always told her she was all the excitement he needed. She knew better every time she'd swung in behind him on his Harley and he zigzagged through city traffic heading for the open road. Tony Machado was her thrill seeker, and she still missed him.

As she took the warm clothes from the dryer and began folding them, she thought, How prophetic that little nonsensical conversation had been—that Tony would name his successor. That was the reason Jared popped up as the man in the dreams—because Tony had planted the seed. Now that she'd figured it out, she just wished the dreams would stop.

She glanced at the clock and realized she had less than an hour to shower and meet her friends. She sprinted up the back stairs to her bedroom.

Six hours later Georgia returned home, disarmed and then reset her alarm, and set her keys on the hall table. She took her letter mail and the paper upstairs with her to get ready for bed. The movie had been lackluster, but the dinner and conversation with her three crazy friends made up for it. She needed that girls' night out and hadn't had one in months. Fun time was the first casualty of professional black women trying to coordinate a balance between work and pleasure. She took off her clothes, laughing at how the conversation always turned to men in general, and Jared Jaymes in particular. The threesome were always disappointed that Georgia had nothing in the way of information to give them. Her friends had more social interaction with her boss than did she, which was as it should be. One friend said she finally had the nerve to ring the doorbell of his house in the Hamptons only to be confronted by his parents. Georgia'd remarked that it was probably his parents' house, when her friend quoted a *Black Enterprise* article, which reported that he'd bought that house four years ago; her friend lamented how she was still renting but "brother-man owns." Georgia couldn't imagine when Jared had time to use it. He was always working or on some sociopolitical jaunt to further his career.

Georgia washed her face and chuckled at how another friend said she had to go all the way to Washington, D.C., to meet him at a Black Caucus event. She'd given Jared her number, but he never called her. He was surely still dating Courtney last fall. Georgia didn't know everything about her boss, but he was notoriously monogamous and it wasn't his style to pick up women at an event, out of town or otherwise. Georgia brushed her teeth and put on a toothpaste smile for the mirror, remembering how her girlfriend finally admitted that she'd slipped her number in his tux pocket.

She spat, rinsed, and said to her mirrored image, "Hoochies. My girlfriends are hoochies."

She ran her shower and soaped her body as their words echoed around the shower stall.

"All I know is that if I was around that fine specimen of a man twenty-four-seven like you, Georgia Mackenzie, I'd make things happen. And when that relationship with Courtney crashes and burns, I got first dibs. One of us should get him. And if Georgia doesn't want him, I got next."

Georgia toweled off and applied lotion, agreeing with her girlfriends on one thing: at least Jared, who was at the top of his professional game, didn't think he should accessorize his success with a nonblack woman. They had toasted that revelation with a "Hallelujah," an "Amen," and another round of apple martinis.

You got to respect a man like that, Georgia thought. It gave her girls hope. *Dance with the one who brung ya.* "My crazy friends," Georgia said aloud as she put on a camisole top and silk pj bottoms. She hadn't mentioned Neal's claim that Jared was available to them, just in case he wasn't. Neal would say almost anything just to get reactions out of people, and Georgia wouldn't dare raise her girlfriends' expectations for naught. She flicked on the television for company and rifled though her mail. She opened the paper and there was her boss with the mayor and police commissioner with the headline WHY WON'T JARED RUN?

Georgia skimmed the article, which predicted, as they always did, that Jared Jaymes was a shoo-in for mayor if he'd just throw his signature black fedora into the ring. It speculated that either Jared was too good a friend of the current mayor and didn't want to put him out of a job, or Jared loved being a state attorney for Philadelphia.

Georgia tossed the paper aside knowing that if Jared wanted to run, he would. Something else was holding him back and it wasn't his friendship with the mayor or that he loved being the DA. She absently wondered too why he hesitated. She didn't know exactly what was keeping him from running but, if/when Jared Jaymes decided to run, he had her vote.

Georgia set the alarm, got between her sheets, and thought, *Parents?* She'd never thought of Jared Jaymes as having or needing parents. It was like he came into this world fully grown, teeming with integrity, composure, and the capability of achieving anything he put his mind to. But of course, his parents were the ones who inserted the silver spoon into his mouth and gave him his push into the good life. So Jared Jaymes hadn't wasted time with cashmere when the more expensive, rarer Peruvian alpaca coat and the vicuna sweaters were better suited to the University of Pennsylvania, top-of-his-class graduate. Jared Jaymes bought his stone Victorian house in the historically established neighborhood of University City, avoiding the trendy upscale section where most upwardly mobile buppies showcased their conspicuous consumption. She'd only visited his house once, for a Christmas party, and was immediately impressed because it was not the razzle-dazzle ostentation of "new money" set to modernism; Jared Jaymes's house was stoic, classic, and traditional with the understated elegance only plaster walls and a mansard slate roof could provide. But Jared Jaymes had nothing to prove and nobody to impress. He had the trendy votes and the only way to get the elitist votes was to live among them and show that he was just a regular Joe with family values, unflinching honesty, and a reputation as solid as the slate-black Hummer he drove.

"Like I said, you got my vote, boss," Georgia repeated, and grabbed the remote to begin channel-surfing for something that would soothe her to sleep.

That night she slept deep and hard and the uninvited dream came. But that night she had expected it. That night when Jared took her into his powerful arms at the swimming hole and said, "I've been waiting for you," Georgia Mackenzie said, "I know."

Chapter 2

Jared addressed his team of assistant DAs as they sat around the conference table for their usual Monday morning case reviews. He seemed nonplused and normal, and Georgia was relieved. She tried making as little eye contact with him as possible, yet every time she did, his bittersweet, espresso eyes seemed to drink in hers in the most unnerving way. She was at work; besides home, it was one place she was able to garner control and maintain her professionalism. She didn't want to be unnerved here.

How long is this going to go on? she asked herself as she reported on the status of her cases. She looked at Neal and the other team members, intentionally avoiding the man at the head of the long conference table. The one time she looked into his waiting eyes, she lost her place. Momentarily, anxiety crept in, but her voice stayed steady. Once she finished her report she slid her chair back a little under the guise of having enough room to cross her legs. By doing this, she was only subjected to Jared's comments and questions, but could not see him. She just wanted this craziness to pass. She couldn't control dreams, but she could manipulate reality.

When the meeting was over, Jared sat perched on the corner of his desk as he usually did. They all headed out the door.

"MacKenzie. A moment please," he said.

Damn! she thought, but turned and said, "Yes?"

"Are you all right?"

"Fine. Why?" She met his gaze, trying not to be absorbed by his pools of liquid darkness.

"Need any help with the Cusamano case?"

"No. Like I said in the meeting, I have two more witnesses. Then I'm ready to close."

"I didn't mean anything by it," he said with a quick, dismissive smile.

"Sure. Is there anything else?"

His intercom buzzed. "No," he said, leaving his perch to answer it.

She went into her office and began to work on depositions in another case. Involuntarily, her eyes drifted though the two sets of plate-glass windows across the hall and rested on Jared. With papers sprawled across her desk, her hand brusquely under her chin, and her pinky finger lodged between her lips, she wondered why she was so suddenly intimidated by him. Nobody but nobody intimidated Georgia MacKenzie. While looking at him, she noticed how his white shirt fell over his broad shoulders without wrinkling; how his tie, slightly loosened around his neck, gave him a casual, sexy look. He wasn't tall like Tony. Jared was probably only five feet ten or eleven, but what was there was prime, proportioned, and formed an inviting athletic V shape. He had a way of commanding attention just by entering a room. She'd seen him do it in court, or walking down the court's halls, at press conferences on television, and according to her girlfriends, he was no different at parties or social events. Charisma oozed from his pores without him opening his mouth. Political pundits, men and women, labeled it "power," both personal and professional. It just wasn't that he was handsome, an impeccable dresser, or had been born on the right side of the tracks, but there was a confidence bred from a series of successes in his life—the result of his setting goals and achieving them, then setting and achieving more. She wondered if he'd made a pact with the powers-that-be, who'd anointed him with a spotless record and reputation, deeming that he could remain "top dog" as long as he continued to be a role model by example—guys wanted to know and be like him, and women wanted to date and marry him.

Well, not her of course, she thought quickly, watching him stroke the back of his neck as he talked on the phone. But she was probably the only single woman in Philly, on the entire eastern seaboard, who didn't have designs on Jared Jaymes.

He swiveled his chair around and faced her direction. Georgia immediately busied herself with papers, clearing her throat to harness her thoughts and redirect her mind. She'd made peace with the dreams knowing they didn't mean diddley, and like a school yard bully, if she didn't give them power, they'd pass soon. She ran the dream's antidote, the "commercial" tape of her brain again—Jared was the natural candidate to be the personification of Tony's replacement in her subconscious; she saw Jared every day and he was the only available male she currently knew who matched Tony in integrity.

And like Tony, she reminded herself, Jared was unreachable, untouchable, and beyond her grasp—he was her boss. "Don't sleep where you earn your meat," her daddy'd told her. As soon as she found a real flesh-and-blood man to take Tony's place, this thing with Jared would evaporate into thin air as easily as it had been fabricated. Until she found that man, her subconscious would default to Jared. "Nothing for me to worry about," she concluded.

She decided she'd take Neal up on his tennis foursome this weekend. She needed another male distraction and if he'd just replace Jared in her dreams, that would be an enormous feat, and then things could get back to normal. Maybe she'd even call Pernell—the harmonica-playing hick from her neck of the woods. He might be just the diversion and entertainment she considered necessary. Georgia stacked papers and smiled, thinking, *Pernell sounds like he has a part down the middle of his hair and wears a bow tie.* No, she wouldn't call Pernell unless she became really desperate. As desperate as her girl-friends, she thought, and flipped open the Cusa-mano case file.

* * *

Georgia embraced the weekend for what it was, a reprieve from work and Jared's looming existence. Luckily, in the last few days she'd been too involved with her cases to be distracted by Jared's presence or absences and she relished getting away from him and the Cusamano case. The brilliant autumn morning had an early crispness in the air, forewarning of a cold winter as she drove to join Neal and Brenda for a good, strenuous tennis match. She parked her sporty red Lexus coupé, grabbed her racket, and sauntered toward the happy couple.

"I know you didn't just come here to show off those pretty caramel legs," Brenda teased, opening her arms for a hug.

"Hey, at least they're not white," Georgia said. "It's after Labor Day." The two women finished together, peeling into giddy laughter. "Hey, Daddy," Georgia greeted Neal, and looked at Brenda's belly. "How's that big, bald-headed little boy in there?"

"As you can see I'm partial to bald heads." Brenda rubbed her husband's head playfully. "But it's a girl."

"Here we go," Neal said, wearily. "It's a boy. Now let's play tennis, ladies."

Georgia turned toward the gate and, through the fence, saw him. "Oh, damn!" she said at the sight of Jared on the other side of the chain links. "What is *he* doing here?" Automatically her eyes quickly combed the courts for Courtney. Georgia still had not confirmed that Courtney and Jared had really broken up. Georgia would not give Neal the satisfaction of asking again.

Courtney was probably in the bathroom putting on lipstick.

Neal and Brenda exchanged quizzical looks.

"Listen, let's just say hello and keep moving," Georgia instructed them. "I see him at work and don't need to see him on the weekends too." She led the threesome around the fence.

"Hi," Jared said brightly, approaching the trio. "Glad you could make it," he said to Georgia. "I hear you're pretty good."

Georgia froze as her mind worked feverishly to decipher what he had just said. Was he speaking English? It was early on this Saturday morning, but she finally realized that *she* was expected. *She* was the fourth of this already formed threesome.

Georgia's eyebrows knitted in betrayal and she shot Neal the look she'd used on him in law school when he'd messed up on a joint assignment.

Neal accepted the visual scolding from Georgia as he greeted Jared, "Hey, man."

Damn, was all Georgia could think. *I could be home sleeping late, washing my hair, grocery shopping, be anywhere but here . . . with my boss on the weekend. Ambushed.* Hoodwinked, like a virgin being told she can't get pregnant on the first time. Georgia was so upset with the situation she could barely listen to the pairings as her head spun. She backed up and accidentally bumped into Jared. He grabbed her at her waist. An electrical shock sparked between them. His hand at her waist felt as warm and comforting in real life as it had in the dream.

"Sorry," Georgia mumbled, unable to concentrate on anything but the nearness of him. It was the first time since the handshake at her initial interview with him over five years ago that he had touched her. His hand lingered at her waist. *Remove your hand from my waist,* her brain screamed.

"You okay?" Jared asked as his coal-black eyes sparkled.

"Yes. Let's play." She stood frozen in place, wanting to walk away, willing her feet to move, yet waiting for him to release her. Finally, he did.

He played backcourt and Georgia was grateful she didn't have to look at him—the way the off-white shorts contrasted with his Hershey's milk chocolate skin. The way bands of color cuffed his wrists just below his powerful forearms. The way wisps of chest hair peeked from the top of the knit shirt that clung to his muscled torso, and his bare legs—had she ever expected to see her boss's bare legs?

"Concentrate," she ordered herself.

The couple played well together and Georgia began to relax and enjoy the game. After a few sets, Brenda said she was tired and asked Neal to take her home.

When they all went to the side bench Neal said, "We have the court reserved for another hour. Why don't you two stay?"

"Sure, I'm game. Mackenzie?" Jared's eyes questioned hers.

Her mind spun. She wanted to tell him, "No. I don't want to play. I don't want to see you outside of the office." Yet she wanted to tell him to call her "Georgia." After all, they weren't at work.

But she didn't plan for this to be a habit so "Mackenzie" it remained.

"Sure," she finally answered with the cool of a woman in control—which of course she was not.

"Is there anything we can do?" Jared asked Neal and Brenda.

We, Georgia thought. *Who is "we"?*

"Nope. Once I get home and take a little nap I'll be as good as new. In fact you two stop by later for tacos and margaritas," Brenda offered.

"She's not drinking," Neal clarified. "But I still do."

"Thanks, man. We'll see how it goes. Take care," Jared said.

"We" again? There is no "we," and there will never be, Georgia thought. She did not appreciate being placed in this awkward situation by a so-called friend who knew how she felt about socializing with her boss. Neal would hear about this later. Right now she had to fight with the image of Jared's masculine form assaulting her eyes.

As Jared went to claim the other side of the net, Georgia shot Neal her signature ticked-off stare.

"Your serve," Jared said, and tossed Georgia the ball.

She caught the ball in one hand and bounced it a few times, struggling to distract herself from his imposing physique across the net. The sight of him like this was not going to get rid of those dreams, she thought. There they were again, his slightly bowed, built legs supporting his muscled upper body, which was hunched down at the ready. She could see the power and definition of his athletic build in the shorts and knit top the way she could never see them in a suit and tie. She bounced the ball a few more times, trying to steady the inner havoc the vision of him was causing. She breathed deeply a few times, tossed the ball in the air, and *Thwack*—the competition began. He won—she won—he won—she won. Then their time was up.

"You two are really good," the next couple waiting said as Jared and Georgia went to the bench to wipe off their sweaty faces.

Georgia didn't speak.

"Thanks," Jared said to them, and then to Georgia, "You are surprisingly good, Mackenzie. But then you're good at everything you do."

"Thanks. You too." She drank almost an entire bottle of water in one gulp.

"Guess we better enjoy the last of the warm weather." He watched her drain the plastic bottle of liquid. "You think Brenda's okay? Should we check on her?"

Georgia almost strangled. *We?* Again. "I think her husband is taking good care of her." *And I'm not going anywhere with you,* she thought.

"Tacos and margaritas would taste good about now. Replace our salt. Unless you'd like to go somewhere else."

What? her incensed inner voice questioned. "Thanks, but I've got some errands to do." She wiped her face, gathered her racket, and backed away from him. She had to put distance between him and her. Not only was he all out of the box labeled "boss," but he was awakening feelings she thought, after two years, she was ready for, but apparently wasn't—at least not from him. "But you go on. I'll call them later. And I'll see you in the office on *Monday*." She stepped on the grassy, uneven threshold between the gate and the cement. Her ankle twisted. "Ow!"

Jared sprang to her rescue and grabbed her arm. The sensation she felt in her ankle was rivaled by his touch on her arm—firm but tender. "C'mon and sit back down." He led her to the bench.

"I'm fine." She couldn't help but inhale the intoxicating aroma of musk, faded aftershave, and—man.

"Will you let me see?" he said in his official "boss" tone.

Reluctantly, she sat down on the bench and thought, *This is why you and your boss should not go out socially.* She couldn't just tell him to "buzz off." He might hold her attitude against her at appraisal time and deny her a most deserved raise. Unnecessary complications.

He knelt before her and gently lifted her leg so that her ankle rested on his thigh. He undid her shoe and removed her sock before she could protest. His touch sent an electric shiver up her spine, which radiated to all parts of her body.

"Cold?" he asked.

"No."

Her stomach flipped and her body warmed. No man had touched her like this since Tony. She hadn't realized how much she missed it until now. Jared's touch was both new and nostalgic. It was skin-to-skin as his hands slid up and down and over her ankle; she was not prepared for the sight or sensation of his hands on her bare skin. She tried to divert her attention by focusing on how long and tapered his fingers were; how his nails were clean, manicured, and buffed and he had a small, flat mole embedded in his thumbnail. But the sight was overrun by the tactile sensation of his warm, soothing fingers pinching, then caressing her Achilles tendon. He unintentionally tickled her arch.

She giggled.

He smiled. "Ticklish, huh?"

She couldn't breathe. *Just get me out of here. I can't believe this is happening to me.*

Then he looked up at her with those espresso eyes, hooded by long eyelashes. The setting sun cut across his chiseled features. Over the past few years she must have looked at him a million times. But now for the first time, she really *saw* Jared Jaymes—up close and personal. Not as her boss, but as a man. His eyes were piercing and intelligent. His nose complemented his high cheekbones framed by a strong jawline, all set in smooth, clean-shaven milk chocolate skin. And his lips were full, luscious, and inviting. She couldn't tear her eyes away from them, and the strong desire to kiss them suddenly overwhelmed her. She wanted to feel them kiss her. She wondered how he tasted. *Well,* her conscious mind thought, *what do you know? Jared Jaymes is a hunk.* Was this what her girlfriends saw when they looked at him? Was this what she had missed by *not* looking at him all those years?

"You all right?" he asked.

"Yes. Yes, I am. Thanks." His smile was thawing the protective block of ice around her heart.

"It's not broken. Can you drive?"

"Yes."

His hand was resting on her foot and she was glad she'd painted her toenails last night. She liked the visual contrast of his milk chocolate skin against her mocha, mimicking the color of the Reese's peanut butter cups he kept in his office.

Gently, he put her shoe back on. "C'mon. Lean into me."

"This is silly."

"C'mon, Mackenzie."

She obeyed as he walked her to her car and helped her in.

"Still feel okay?" He closed her car door.

"I'll be fine. I'll ice and elevate it when I get home, and it'll be as good as new. Thanks." She started up her ignition, but she really wasn't ready to go. Her eyes fixed on his luscious lips again. She tucked in her own lips between her teeth and breathed deeply, trying to quiet the fire he had ignited. His laugh lines framed either side of those luscious lips and formed parentheses that punctuated how perfect his mouth was—perfect for kissing, for exploring—

The Spinners singing "Could It Be I'm Falling in Love?" blasted from her radio. They chuckled, and she turned the volume down.

"Freckles," he said to her, wanting to tweak her nose playfully, but, thinking better of it, he crossed his arms upon themselves the way he did in meetings. *Freckles*, he repeated to himself, conjuring up thoughts of the first time he'd seen them when

she was jogging in the park and she was with Tony
and he with Courtney. But now it was years later
and just the two of them.

"Yep. Freckles."

"See you Monday . . . Georgia."

Georgia. She smiled like a second grader who'd
just been given the lead in a school play. Had he
ever called her *Georgia* before? "Bye."

She liked the sound of her name falling from
those beautiful lips set in a parenthetical smile,
capped with the soft bedroom eyes. She backed
out, gave him a wave, and drove away with his
image consuming her rearview mirror.

A few miles down the road she felt another
cold shiver go up her spine. This time she recognized it as her father flipping over in his grave.
She could hear the echo of his reprimanding
words in her brain. *He is your boss, Georgia.*

She'd been raised with a litany of MacKenzie
mottoes, but those most often repeated were
always do your personal best, give back to your
community, and never sleep where you earn your
meat. The latter was the last one to take hold of
an adult Georgia. As a child she couldn't understand why her father would put a bed at the mill
or her mother put one in her third grade class-
room. When she was a child, the maxims were
spouted long before there was any understanding
or practical application. An eight-year-old Georgia sitting in a fishing boat with her dad, live bait,
and a snack of fried chicken and boiled peanuts
had no idea what a "workplace romance" was. All
she knew was how passionately her father felt on
the subject based on his experience, first as the

foreman, then supervisor at the mill, where he witnessed capable women "giving up their good sense and good jobs" by dating the wrong men— their bosses. His lectures were laced with grown-up lingo about "double standards," "no control," and "ruined reputations," situations that were incomprehensible to a young Georgia. Her father would conclude that these women, not the men, lost their jobs and dignity, and it wasn't going to happen to his daughter.

As with all family mottoes, children mature and recognize that these parental edicts were developed to form value bases and to protect them through adolescence: don't eat with your elbows on the table, don't ride in the car with boys, and don't talk to strangers. As children mature they qualify and amend family traditions, realizing that if they are in a strange town and need directions, a stranger is the only person to ask. Georgia's mother had piggybacked her father's edicts by pointing out many an "unfortunate girl" of easy virtue she'd taught in her third grade class who made stupid, irrevocable choices by high school: girls whose raging hormones, poor judgment, and bad choices got them into compromising positions and hot water, and their "good names" were never restored. It wasn't until Georgia's summer internship at D.C. Superior Court that her father's "never sleep where you earn your meat" came to fruition. In just ninety days, Georgia had witnessed many a warm hello filled with the promise of possibilities turn into a sad good-bye with regrets and should-have-known-betters. She saw women date their bosses, and in the end, the women lost all respect and credibility while a double standard applied to the men boosted their Lothario reputations. What she saw in D.C., and since, had verified her father's axioms. "The walking's easy when the road is flat"—and it was easy to adhere to family beliefs when you were not attracted to your boss and there was no chance of any alliance. But Jared Jaymes was the first man to present a possible challenge to the MacKenzie maxims. However, if she quashed it now, there would be no problem. No unintended consequences or unnecessary complications.

Georgia had spent too many years building a reputation and a flawless conviction record to have it sabotaged by the likes of Jared Jaymes. He was her boss, not worth the gamble, and that was it. She didn't know what that flirtation was with Jared, but it wasn't going to happen again. You can be attracted to anyone of the opposite sex, but not act on it—that's the definition of flirting, but even that is not a positive if the man is your boss. The act alone could detrimentally affect her career. She would institute safeguards to make sure it wouldn't happen again, and they would start with Neal. She didn't need a so-called friend who ignored or disregarded her beliefs, whatever they might be. He set up to ambush her ideals and Georgia did not appreciate it. She would never do that to him.

By the time Georgia reached home she was over the temporary insanity that allowed her to think of her boss as a man. The possibility of Jared being haphazardly thrown into her dating pool had turned into fury. She hopped through the living room and dining room to the kitchen, grabbed a bag of frozen peas from the freezer, and limped to the den's couch. She put her ankle up on the pillows, laid the frozen peas over it, grabbed the phone, and punched in the familiar number.

"Hello," the male voice answered.

"Is Brenda all right?" Georgia asked.

"Yeah. She came home and took—"

"What was that?"

"What?"

"Jared. Tennis."

"C'mon, Georgia. Truth be told, you were the odd one out."

"Excuse me?"

"We had a planned foursome and one of the players bailed."

"You mean Courtney bailed and you thought of me. What am I, her damn substitute?"

"Whoa. No one thinks of you as anyone's 'substitute.' And I told you they broke up."

"So you said."

"Ask him."

"Oh, Negro, puleeze."

"Jared's brother had an emergency. He's a doctor. No one knows better than me how you feel about mixing work with personal life, but you are good at tennis. I thought better of it but Bren said you were a 'big girl' and to go ahead and call you."

"I do not expect to see my *boss* on the weekends, Neal. Is that so hard to understand?"

"Okay. I get it, Mac," he sighed impatiently.

"Apparently not."

"I think that Cusamano case has got you riled."
He knew how to get her off the subject.

"Oh? You wish. The day hasn't dawned when a
case can get me 'riled.'"

"Just because your name is in the papers every
day and they said you made mincemeat of that
surprise witness—"

"I believe the exact words were that 'the defense threw a surprise witness at ADA Mackenzie
and she proceeded to discredit him with the skill
of a fishmonger skinning a tuna and picking the
bones.'"

"Oh? Do we have a scrapbook?"

Georgia chuckled. "Jealousy doesn't become
you."

"But a little professional rivalry among friends
does whet the judicial appetite. Everybody wanted
the Cusamano case, but it was your rotation . . .
and I have to give you your props. You do make
our office shine."

"Jury's not in yet."

"Fake modesty doesn't become you, my sista.
So you been sending your mom and Grandma
Mac the articles from the paper?"

"Nah. They'd just worry about his connection
with the Caprese crime family. They don't understand 'the Mob,'" she added dramatically.

"The Cusamano/Caprese connection is no
joke, Mac."

"It'll be over in a couple of weeks. I'm not
pressed." She eyed her ankle. "Let me go. I'll talk
to you later." She hung up.

She touched her ankle and saw how the intense cold was causing the swelling to go down.

Her touch didn't feel half as good as Jared's. Absently her mind returned to the comfort and caress of Jared's hands on her bare skin.

"Cheez," she self-chastised aloud, "simmer down."

She grabbed the remote and clicked on the television for any noise that would fill her head and keep her from thoughts of him. A commercial advertising "old school" music flashed on the set. The Spinners sang, "Could It Be I'm Falling in Love?"

"It's an insane conspiracy," Georgia lamented, and clicked the set off.

Chapter 3

Georgia grabbed her mug of green tea and assumed her usual seat at the conference table with the other ADAs and administrative assistants. She unfastened the last button of her suit jacket, crossed her legs, and popped her pen before placing it over her pad, ready to takes notes if necessary. Jared removed his suit jacket, draped it over the high back of his desk chair, hung up the telephone, took his seat at the head as he rolled up his sleeves, and commenced the Monday morning case reviews. Georgia expected awkwardness but was met with Jared's classic professionalism.

Maybe I'm making too much out of it, she thought as he took his staff through the usual Monday morning paces. After everyone reported on the status of their cases, Jared offered his comments and recommendations and dismissed his ADAs.

"Mackenzie," he called.

She rather missed his addressing her as *Georgia*. "Yes?" she replied evenly.

"How's the ankle?" he asked perfunctorily as he rounded his desk and sat down.

"Fine. Thanks for asking." She returned his offhanded blaséness.

"Good." His administrative assistant buzzed. "Don't hesitate to use Harris if you need him for the Cusamano case." He punched the blinking light, yanked up the telephone. "Jaymes," he spoke into the receiver.

Georgia left his office feeling . . . strangely. Jared had asked her about her ankle as he would have asked any other DA. His only interest was how it would affect her ability to do her job. Wasn't that what she wanted? Or did she want him to show more concern? Did she want people to know that they had played tennis over the weekend? What did she want? And why did she want it, and from whom did she want it? When she reached her office she glanced at Jared through two sets of glass, behind his impressive desk, carrying on business as usual.

She felt dismissed.

Thankfully, the week passed swiftly, uneventfully. A few more weeks like this, Georgia thought, and everything would be back to normal: boss and subordinate, no inappropriate, private-life conversation. No more dreams.

On Saturday she rose early, washed up, dressed in jeans, tennis shoes, and a Georgetown Law sweatshirt. She pulled her hair through a barrette into a ponytail, donned a Cancún cap, swallowed a boiled egg, bagel, and juice before jogging down the steps to her red chariot. She drove south, breathing in the sharp autumn air and relishing the opportunity to work at Homes for Humankind. She hadn't been in well over a month, couldn't go next weekend, and the following weekend was Brenda's baby shower, so volunteering today was going to be it until next month. She'd worked on seven homes and the MacKenzie maxim of "giving back to your community" so people could live in brand-new homes was not only tradition, but rewarding. She just wished she had more free time.

"Hey," she greeted her foreman.

"Hey," he greeted, hugging her momentarily. "I couldn't believe it when I saw your name on the roster. It's been a while. Welcome back."

"My pleasure. Where do you want me?" Georgia asked, looking around the project.

"You have your specialty. Drywalling."

"You know I love that hammer and nail."

"With your job—I can only imagine. Go 'head in . . . some of your old friends are inside."

"Great. Thanks."

Georgia bounced in, greeted everyone, and started to work. She and her partner had a cadence going with the placing and nailing. It freed her mind to think about the defense in the Cusamano case although it constantly drifted back to Jared. She didn't know why, but she was still irked that he was so nonplussed. It just showed her that she had overdramatized the entire encounter. "Cusamano case," she said to herself, redirecting her thoughts.

Everyone made a big deal about all the press, the curious, the thrill seekers, and the bored who crowded into the courtroom daily to witness the trial of the Mob hit man, but Georgia wasn't there for them. She was there for the victims' families. She was there to prosecute Rocco Cusamano to the full extent of the law for the heinous crime he had committed. Like a 1930s gangster, he had sprayed a bus stop with bullets to get his intended mark, but in the process had killed innocent, everyday people: a mother and child on their way to the clinic, whose husband was in the courtroom every day; an elderly man on his way to fill a prescription for his wife, who now appeared daily in the court; a seventeen-year-old with a bright future on his way to basketball practice and college on a scholarship, whose parents sat three rows behind her each morning. These were the folks for whom Georgia worked. These were the people to whom she felt an obligation to prosecute Cusamano, Cusamano types, and Cusamano wannabes. Her small part of the big puzzle was to send the message that there are consequences for bad behavior, and to make Philly streets and bus stops safe for everyday folks. It was her job to help the victims' families heal and begin to rebuild their shattered lives, which were forever altered because of Cusamano's lawlessness.

Georgia was impatient. Usually her cases had a rhythm to them, but the pacing was off. Something wasn't right, but she couldn't put her finger on it. The defense lawyers seemed ill-prepared and nervous, and the judge was too lenient with defense rulings to suit her. She had no doubt she could nail this thug to the wall, but it was taking much longer than she had anticipated. She and the victims' families just wanted it over.

Georgia hammered near the window casement, and as she reached the sash, a male hand held the woodwork in place as he worked from the outside in. She looked at the hand. The long, dark, tapered fingers with manicured, buffed nails and a small, flat mole in the thumbnail. The last time she saw those hands they were massaging her ankle.

"Hi."

Georgia looked up into the coal-black eyes of Jared Jaymes.

"Fancy finding you here." He smiled at seeing her unexpectedly. Had he ever known she performed community service?

"Isn't it?" she said surlily.

"Not a morning person?"

"Not a person used to running into her boss during her free time."

"Counselor. If I didn't know better I would think you thought this was by design."

"Isn't it?"

"Well." Jared was taken aback. "Someone has a mighty high opinion of themselves." He let go of the window sash. "If it's really an issue, you can check the roster either here or online and see that I do this twice a month when I have time. It's public record." He looked at her for a few moments and added, "No apologies necessary."

"Speaking of 'high opinions of themselves,' I won't be apologizing to you in this lifetime."

"Well, you have a good day and enjoy the rest of your weekend," Jared offered evenly like a true politician.

Jared had spent the better part of his free time

thinking about Georgia. Trying to decide if pursuing her on a social level was anything worth entertaining. After all these years, he'd thought that continually bumping into her lately was perhaps a sign that he should reconsider his dating edicts. Should he call her? But what would be his excuse for doing so? If she wasn't interested, it could be awkward and messy. If he asked her out, later she could claim he'd made unwanted advances. All of which simply reinforced for him why he didn't date *anyone* in or around City Hall. If he was wondering before, his query had been answered today. He knew that Homes for Humankind ran several sites around the city concurrently, and from now on, he'd make sure they never crossed paths again during her free time. Even during his ethics reevaluation, he'd suspected deep down that dating her was a bad idea from the start. It was easy to let this potential relationship go. Now his life and free thoughts could return to the usual. He had quite a full plate and he didn't need a helping of Ms. Georgia MacKenzie.

Georgia continued working, not knowing why she was so ticked. Jared was just popping up everywhere and she didn't like being unable to control his sightings. She put him in a compartment labeled "boss—Monday–Fridays." She didn't appreciate him overstepping his boundaries into her Saturdays and Sundays. When she finished up her assignment and went to get another one, she saw Jared climb into his black Hummer and drive away.

Good riddance, she thought, and began reclaiming her weekend.

On the way home she stopped at a grocery store near the site and parked. Despite her best efforts, seeing Jared had taken the fun out of her Saturday afternoon. She hated that. She headed for the dairy aisle and there, holding court in the middle of a knot of people, was—Jared. *It is a conspiracy,* she thought, *he should have been home by now.* She ducked around to the produce side before he could see her and picked up tomatoes, garlic, and avocados. The last thing she needed was an inane conversation with him and his groupies. *Being in the public eye must be a real drag,* she thought. In that one glance she could tell that Jared didn't know those people personally, but he felt compelled to be politically charming and engaging. *Who needs that?* Georgia thought. *Being nice when you just want to get groceries and go home?* She passed the bakery, picked up ciabatta rolls, headed for the checkout, and sighed. *It's one thing to have him pop up in dreams,* she thought, *yet quite another to see him in reality.* This lack of control on either front was really bugging her. She wanted this entire Jared thing to calm down and return to status quo. She didn't think that was asking too much.

Once at home, she listened to her messages as she put her groceries away. She then showered, flipped on a vintage Babyface CD, and jumped into her drawstring pants and tank top. She went down the back stairs to the kitchen, began to cut up veggies for a pot of stew, called her girlfriend, and talked while it simmered. Once done, she ate, cleaned her kitchen, and then took the back stairs to her office outside the master bedroom. Done in a vibrant bougainvillea-pink with white shutters and white built-in bookcases, her office housed her computer and most of the books needed to complete work at home. She liked the look of the room because it reminded her of the Caribbean, except for the treadmill right beside her desk, which she used when she got stuck and had to move around to get her energy peaked. She lived in this home office, her bedroom, kitchen, and den. The rest of the house, the living room, dining room, upstairs guest bedroom, and bath at the front of the house, was seldom used.

Georgia relished the contrast between her colorful office and her soothing bedroom. Her iron-filigreed queen-size bed sat on cream-colored carpeting, cater-corner to the window with the window seat and the small balcony overlooking her backyard garden, the same view she saw from her bathroom. A richly carved armoire between the window and the balcony hid the television and other media equipment. Her clothes were either hung or placed in built-in drawers in her walk-in closet, so her bedroom was airy and full of space where she often exercised or did yoga unencumbered. Her house was her comfort and her bedroom her sanctuary from the harsh reality of the courthouse. This was now the only place where she was sure Jared Jaymes would never be.

* * *

Georgia danced with the Staple Singers, joining in with Mavis's vocals on "Respect Yourself." She blasted her favorite song as she crowned her buttery-soft, brown Italian leather pants with a cable-stitched, cowl-necked orange sweater. She smiled approvingly at her outfit, and although it was only October, she knew Neal kept the Ice Palace cold year-round. *Certainly Neal would warm up the house when the baby came,* she thought.

A baby. Neal was having a baby. As much as he had run the streets of D.C., Georgia thought she would be the first one to settle down, marry, and have a baby—but Neal had beaten her to it. She picked up her shoulder bag, the first of many gifts for "Baby Preston" from Auntie Georgia. She sauntered down the back stairs to the kitchen, where she packed up her requested macaroni and cheese and jambalaya, grabbed her leather jacket, picked up her car keys, and headed out the front door. She spoke to her downstairs tenant as he trimmed his topiary on this gorgeous fall day. Thanks to converting her basement into a separate apartment and renting it to him, she could easily afford her house and certain indulgences in her trilogy of "Something for Everybody" baby shower gifts: the silver cup to be engraved with the baby's name once he/she was here, the head-to-toe spa day for Brenda complete with Georgia's offer to babysit, and one month's catering from Carolina Catering for the family.

Life is good, Georgia thought as she drove to the Preston home.

Neal answered the door with a big smile and

an announcement, "Here's the jambalaya that not only nourished but inspired me through three years of law school."

"Hello to you too," Georgia said as he took the dish from her.

"Crazy man. Hey, Georgia," Brenda said, and kissed her husband's best friend.

Georgia greeted the usual suspects and helped with the final touches on the ornate shower umbrella, poured the ginger ale over the lime sherbet, and announced, "Frappe's ready."

"Not for us," Neal said as he took a case of beer under his arm and began descending the stairs to the basement.

"Vying for attention already. Had to have your own party? Gotta have some boys over 'cause the girls are having a shower, huh?" Georgia called after him as his bald head hit the bottom step and he turned the corner.

The doorbell rang.

"The first guest. Let the baby shower begin!" Georgia decreed.

Once all the shower guests were present, Georgia let Neal answer the door and shepherd his boys downstairs to the basement, leaving the first-floor family room to the ladies.

Neal returned to the kitchen for reinforcements and Georgia teased, "Why not be like most ordinary, respectable fathers-to-be and vacate the premises?"

"You ought to know there's nothin' ordinary about me or my baby," he said, returning downstairs. "When you're finished up here, c'mon downstairs. We need a bar wench to serve."

"In your dreams." Georgia took more shrimp salad to the shower table. In a single, flashing millisecond, Georgia wondered if Jared would be invited to join the basement boys' party, a notion she dismissed; tennis was one thing, but Neal wouldn't do that to her or invite their boss to his home.

Once the silly baby games had been played, the gifts opened, the food devoured, and the cake cut, Georgia meandered downstairs to see what the menfolk were up to. As she descended the stairs she heard the trash-talking, glanced at the table, and walked to Neal, who was tending bar.

"Ah, the bar wench has arrived," he teased.

"Lost all your money already?" she asked Neal, and looked at the table of poker-playing men.

Then she saw him.

The sight of him stole her breath. "What is *he* doing here?"

"Who?" Neal asked.

"Who do you think? Who over there is not in a suit and tie and not at work?"

"Jared? I invited him."

"Why?"

"Because he's a good bid whist and poker player who is currently winning all the money."

"Cheez," Georgia said with a shake of her head.

Despite her exasperation, Georgia eyed Jared and couldn't help but notice the way the black knit sweater clung to his upper torso. He was so busy selling wolf-tickets he hadn't seen her yet. *Jared in the Box*, she thought. Just keeps popping out of his confines and all over her private life.

"Aw, JJ, man." A tall handsome man referred to Jared.

"Who's that?" she asked Neal of the only other stranger at the table.

"Jared's brother. The doctor."

"Of course, his brother the doctor. Doctor, lawyer . . . no Indian chief?" Georgia said sarcastically, referring to the nursery rhyme.

Jared called his brother and then threw his cards on the table with a winning flair. "Bam!"

"Ooooh," all the men yelled in unison. "You got nothin' . . . you bluffin' mother—"

"Hey, hey—lady in the house," Neal announced from the bar, and everybody turned to greet Georgia.

Jared smiled at her as he raked in the pot. She could feel the heat of him from across the room. She swooped hair behind her ear as his brother got up and came toward her.

"So you're Mac," he said, his face breaking into a smile that resembled Jared's. "I've heard a lot about you."

"Really?" She felt herself blush. She'd been discussed.

"Yeah, Neal told me all about your days in D.C."

"Oh." Georgia tried not to show her disappointment that it was Neal who'd done the discussing, not Jared.

"They must have been some wild times."

"Yes, they were." Her frozen, insincere smile stayed in place. If she didn't know better she would have sworn that Neal and Jared exchanged glances and shared a private joke. She didn't like this newfound friendship that seemed to have sprung up between the pair. She wasn't used to and didn't like being on the outside.

"You in or out?" Jared called to his brother as he began shuffling the cards.

"Let me see if I can win some of my money back from big brother."

Georgia turned to watch her boss act like a man—a crazy, funny, unpretentious, handsome black man. Had she ever thought him capable of being ordinary and down-to-earth? With his wealth, privilege, and pedigree of a white boy, she was now treated to a version of the Princeton and U Penn law graduate she didn't know existed. Apparently, Jared was comfortably fluent in both worlds.

"So, how long has this been going on?" Georgia asked the bartender. "This Jared thing?"

"We call him 'JJ' away from the office," Neal said to irk her.

"What am I, the last to know?"

"Ain't that always the way?"

Georgia cut her eyes.

"Jared and I ain't dating, Mac. We're both happy, hetero men." Neal laughed.

Georgia didn't. She stared at Neal in that disarming, pissed, no-nonsense way.

Neal caved under her gaze. "I don't know. When you begged out of the Barristers' Ball."

"Last year? How could you keep this from me for a whole year?"

"A little over a year. After your thirtieth birthday. It's a natural alliance—two good-looking, intelligent, handsome brothers who can ball and play cards." He hunched his shoulders. "It's like we've known each other longer, really. We thought it was time."

"Who thought it was 'time'? Time for what?"

"Brenda and me and that's all I'm saying or I'll ruin it and she'll have my hide," he said in his no-nonsense, you-ain't-getting-another-thing-out-of-me way.

Georgia rolled her eyes.

Neal poured her a beer and slid it to her. "His being here doesn't compromise your work situation. Hell, you didn't know Jared and I hung out after hours, and nobody at work knows either. It's called discretion."

The men roared again as Jared won another hand. The most infectious smile claimed his face. It began crinkly and warm behind his dark eyes, launching into that full-blown smile that offered those luscious lips. Had she ever seen him smile like that? He glanced her way, she involuntarily returned his smile, and he hunched his shoulders playfully.

"Hey!" The other women from the shower came down to claim their husbands and men. "Put those cards up, it's time to party!"

"So, where's Courtney?" Georgia asked Neal casually, fishing for confirmation of their breakup, and not that Courtney was just in Paris for her usual shopping trip.

"I don't know, I don't care, she can kiss my underwear." They chuckled at the childhood rhyme. "Hey, if you can do 'doctor, lawyer, Indian chief,' I get to do one too."

"You nut."

"Courtney's not a friend of Brenda's, so she

wasn't invited. Besides, I told you they broke up."
He offered a big, cheesy, insincere grin. "And
why should that matter to you?"

"It doesn't," Georgia answered too quickly,
and went upstairs to start cleaning up.

When Georgia returned to the basement, she
descended into the throngs of a full-fledged
party. The women had been successful in claim-
ing their men and they were dancing up a storm.
Georgia's body responded to the rhythm of Lake-
side's "Fantastic Voyage."

"Old school!" Neal yelled over the din. "Party
over here!"

The sight of so many happy black people giving
their bodies up to the beat made Georgia laugh.
When was the last time she'd been to a house
party? When the Cha Cha Slide came on, Georgia
jumped in and let the syncopated groove take her
away. When she did the third turn, Jared was
by her side. She didn't care, she was having too
good a time to let her boss ruin it. The Booty Call
and Cuban Shuffle followed and she and Jared
matched steps to perfection. He was shattering all
her perceptions of him. Had she ever thought he
had a brother, played cards, or could dance like
he was dancing now? He didn't learn this as an Ivy
Leaguer. His body held controlled energy as
his muscles rippled subtly under his black knit
shirt, and his feet kept perfect rhythm. He was the
personification of "cool." He smiled. He had a
dimple on his left side. Had she known that?

When the Spinners volleyed into "Could It Be
I'm Falling in Love?" Georgia and Jared broke
into laughter as he grabbed her hand and began

hand-dancing. Georgia hadn't been dazzled, turned, and spun around like this since her dance buddy Gerald Shamwell at Roosevelt High in Evelyn, Tennessee. The crowd had to give them space and Georgia basked in the sheer exhilaration of showcasing her dancing prowess with such a skillful partner. They owned the floor.

The pace slowed when Isaac Hayes crooned "I Stand Accused" and, as naturally as if they'd done it a million times, Jared slid his arm around Georgia's waist and she leaned into him. She panted from the last four fast records, or was it the nearness of Jared that made her breathless? Isaac's deep, sexy, mellow voice silenced everyone, who was happy for the slow-drag reprieve. All that was missing was a blue light in the basement and watchful parents upstairs in the kitchen. Jared held Georgia close. She felt the rise and fall of her breasts against Jared's chest. His hands spread across the expanse of her back, and though he kept a respectful distance, her cheek nestled into his. She could feel his breath on her ear, and like in the dream, it felt like mentholated cool. He smelled like a man who'd bathed and splashed on aftershave earlier, but the aroma had been replaced by a good time . . . a natural, seductive earthiness. As Isaac declared he was "guilty for loving you," Georgia's eyes closed and her body melted into the rhythm established by this man. Not her boss—this man. It had been such a long time since she'd been held with tenderness and authority. She gladly surrendered herself to his adept movements as their hips rotated against each other's, their legs straddled, forcing their thighs to rub against each other's. Luther Vandross took up where Isaac left off, singing about how "amazing" love was, and the connection between Georgia and Jared remained unbroken.

In too short a span, James Brown yelled, forcing their eyes open and yanking Georgia back from the fanciful edge with "The Big Payback." Reluctantly, Georgia and Jared separated and began snapping their fingers to get their feet to move into a fast dance. Georgia could not meet Jared's eyes. She didn't want to see what was there, whether it was deep desire or casual flirtation. She told herself she was ready for neither; especially from her boss, who was probably still attached. She needed to center herself again, get her defenses up again. So regardless of what she saw in his eyes, she could handle it. She needed to keep him at bay and put this dalliance in perspective. James then belted out "I Got That Feelin'" next and it was cathartic for her to chant "baby, baby, baby. Baby, baby, baby" with everyone else.

At the end of that record, Neal cut the music off and Brenda joined him. Jared stood behind Georgia. She thought they looked too much like a couple, so she walked to the other side of the room away from Jared. As Georgia struggled to regain her composure, Neal thanked everyone for coming, talked about the importance of good friends, and thought this was the best time to announce the godparents he and Brenda had selected.

"In one way it was easy, 'cause some of you are

really triflin' and I wouldn't let you be godparents to my dog—if I had one," Neal joked, and they laughed. "In another way, it was hard, 'cause you have to pick someone you wouldn't mind raising your child if something were to happen to Brenda and I couldn't cope."

"Ah! Kill me off?" Brenda protested playfully.

"Someone with good values, good sense, good heart, and money enough to raise my kid in a fashion we couldn't."

Everybody laughed again.

"Unfortunately, we couldn't decide on a couple, which would have been ideal, so we picked individuals. Which is good because when they marry other people—that means my little guy—"

"Or girl," Brenda interjected. "Okay, you're rambling—"

"Godmother is Mac," Neal said, and pointed.

Georgia gasped, totally moved by the honor.

"You've been though thick and thin with me," Neal said to her. "Told me that Brenda was the woman for me before even I realized it. Next to Bren, we couldn't think of a better woman in our child's life. You'll be an excellent godmom since it doesn't look like you're going to get to be a mom on your own."

"Oooooh," the crowd chimed as Georgia punched his arm.

"Maybe we should rethink this," Neal said to Brenda. "She's kinda belligerent."

"I love you guys. Thanks," Georgia said as she fought back tears and the three hugged.

"Okay, enough mush," Neal said. "Now goddaddy. My old male friends are tired. You know you are. I'll keep you when I become rich and famous, but you're not good enough for my kid. So I went with someone I haven't known for a lot of years although it feels like it. He's a stand-up guy, has great values, and is already a role model for plenty of folks . . . so why not my kid? JJ. Jared Jaymes."

Obvious shock registered on Jared's face as he accepted back slaps from folks nearby.

But he was not as shocked as Georgia.

"Do you accept?" Neal asked.

"I'm honored, man," Jared said, his face breaking into a huge smile as they exchanged the black-brother handshake. "Thanks."

"Cool. Okay, let's get back to partying." Neal put the music back on.

Damn, Georgia thought. Was there no relief in sight? She was going to be tied to Jared at work not only for as long as she remained an ADA, but now, forever after in her private life as they shared a godchild. It was like cold water thrown on a best moment. She wouldn't let her reaction ruin this for Neal and Brenda, yet she couldn't stay and participate. Saddled with JJ all her life? Georgia had to go.

"Congratulations, godmother," Jared said with a smile.

"You too."

"I've been an uncle but never a godfather."

"Imagine. I got to go."

"What? It's early."

"I have to get up and go to church tomorrow," she lied, hoping God wouldn't strike her dead.

"Oh, what church?"

"Why? Are you going to show up there too?" *And just where is Courtney?* was on the tip of her tongue. If Georgia could just confirm that her boss and Courtney were still involved and on their way to marriage, that would guarantee that Georgia would have no opening to pursue him as she would never be attracted to an attached male. A Jared and Courtney coupling would quiet her heart, which was raging against the common sense of her mind.

Georgia didn't like the feel of any of this and suddenly she felt disgusted and ill. An orgy of colliding emotions fueled by alcohol, heat, and Jared being so close, violating her space, made her feel faint. Like Tourette ticks that burst forth with no rhyme or reason, questions and feelings swirled around her, taunting her with obscure absurdities. If Neal was teasing, and Jared and Courtney were still an item, did this mean that Jared just wanted someone to play with while his girlfriend was away? Was Jared trying to cast her in the role of the "other woman"? Why did it feel like he was married, but was looking for a convenient work-thing, on the side? A change of pace, like ice cream for breakfast, and once the novelty wore off he'd return to his basic sustenance of bacon and eggs—he'd return to Courtney. Georgia was no man's dessert; she was the main meal or he could just starve. None of these scenarios were what Georgia wanted. All were just what Georgia swore would never happen to her—never date her boss, never date an attached male, never be anyone's backup woman or booty call. As she began threading her way toward her hosts to say good-bye, she remembered the old saying—what you truly fear, you will create.

What have you learned from this situation? she mentally quizzed herself, trying to restore reason and control and make sense out of nonsense. Her heart answered that, now with Jared so close, so attentive, so gorgeous, at least she understood how some women could be seduced into the worst role of their lives—second best. But not Georgia MacKenzie, her mind retaliated. Not in this life.

"I'll walk you to your car," Jared was saying over her shoulder as he followed her through the crowd.

"That's not necessary," she threw back at Jared. "Thanks, you two." Georgia reached and hugged Neal and Brenda.

"You all leaving already?" Brenda, wrapped in Neal's slow dance embrace, asked.

"No. *I'm* leaving now. He seems determined to walk me to my car like I'm helpless and have never been alone."

The three of them looked at her. Only Jared had a bemused expression on his face.

"Godfathers need to protect godmothers," Jared said. "We're almost family."

"Godmothers can take care of themselves. Neal, can I get that Holmes brief?"

"Now?" Neal asked.

"Yes. I'll work on it tomorrow afternoon."

Georgia followed Neal upstairs to his office off the kitchen.

Neal knew his strong-willed friend would be

upset with his choice of godfather, but he'd hoped he wouldn't have to deal with it tonight.

Georgia closed the office door behind them and assaulted him. "Would you introduce me to a married man to date?"

"Of course not." Neal scowled indignantly.

"If I were an atheist and you a Christian, would you hound me to go to church every Sunday?"

Neal shook his head in response.

"As a nonsmoker, would you encourage or offer me cigarettes? Serve me red meat if I were a vegetarian? Give me sugar if I were diabetic?"

Neal had stopped responding in defeat.

"Then why the hell do you keep pushing Jared Jaymes into my private space when you know how I feel about office relationships? You stomp on my beliefs. What kind of friend does that, Neal? Jared is bad for my mental and career health." She stopped to rephrase her statement. "Getting involved with my boss on any level other than professional would be out of the question. It's unethical."

"I disagree. Stupid, but not unethical."

"You don't get a vote, Neal. I didn't ask your opinion. I am not confused on the subject. These are *my* principles. *My* values you are trashing. I would not do that to you. Friends are supposed to support friends."

Neal did not like his loyalty attacked and snapped, "So I'm supposed to deny my kid the two best people on the planet as godparents because one does not like the other."

"You know that's not the issue. I respect and admire Jared as my boss. I've learned so much from him. But I do not and will not know him as a man."

"Then don't. That's not up to me, Mac," he sniped. "Hold up, so you're telling me that you don't have enough self-control around him and I have to police your emotions?"

"Don't get it twisted, Neal."

"So you're willing to give up being godmother 'cause of Jared?"

"That's ridiculous."

"It's all ridiculous, Mac. By the time my kid can walk, Jared will be mayor and you'll probably be either a judge or a DA of Philly. You'll both marry other people and the whole thing will be moot in five years."

Georgia didn't know what to object to first, his personal or his professional attack. If, who, or when she married, taking a judgeship—and she never wanted Jared's job.

Georgia and Neal glared at each other—both stubborn, and hopping mad; she at his betrayal and he at her audacity. Both seething and neither of them daring to budge.

Moments passed then Neal relented and said, "Dead right."

It was a truce they'd established in law school when they were on opposing sides of an argument and neither would give in. They both thought themselves "right" about an issue and for the sake of their friendship, the issue would be "dead" between them. Georgia didn't want to agree to disagree about an issue so important to her. In that moment, she felt a little of their relationship die. That he would choose to dismiss her principles for his own selfishness showed a true color she didn't know he had on his palate. That he'd picked newcomer Jared over her long-standing values hurt. As his friend she would never have challenged any ideal Neal so vehemently believed in. *But, unfortunately, we are not our own best friends,* she thought.

"Dead right," Georgia finally agreed. Neal handed her the file and she opened the door just as Jared was coming up the steps.

"Ready?" Jared asked Georgia.

She grabbed her pocketbook and sprinted out the front door like Cinderella scurrying home to beat the clock's midnight strike, when all her vulnerabilities would be exposed. She walked toward her car. Behind her red sports coupe was the imposing slate-black-on-black Hummer H3.

"Look at that!" She pointed out their cars to Jared, and thought, *We are so wrong for each other on so many levels.* That truck could run right over her little car, smash it, and leave it devastated in the H3's wake without even putting a scratch on its black finish. Jared could do that to her. Run her over, smash her up, ruin her career, marry Courtney, be mayor, and what would Georgia MacKenzie be? The brunt of behind-the-back whispers, "she was ADA who used to date Jared Jaymes. The girl who used to have a brilliant career ahead of her before she dated, and was dismissed by, Jared Jaymes." Georgia wasn't raised to be a footnote in anybody's life.

"What?" a perplexed Jared asked. "My truck and your car?"

Obviously, he didn't get her reference. She

didn't want to explain it to him. She couldn't explain it to him. She tried to gather her fragmented thoughts. Why did he rattle her so? She breathed deeply and told herself that he was just a coworker walking her to her car. He was her boss. Jared would walk any woman to her car, he was raised that way. He probably thought she was crazy or just PMS-ing. But feelings when he held her close had happened tonight that she hadn't expected, and she needed to regroup. She struggled to be cordial and professional. She still had to work with the man. He still controlled her work flow, case assignments, pay raises, holiday leave, and vacation time.

"Listen. Thanks for walking me to my car. And . . . I'll see you Monday. Good night." With that she started her car and drove off. She was shaking. In her rearview mirror she watched his image get smaller and smaller until he was out of sight. But he might as well have been sitting on her hood, butt-naked. The dreams about him had become fewer, maybe because her subconscious no longer needed to bring him to her— her consciousness had taken over. She'd have to back Mr. Jared Jaymes up into his place every time he overstepped his bounds.

It takes two to tango and he'll be out there on the dance floor by himself, she thought. She was on her own. Clearly, Neal didn't feel any responsibility to her. She punched a smooth jazz station. The sound of a sexy soprano sax filled the car, Kenny G or Najee, she didn't know which or care. She didn't want any lyrics or reminders on her ride home, just soothing sounds, fresh air, and controlled breathing.

As she drove, her disappointment in Neal remained the same, but, she had to admit, he was right. In five years this all would be moot. She and Jared and his wife would share godparenting duties for birthdays, graduations, and holidays. In five years—in five years she'd be thirty-six. In five years she'd be—

"Holy moly," Georgia said aloud.

In five years where would she be? What would she be doing? What did she want to be doing? At this point, all she knew was what she did not want. She didn't want a restrictive judgeship or the unpredictable, gargantuan responsibility of being DA or to be the wife of a public figure . . . like mayor.

But what do you want, Georgia MacKenzie? she asked herself.

It was with a sudden, jolting clarity that she realized that she'd been working so hard doing her job and living that, for the first time in six years, she had no five-year plan. How was that possible? How had she let something so important slide? That was why she felt so out of control, adrift, and scattered. That was why she didn't feel anchored because she had no plan with specific goals in place to work toward. She was career-oriented enough to know that once she established goals it would be clear to her what the course of action would be—to achieve said goals. It had been that way all her life . . . from being "Willow" in preschool to law school to the DA's office in Philly. Now what?

After winning a few high-profile cases she'd been offered positions at prestigious law firms in both L.A. and New York City, but neither appealed to her at the time. L.A. and New York were polar opposites of the same spectrum— L.A. too laid-back and New York too intense. She liked Philly, this City of Brotherly Love. And while she wasn't ready to jump out there on her own, she relished the idea of joining a downtown law firm where she could do pro bono work: take on tobacco conglomerates or HMOs or sink her teeth into environmental law. Her ideal firm would be a family-friendly position, which would allow her to marry, have children, volunteer for their field trips, and be home by three in time to meet the school bus. Or maybe she'd teach at one of the universities once the children came, or be a legal analyst for one of the network news stations.

Georgia laughed out loud with relief. Exploring her options both excited and calmed her. After her Cusamano win she'd turn her attention to seriously perusing her options.

Unexpectedly, all the weirdness lifted from her mind, body, and soul. All this time she had thought her restlessness and uncharacteristic lack of control, the dreams, and all the other craziness had to do with Jared Jaymes—and it didn't. It was all her—her lack of direction and her need for another career challenge. Neal was right, in five years it wouldn't matter—well, in five minutes it hadn't. She went home, showered, prepared for bed still giddy from her epiphany.

It had nothing to do with Jared, she thought again as she cut out the light.

Georgia was thankful she didn't pursue a relationship with him. What an occupational mess that would have been. To have been on a few dates and discovered that there was nothing there . . . but scatterbrained boredom and internal chaos. How do you ease out of that dilemma, rejecting your boss with "Oops, my mistake. I'm not attracted to you after all. Sorry"? Yet another reason you should not date your boss. Having not gone that route, she could now use him as a reference for future positions. She smiled into a stream of moonlight.

That night she slept like an innocent child— deep, satisfying, and dreamless. Her lost mind had returned, and arrogantly assumed its rightful place at control center.

Her heart, on the other hand, chuckled.

Chapter 4

Jared watched Georgia's car pull away from the curb and blend into the darkness. He looked up at the clear black night with the full luminous moon and inhaled the cool air lightly scented with smoke from someone's fireplace. On this evening his feelings about Georgia MacKenzie had done a 180. He didn't know what to name the connection he felt to Georgia, but naming it or not, it was clearly there. He only wondered if it had been there all along buried beneath the surface. He wondered if the feeling was the reason he couldn't totally commit to Courtney, or was this feeling with Georgia brand-new—a natural progression borne from respect and propinquity?

He shoved his hands into his pockets and walked back toward Neal's house. After tonight he knew a few things. Like it or not, he knew how he felt about Georgia MacKenzie. When he took her in his arms on that slow dance and held her . . . he knew. She felt like "home," like no woman had before her and no woman would hereafter. Her warm, tender body fit perfectly into the contours of his, like she belonged there. When Isaac Hayes's lyrics accused Jared of loving her— Jared knew he was guilty. He didn't know for how long or when it had happened, but it could not be denied. When Neal announced them as godparents, Jared knew that some cosmic force was sealing them together forever. Jared couldn't have planned it any better; he was ecstatic and leery.

After five years of working with her, he also knew Georgia MacKenzie. He knew she would resist any feelings she had for him because he was her boss. That was evident in the way she scurried to the other side of the room after they danced, and the way she sped away from here just moments ago. She had her principles on office dalliances, principles he had shared until Georgia MacKenzie tested, and then mocked them in the sweetest way.

Jared knew that his entire world had changed and Georgia MacKenzie was the last piece of his life's puzzle. Years ago he had questioned whether he really wanted to be mayor. He had the drive to get there, but not the interest to stay there; his ambition was compelled by the journey, not the destination. As it was, outside of work, he had little time for anything else but the pursuit of the mayor's office and he wanted more. At the time he had a woman who wanted him to be mayor even more than he did. After being privy to the never-ending demands of the office, he had cooled on the notion, and her, and their relationship had limped to its inevitable end about two months ago. Since then Jared had enjoyed the little pleasures of a commitment-free weekend—

washing his truck, cutting his own grass, leisurely shopping at the grocery store, performing community service, playing racquetball and cards with friends. Now that his weekends weren't submerged under "sociopolitical, meet-and-greet obligations," on Saturday nights he looked forward to falling asleep in front of an old movie he'd seen a thousand times. He savored waking late on a Sunday morning and reading the paper from front to back before cooking, then eating his own meals. He relished playing the piano all day until his fingers ached. He valued being an ordinary Joe, enjoying his own house, playing his music loudly, and even thought about getting a dog or going on a vacation. Originally, after being mayor for a term or two, he had planned to set up his own downtown practice and give Willie Gary's and Johnnie Cochran's offices a run for their money. As of late, he'd outgrown any mayoral interest or aspirations and fast-forwarded to establishing his own law firm. Yet with all his enjoyment and plans he hadn't moved on it. Something was missing—*someone* was missing and her identity became crystal clear to him on this night. It was like what the Wizard of Oz told the Tin Man—who and what he wanted was there all along.

Georgia MacKenzie rounded out his wish list. She was the woman who was missing from the quiet evenings at home. She was a woman who respected, not only a balance, but a separation of home and work. On a wintry Saturday night, she would be content nuzzling in front of a roaring fire and not want to be someplace else. She was a woman who'd want to raise her own children, not leave them in the care of nannies before farming them out to prestigious boarding schools. She would want to attend PTA meetings, volunteer for field trips, and make cookies for the bake sales. She was a "death do you part," "through thick and thin" woman. Jared wanted her to be his woman, his wife and life partner. There was nothing else in the world he'd rather do than wake up to Georgia sleeping beside him. When he was ninety years old, he wanted to die loving Georgia MacKenzie. That would be his greatest accomplishment, privilege, and joy.

Clearly, he could not challenge, push, or even cajole himself into Georgia's life—she could be stubborn, willful, and decisive. He'd have to woo her. He'd never wooed a woman before. But then, he'd never felt so unambiguous about his feelings for a woman before; at least that was how he felt now. He hoped his feelings weren't the result of a magical night with good food, good friends, good wine, and a good woman to whom he was suddenly and unequivocally attracted. He didn't think so, but time would tell. He smiled and walked back into Neal's house.

"Mac get off okay?" Neal asked.

"Yeah," Jared replied. A smile claimed his face at the thought of her.

"Interesting woman, huh?" Neal broached.

"One of a kind."

"I object." Georgia sprang to her feet demanding the attention of the judge, defense lawyers, jury, and spectators. "Yet *another* surprise witness, Your Honor?"

She listened to the defense attorney explain how this person had just come forward and heard the judge allow it. Her impatience was showing and when it came time to cross-examine, she questioned how he could be Cusamano's alibi when the witness was locked up in County on a robbery charge at the time. Georgia had successfully discredited another witness and was insulted by the elementary delay tactics that anyone who'd watched one episode of *Perry Mason* or *Matlock* could figure out.

At the day's end, Georgia gathered her notes when the lawyer for the defense approached her. "Perhaps you shouldn't dismiss the surprise witnesses so quickly, Counselor."

"Then give me credible witnesses," Georgia dismissed, filing papers in her attaché.

"You do know that Cusamano is Carmine Caprese's nephew."

Georgia stopped and looked him in the eye. "Are you giving me a genealogy lesson?" She raised one eyebrow. "I certainly hope so. I would hate to think that you are threatening an officer of the court," she said loud enough for everyone within earshot to hear. "Because if you are, that is a federal offense and you will be needing a lawyer as well." She cut her eyes, yanked up her briefcase, spun around, and let her heels punctuate her exasperation on the marble floor.

Following her from the courtroom, Neal asked, "Should you be antagonizing the Caprese family?"

"Inept lawyer, a soft judge apparently intimidated by the Caprese connection. Face it—Cusamano is a sacrificial lamb. He was apparently freelancing, trying to impress his uncle, when he killed that man and the innocent bystanders. The Capreses are not going to back him—DNA or no."

"I dunno. You never know when the Mob sister starts crying on her Mob brother's shoulder about her baby boys . . . anything can happen."

"Not with that shyster defending him. We need to stop wasting everybody's time and the taxpayers' money. These victims' families need closure."

Later that day, Georgia was finishing up research on another case. She massaged her neck and looked through the double panes of glass. Jared was still in his office. She kept working. When darkness claimed her desk and the skyline lit up behind her, Georgia clicked on her desk lamp and glanced over at Jared again. He was preparing to leave. She went back to work, hoping he wouldn't come by to say good night. The only recipe for maintaining a professional relationship with him was keeping her distance until this strangeness blew over. She heard claps of thunder as rain pelted her window. Lightning sizzled across the black sky and she hoped the building wouldn't lose power. She didn't want to be stuck here at night alone. When she checked her flashlight in her top drawer, she noticed that Jared's coat and hat hung on the rack, but he wasn't in his office. Her lamp flickered and she decided to use this opportunity to beat him out. She gathered her coat and briefcase and spirited to the elevator. After what seemed like an eternity, it finally came with a loud *ding*. The door eased open. She got on. Then she heard his voice, "Hold the elevator, please."

She didn't move a muscle. "Close. Close," she prayed.

He held out his hand to stop the door. "Thanks."

Was he being sarcastic? she wondered.

"It's really raining out there," he said as he punched the first-floor button.

"It's that time of year."

"When you work late like this, you should have the guard walk you to your car."

"I've been doing this for almost six years." *And you've never been interested before*, she thought.

"Doesn't make it right. You've been lucky."

"Lucky me."

She watched the numbers light up as the elevator descended. Being surly was the only way she could keep her feelings about him in the box labeled "boss." Despite her antagonistic stance, her all-too-smitten heart was happy to see him. She felt all four chambers swell at the sight of him and Georgia was pissed at her wayward emotions. She'd decided that it was her lack of a five-year plan that had caused her the temporary insanity, yet all her eyes needed to do was see the man and her heart took off again. Like babysitting a child who'd just blurted out a confidence, she felt betrayed, but in control.

With a jolt, the elevator stopped.

Jared punched the first-floor button but there was no movement.

"Well, looks like my luck just ran out," Georgia said with a sigh.

The elevator went black, and then a dull amber light shone as Jared picked up the emergency phone. Georgia listened to him report the problem and noted how, after ten hours of work, his shirt collar still looked starched and fresh. His back was expansive, his posture superb, and even in a crisis, he was cool, calm, and composed.

"Well, it'll be a while. Might as well get comfortable," he said, setting down his briefcase and loosening his tie.

Georgia breathed out deeply. She was not ready to test her resolve with Jared and her five-year-plan-theory. "Is it hot in here?" she asked, setting her briefcase down and taking off her coat.

"It's a little close."

"I'm not a lover of tight places." She turned her attaché on its back and sat upon it. She kicked off her heels and crossed her ankles in front of her.

Jared couldn't help but notice her shapely brown legs as he removed his jacket and slung it over the rail. He sat on his attaché, put his hat on his knee, and recalled when those pretty caramel legs were crowned with white tennis shorts and rested on his thigh. He still had her sock. They sat in opposite corners of the small cubicle, but their long legs almost touched in the center.

Despite her best efforts, images of Jared holding her ankle whirled in her head. The dim light of the elevator provided an intimacy that made her equally uncomfortable; they could have been sitting at a table for two in a small jazz club waiting for a set to begin. She closed her eyes so she couldn't see him, but she could feel his presence, smell the remnants of aftershave, hear his breathing, and remember how he had held her when they slow-dragged in Neal's basement. How his solid body felt against hers. How his hands caressed her back. How his breathing timed with hers.

Her stomach growled.

They chuckled and he asked," Hungry?"

"Always."

From the inside pocket of his expensive suit he fished out an Almond Joy, opened it, and offered her half.

"My favorite. Thank you."

"I thought Snickers were your favorite." He looked at her casually and smiled.

Georgia chuckled and said, "Okay, my second favorite." He had a way of disarming her—of looking like a viable, available man. She bit into the chocolate and coconut, and crunched on the almond. "Ummm. Nectar of the gods."

"Ready to wrap up the Cusamano case?" he asked, trying to keep his composure as he watched her skirt rise above her knees and inch up her taut thighs.

"Been ready. Should have been open and shut but the judge sucks."

"That's judicial terminology I'm not quite familiar with."

She laughed, happy to dispel some of the tension.

"That would be a Brody-Mac-Jr. term," she

offered laughingly. "And you have to say it all in one word like that. Because just plain Brody or Big Brody Mac would be my dad."

"Is he? Big?"

"Yes, he was. Big physically, spiritually, big of heart—until it failed and the doctor promised him one, but the hospital gave it to somebody else."

Jared then realized that her father had been the reason she'd been so uncharacteristically passionate about the "breach of promise" argument that had begun this odyssey of new feelings for him. He imagined Georgia arguing in vain for her father to get the promised heart. He wondered how old she was when her dad died. Was that the impetus for her to become a lawyer? There were so many things he wanted to know about her. What her dreams were. What turned her on—what turned her off. What she slept in. What was the last thing she thought about at night, or her first thought in the morning. What sounds she'd make when they first kissed or made love. *All in due time*, he told himself. *Slow and easy wins the race.* He'd like to think that maybe Big Brody Mac started the argument between them so something could happen to change their lives and bring them together. He hoped Big Brody Mac was on his side, pulling his daughter's heartstrings from above. He needed all the help he could get.

"It was hard," Georgia continued absently, "to watch a big vital man reduced to a raisin on a white hospital sheet. In the end, he didn't resemble my daddy at all."

"But his spirit is always with you."

"Yes." Georgia smiled thinking of her daddy. "Yes, it is." She rested her head against the elevator's back panel and thought, *That was a nice thing for Jared to say.* Her stomach grumbled again. "Let's see what I have." She jumped at the distraction and found a Snickers in her purse. "Voilá!" They laughed. She unwrapped the candy bar and offered him the top part. "Now if we just had a couple of swallows of bottled water—this would be a gourmet meal."

"Best meal?" he asked her playfully.

"Besides now? Let's see. A succulent leg of lamb, roasted asparagus with olive oil, and a sprinkle of Parmesan cheese. Oh, no, wait. A big, juicy hamburger," she said with a wide smile. "Right off the grill with a toasted bun. Nothing says summer like a hamburger right off the grill. And with winter bearing down upon us—I want to hold on to a little summer."

"A woman who still eats beef. Novel."

"I'm a carnivore. How about you? Best meal?"

"Steak, medium rare, au gratin potatoes, Caesar salad, my grandma's iced tea, bread pudding, and divinity."

"Divinity?" Georgia chuckled. "What does an uptown, Ivy League northern boy know about 'divinity'? That's a southern, sweet rot-your-teeth candy—"

"I know what it is."

"What'd you do, *read* about it?"

"I was born in the South."

"Oh, c'mon. You were not. When'd you come up here?"

"When I was two . . . but my brother and I went back every summer until middle school."

Georgia laughed and surmised that his traveling south each summer was the reason for his genteel manners.

"Then it was karate and music lessons, swim clubs, tennis camps, and golf clinics," Georgia said.

"How'd you know?" Jared looked over at her sideways and smiled.

"I *read* too," she said with a laugh.

"So you believe me when I say my grandma Hattie Mae makes the best divinity?"

"You have a grandma Hattie Mae?"

"Hattie Mae Jaymes," he said proudly.

"Well. I say we have to have a Christmas bake-off. Your grandma Hattie Mae and my grandma Mac send their divinity up here for a taste test."

"You're on."

A smile split those luscious lips and Georgia watched his temperamental dimple appear. She supposed he reserved it for special times.

"I don't know, Jaymes," she said. "I may have to rethink some things about you."

"Is that a good thing?"

"Well, you don't appear to be the stuck-up preppie, bourgie man I thought you were. I figured you fell asleep on the Weather Channel and awoke to *Mozart in the Morning*."

"I do," he teased, "but I also cook, iron, and have a seasoned cast-iron skillet that makes the best fried chicken in all of Philly."

"Oh? I'll be the judge of that."

"Will you?" He stopped laughing and caused her to do the same.

His dark, ebony eyes gleamed in the dim amber light and seemed to cradle hers in his gaze. She looked at the way the pale yellow light painted the ends of his long lashes gold. It was hot and quiet and they were caught in a controlled environment where real feelings ricocheted off the fake wood grain of the cubicle. It was one of those organic moments in time when almost anything was possible—if you just let it happen, naturally. She felt relaxed, content, and easy. She sensed her mind had deserted her some time ago, leaving her heart to celebrate in reckless abandon, and fully buy his masquerade as a handsome, available man.

The elevator rattled, a door opened three floors above them, and a voice yelled, "Mr. Jaymes?"

"Yes," Jared said, standing, placing his fedora on his head.

"We'll get you out in a second, sir. The fire department is here."

"Thank you." He extended his hands to Georgia and lifted her to her feet and into him.

"Fire department?" It was hot. She was hot. She could use the fire department to extinguish all the heat he was generating in her. She melted physically and mentally, dissolving in his gentlemanly embrace—a slow dance without music. Their lips were inches apart. Desire whirled around them like a breezy maelstrom and she wanted to kiss him. She wanted to be kissed by him. She leaned into him, feeling every inch of him on every inch of her, but he made no effort to meet her halfway. "Thank you," she managed huskily, and stepped away from him to get her shoes and coat.

With all the restraint he could muster, Jared fought the impulse to grab and kiss her. It was too soon and he didn't want to jeopardize the connection they'd just made. He wanted to build on it. He put on his jacket, pulling his French cuffs through the sleeves. As the elevator began to move he asked as casually as he could, "How about a bite to eat?" He went over and straightened her coat collar and saw trepidation in her eyes. "Nothing fancy. Let's see if we can find you a grilled hamburger."

Georgia looked up into his eyes and smiled. "I'd like that."

He tossed his patented smile at her in answer, then said, "Good."

The elevator door slid open and a flood of flashing lights from the press blinded them both. Automatically, Jared tried protecting Georgia from the attack of the media's lights.

Courtney bounded in. "Jared!" She embraced the surprised DA in view of the bright cameras, posing perfectly for a few shots.

"Slow news night, fellas?" Jared asked as he unhooked Courtney's arms from around his neck and watched Georgia as she slid off to the side, past the reporters, and down the stairs to the garage.

"And there she is. Courtney!" Georgia said as she entered the parking garage. *I knew it wasn't over*, she thought. *I knew she wouldn't give up on a guy like Jared Jaymes. She gave him a month's space, time to really miss her, but now she's come back for the kill and claim.* That is, if what Neal said was ever true. They probably never broke up.

"Wise up, Georgia," she said to herself as she made her way down the rows to her car. "Just keep your distance. Tomorrow's headlines will read 'DA Jaymes Trapped in Elevator.'" *They dog that man's every move,* she thought.

Georgia reached her car. She dropped her keys, bent to pick them up, and when she did a man grabbed her from behind, slammed her against the car, and choke-held her with a knife-point at her throat. She dropped her attaché as she struggled to breathe and spotted the Born To Kill tattoo on his forearm.

"You don't know me, lawyer lady." His foul, funky breath assaulted her. "The name is Cusamano and I'm here to tell you that the next surprise witness we throw your way, you better take. If not, I may have to kill you 'cause my brother ain't going back to jail. *Capishe*?"

He held her so tightly around her neck that Georgia didn't have enough room to nod her head in agreement. Her eyes scoured the vacant garage for help as she tried to pry his arm from around her neck so she could breathe.

"If my brother don't get off, I'm going off—on you. I might die, but you'll die first. That's a Crazy Cusamano promise."

The door swung open at the far end and two firemen entered the garage to check the elevator at the ground floor.

"If I only had a gun I could kill 'em both," Cusamano whispered, unfazed by her or them.

"Don't forget what I said, lawyer lady. Or it will be more than the elevator that gets stuck next time." He released her, retracted his switchblade, and disappeared. She slumped against her car. The free intake of air caused her to cough as she fumbled with her key button to unlock the door. She was trembling.

"You all right, miss?" one of the firemen yelled from the opposite end of the garage.

She waved at him, buzzed herself into her car, threw in her attaché, and closed and locked the door.

Neal followed Georgia into her office after the Monday case review and said, "You look like hell."

"Gee. Thanks." Georgia sank wearily into her leather chair.

"I mean to everybody else you look your usual pulled-together designer self, but I'm not everybody and your eyes look tired. They remind me of the all-nighters we used to pull in law school."

Neal was right. She hadn't slept since the threat last Tuesday. This past Saturday and Sunday, she'd nodded off during the days and jumped at every shadow and noise all night. She was exhausted physically, mentally, and emotionally. She was running on "E" and decided to tell Neal about the threat. "I had a little conversation with Crazy Cusamano last Tuesday night—" she began.

"How's that?"

When she finished, Neal stared at her disbelievingly and said, "Georgia, this threat doesn't go into the dismiss file." He looked her square in the eye. "You have to tell Jared."

"Ugh! I shouldn't have told you."

"The hell you say!"

"I've been threatened before and I'll be threatened again. It's an occupational hazard that comes with the territory. It's been almost a week and nothing has happened. I've discredited another witness and I'm still here."

Neal shot her a wild glare.

"Okay, okay. *I'll* tell Jared. At least let me retain some professional dignity and not have a colleague report it."

"Better he finds out at your funeral?" he sniped sarcastically. "You better tell him or I will, Mac."

"Yet another threat?"

Neal gave her an impatient look.

"*I* will tell him." She dismissed him with a roll of her eyes.

Somehow she thought that if she'd say it out loud, the threat would lose power and go away. She told Neal because she wanted him to say, "Oh, you got threatened again? Me too." But instead he'd alarmed her even more.

Once home she locked her doors and turned on her security system. With the drop in temperature, she noticed the rain had turned to ice and coated the streets in front of her house. *It's a proven fact that crooks don't come out in bad weather*, she told herself. *But what about murderers?* she wondered.

She looked outside again and the car with the man in it was still parked across the street. *Now I'm just being paranoid*, she thought. She cut off the lights like she was going to bed and went upstairs to the front guest room and looked out the window. He was still there. At 1:00 a.m., he was still there. She called the cops. "This is ADA MacKenzie. I've been threatened and there's been a dark maroon car parked across the street since seven this evening."

"We'll send someone right out."

Moments later, Georgia saw the silent, flashing red light up her quiet neighborhood. She watched the policemen approach the man, pull him out then frisk him against the car. The falling sleet caught the red light's glow and painted the naked tree branches crimson, illuminating the entire scene, giving it an eerily festive aura. Georgia then watched them walk the man from the car up her icy front steps. The bell chimed.

"I don't need to meet him," Georgia said to herself as she answered the bell.

She opened the door to find two cops—and Jared.

"Well, at least you had sense to report *me* to the cops. You needed to report Cusamano," Jared began before she could.

"I don't need you to tell me what I need to do and don't do."

"Apparently, you do."

The cops eyed each other and one said to the other, "I guess they know each other."

"If this is going to be a domestic—" the other cop began.

"There is no domestic in this," Georgia spat. "You can take District Attorney Jaymes with you."

"What?" the cop said, and scrutinized Jared. "Oh, I didn't recognize you—in those clothes, sir."

"The judge has ordered twenty-four-hour surveillance to begin at seven a.m. until Cusamano is apprehended. But I want it begun for Ms. MacKenzie ASAP. Thanks."

"Sure thing," the policemen said, and began negotiating the icy steps.

"You can go too," Georgia said.

"I'm not going anywhere unless you come with me. We can go to my house."

"What? I'm safe and sound at home and this is where I'm staying until it's time to go to work."

"Safe and sound? That's why you called the cops on me because you're safe?"

"You're a strange man in a strange car outside my house. I'd have called on a normal night. Now, if you were in that tank you call a car—I would have known it was you and let you stay out there in the ice storm and freeze."

"Obviously, it's a rental—"

"Like those clothes?" She eyed the loud red-and-black-plaid jacket and shirt, and the duck-hunting hat with the flaps in place of his stylish fedora. "We've got a few days before Halloween." She tried to swallow a laugh, but the sight of the impeccably dapper Jared Jaymes looking like Elmer Fudd was too much to bear.

"What? It's my new look. You don't think it suits me?" He began laughing also.

"They didn't even recognize you. You could have been shot. Caught dead in that getup. Who said clothes don't make the man?" Laughter seized her now. She hadn't laughed all week. It felt good.

"Okay. Ha, ha. Not that funny. And if you tell *anyone* I was dressed like this, I'll deny it."

"Ah. They wouldn't believe me. Your secret's safe with me."

"Listen, it's been a while out there in the dark and the cold. Could I use your facilities?"

Georgia was still laughing. "Upstairs, first door on the left."

"Thank you. While I'm getting coffee out of my system, could you see about getting the laughing out of yours?"

When Jared returned, Georgia had put on a kettle of hot water for tea and set two mugs on her kitchen counter.

"I have coffee if you prefer," she said, squelching laughter as she glimpsed the loud plaid shirt and baggy pants.

"Tea's fine." He removed the hat and smoothed over his hair.

She poured the hot water over the tea infuser. "So Neal told you."

"You didn't. He was worried about his child's godmother."

"Listen—"

"No, Georgia, you listen."

He called me Georgia, she noticed.

"You are not alone and you are not Cleopatra Jones. You need help with a crazy man like Cusamano. All the help you can get."

"I appreciate it. I realize that I may be in a little over my head."

"As painful as that might be for a woman like you—"

"Careful, Counselor."

"I know you are a woman used to fighting your own battles. This time you need more troops."

"Agreed." She offered him honey for his tea.

"I'll bunk on the couch."

"What? Oh no. You've called in the troops. They'll be outside—"

"But there is no one *inside*."

"I only have two entrances. If they cover them I'll be fine."

"Our policemen work long and hard. They take breaks and could miss Cusamano from the outside. I'd prefer to be here, inside."

Suddenly, Georgia sobered up and didn't like the idea of Jared being here. In her home—the only place on the face of this earth she was sure he could not invade. *He cannot stay here*, her over-wrought mind screamed. *Get him out of here!* "Thank you. But—"

"When's the last time you've slept, Georgia?"

There it was again. Her name falling from his lips. It sounded like the opening chords of her favorite song and warmed her heart. But she was exhausted. It had been a week since she'd had more than thirty to forty-five minutes of sleep at a time.

"I didn't ask and I don't need anybody to babysit," she heard herself say, and she was five years old and her daddy was agreeing, "That's right. That's my big girl."

"Yes, you do, Georgia," Jared said quietly. "Not always. Maybe never before and maybe never again, but today—tonight—you need somebody to watch over you."

Georgia gritted her teeth as she struggled to keep her composure, attempting to reconcile the independence that was bred into her, and her current need for help. She could call her girl-friends, who'd come to her rescue, but she didn't want to jeopardize their safety. She had no one else she could call or rely on, and she did need someone. She didn't want to be alone with her fears for another interminably long, lonely night. She was *so* tired and Jared was volunteering for duty. Her nose burned and tears brimmed her eyes, but she refused to let them fall.

"To need somebody some of the time is not a sign of weakness, Georgia," Jared said tenderly as he moved toward her. "It's a sign of being human." He forced her gaze to his. "Let me stay. I want to stay. You shouldn't be alone now."

Her world had fallen off its axis and spun out of her control. The last time this happened was when they told her Tony had died. He was on the mend and had been transferred from IC to a regular room and by the time she'd gotten home, his heart had given out. Before that, it was her daddy's death and now this—a man threat-ening her life for doing her job. She had no con-trol over any of it and that was what angered and shook her to the very core. If she could just get one night of sound sleep, just one solid night, she could think clearly again. She could handle it. Jared was offering that—why not?

Jared watched her wrestle internally and said nothing while waiting for her to come to the only logical conclusion. He longed to hold her, but dared not touch her. She looked on the verge of a full-blown cry.

She looked at Jared earnestly. *"Yes"* was on the tip of her tongue. *"Yes, please stay one night so I can get some sleep"* was desperate to be spoken, but her head censored her heart and body in a judgmental vise.

Then the strain and fear Georgia'd bottled up for a week, masked by a brave front, cracked. She swooped her hair behind her ears and, like the New Orleans levee during Hurricane Katrina, crumpled under the pressure. As a deluge of foreign feelings swirled about her—helpless, hopeless, and sheer exhaustion—she fell into Jared's welcoming arms.

"It's okay," he soothed her, holding and rocking her gently. "It'll be okay. It'll all be over soon. Until then, I'm here for you. Trust and believe— I got this."

Had Georgia ever heard a man say three more beautiful words in her entire life? *"I got this."*

She reared back.

Jared looked into the loveliest pair of salty, dark amber eyes; so wide, vulnerable, and scared. Despite all the things he'd told himself about not falling for her—it was again confirmed, for him the fall was over. While away from her or at work, he tried telling himself, it wasn't going to happen, that he'd been drinking at Neal's and must be crazy to even consider this. But—now sober in the midst of a crisis—he knew he was in love with Georgia MacKenzie. No more posturing or pretending, it was crystal clear to him. He could not remember feeling like this about any woman—ever. This was the first time he'd held her since he'd admitted his love for her. Holding her now, he knew, like he had never known before, that he wanted to spend the rest of his living days in the company of Georgia MacKenzie. It would be his honor to love, protect, and care for this strong, fiercely independent woman who, possibly for the first time in her life, was acting human in an inhuman situation.

Tenderly, he wiped the wet from her cheeks with the back of his fingers and to return some of the dignity she surely thought she'd lost said, "Besides, I don't want to get into that rental car and drive across town." His eyes crinkled with a smile. "Now, if I had my truck . . ."

Unable to speak, she returned his smile. When her voice finally cut through all the emotion, she whispered, "I'll get you a pillow and some blankets."

She returned with the linen and began making up the couch.

"I'll do that," Jared offered, unable to stand seeing her doing it for him.

"Okay. Thanks." With glistening eyes, she looked at him. "My knight in shining armor."

"If you let me." His eyes held hers.

Her breath caught in her throat but she managed to say, "Good night."

"Sweet dreams." He watched her disappear up the stairs.

He finished making up the couch and looked around at the tastefully appointed living room: light, airy, and uncluttered with exquisite furniture. He looked at her "old school" album and CD collection and found her tastes as eclectic as his. Images from the fireplace mantel were eyeing him like an intruder, so he decided to inspect the pictures more closely: folks who looked like Georgia, maybe her parents, brother, and grandparents. She and her girlfriends profiling for the camera on a cruise ship. At a birthday party. Making pottery. A couple of Neal and Brenda and . . . Tony, with a dish in front of his image, holding the engagement ring.

Jared looked at the group of pictures realizing what a tribute it was to earn a place on this mantel . . . to live *inside* the love of Georgia MacKenzie. She impressed him as a woman who was hard to get, but easy to hold. Once she took you into her heart—her inner circle—you were there for life. Of all the trophies, plaques, accolades, and awards he'd won, Jared wanted to be on this mantel—not to replace Tony, but to make a place for himself. He didn't want to exist outside with his nose pressed up against the potential of her loving him—he wanted to live inside Georgia's love. What an earth-shattering experience that must be. She was a woman who lived from the inside out. She had her own set of scruples, convictions, and ethics and it didn't matter what the external world thought. "A woman who stands for nothing will fall for anything," his father used to say. That wasn't Georgia MacKenzie.

He'd seen her when luminaries and notables would visit the courthouse and she was cordial but unimpressed by their status or outer trappings.

Yet he'd seen her admire a working-class, single mother or go overboard to intern a college student. In a world where women displayed and gave away their bodies, outsourced their values and morals to the highest bidder for the most "bling," Georgia MacKenzie was refreshing. Georgia MacKenzie was "wife material," as his father would say. The Jaymes family had their "jewels," and, according to his father, there were two kinds of women—the marryin' kind and the fool-around-with kind. Georgia was the marryin' kind. *What's done in the night will come to the light,* had been another Jaymes jewel, which was the reason he'd straightened up in middle school since he knew he wanted to be mayor. Whenever his sister wanted something flashy and trendy, his mother always told her "pretty is as pretty does." She'd explain that the girls with the fancy nails, the hair done, the faddish jewelry, and the latest fashions, who needed all those trappings to glow on the outside, were often bankrupt and hollow inside. That wasn't his Georgia. Not only did he love her, but his parents would too. Not just because she would make their son eternally happy, but in her own right—Georgia was a man's woman—a woman's woman—she was rare and precious. The only irony was that the convictions he admired in her were the very reasons he couldn't have her. Right now he couldn't live with what he couldn't live without. But Jared was used to challenges and getting his way and he'd have to change the circumstances and remove the obstacles so that she'd be free to love him. It would be the most important goal of his life, but he wanted

Georgia MacKenzie till death do them part . . . and he would have her or die trying. He smiled at the prospect.

He cut the light, checked outside for the placement of the cops, removed his clothes, and neatly folded them over the living room's club chair. He climbed between the clean, cold sheets and waited for his body heat to warm them. He listened to her pad around above him. He longed to go upstairs, climb into bed beside her, and hold her body next to his all night long. That wasn't going to happen tonight or any time soon, but at least now he knew it wasn't just the magic at Neal's house. In the stark, sober reality, he knew exactly what it was and who he wanted—Georgia MacKenzie. So he proceeded to count his blessings, which included being in the presence of this woman who was beginning to trust and believe in him and, perhaps, later, the possibility of them. *Nice and easy does it*, he thought, smiling in the darkness.

Upstairs, Georgia glanced in the direction of her stairs. It was dark. Jared was probably fast asleep on her sofa. Her dragon slayer. Every woman should have at least one dragon slayer in her lifetime. A man who loved you unconditionally and would battle any demons for you—be you right or wrong. Her father had been her first dragon slayer. She had three boyfriends in high school. None were dragon slayers. In college she had four boyfriends in as many years. Not a dragon slayer among them. They were more like mackerels in the moonlight; the closer she got to them, the more they stank. In law school she was too focused to ever be distracted by a guy. If it had not been for living vicariously through Neal's exploits, she wouldn't have had a love life at all. There were no "ones that got away" for her to lament over. She had had a crush on a professor who slayed dragons for his wife and kids—as it should've been. After graduation she went to work in Philly for the DA's office for a boss who could have been a dragon slayer, but he was her boss and, therefore, disqualified. Then she met Tony, who was a dragon slayer for a living—he died slaying a dragon, but not for her. And now that disqualified boss who had been ineligible five years ago slept on her couch, and was her ersatz dragon slayer. At least until Cusamano was caught. Who knew? Some girls get none or one—she'd been fortunate to have had three no matter how long, short, or temporary.

Georgia trusted Jared not to betray her momentary weakness by telling anyone she'd been crying. She climbed into her frigid sheets and remembered the warmth of him, the feel of his powerful arms enveloping her, making her feel cherished, nurtured, and secure just like in the dreams. She felt safe with him downstairs. In just three weeks, a man she had known for over five years had suddenly invaded her privacy, turned her controlled, comfortable life upside down, and challenged the very essence of who she was and what she believed. How did things like this happen? What strange alchemy had reshuffled her predictable world, causing such unpredictable chaos? First, being seduced by the caring and good looks of her boss, and second, Cusamano's threat—neither of which she had anticipated.

She knew it was dangerous to have Jared so close to her in a private space she thought he would never be. She could control her mind and body, but she'd have to be vigilant with her renegade heart. Her heart had a history of doing just what it wanted, refusing to be held ransom by logic and MacKenzie maxims. Despite her best efforts, her heart had fallen in love with a first-generation black Latino detective whose parents only spoke Spanish. Her heart was going after Jared—she could tell. But lawyers, like accountants, deal in bottom lines. Bottom line—Jared was her boss. She was a lawyer, and lawyers are in the convincing business—convincing judges, press, and jurors of either guilt or innocence. Georgia had to convince her heart that Jared would never work without disastrous ramifications and repercussions. So what would be the point? Dating a married man, an attached male, or your boss was like rearranging deck chairs on the *Titanic*. Despite the glorious beginning, in the end—guaranteed catastrophic doom; it was history. It was unavoidably inevitable. So it was with the ocean liner and so it would be in any relationship with Jared. So she'd keep her distance and just run the commercial over and over and over again until her heart got the message. Right now, all Georgia wanted was sleep. It was the only freedom she knew.

* * *

Georgia awakened groggily from the first rest-
ful sleep she'd had since the Cusamano threat.
She drew on her shorty robe and sloughed down
the hall to the front bedroom. Pushing the blinds
aside and eyeing the weather, she noted how last
night's ice storm had begun melting with the
morning sun. Rotely, she went down the front
stairs, yawning as she headed for the front door
and the paper. Her brain engaged long enough
to recall that there were policemen guarding her
on the other side of the door. *A respected ADA
should not be seen in her pj's and shorty robe*, she
thought, and started back to get a longer robe.
She stretched as she rounded the corner and
there in a shaft of sunlight lay—Jared Jaymes.

The sight of him yanked her into full wakefulness, yet froze her steps and snatched her breath
from her lungs. The DA was sprawled on her
couch, bare-chested, muscled body with an arm
over his eyes to block out the offending sun. Her
body filled, then pulsed with excitement at the
vision of him.

Omigod, she thought. Her eyes fixated on the
spectacle of him. The way solar rays played in
the silken hair of his chest and dipped into the
shadow of his navel. The way gray boxer briefs
clung to the chiseled contours of his lower body
and hugged his fully awake, morning maleness
seized her. She tried to exhale, tried to look away.
But his body was more exquisite than Michelan-
gelo's *David*, and she swore she heard a Grego-
rian choir chant the "Hallelujah" chorus. She
couldn't tear her eyes away from his projected
male-magnificence straining beneath a thin layer

of gray cotton. His entire body seemed to scream, *What are you waiting for, Georgia? Help yourself!*

Outwardly, she remained still, but inwardly her mind, body, soul, every synapse and cell raged chaotically at the presentation of him. When was the last time she'd made love? Neither her body nor her bed had been used for loving in over two years. She'd repressed or forgotten the need, until this superb reminder dared exhibit and mock all she'd missed. Like a phoenix, this spectacular display of maleness rose from gray cloth and reached for the ceiling. She couldn't move her body, as again, she willed her eyes to look up, look elsewhere—but they remained mesmerized by this spectacular specimen.

Omigod. I could get into big trouble here, Georgia thought. *I could easily go from "hello, handsome, where'd you come from?" to "Lawdy, mercy, what have I done!"*

Like watching a marvel of the universe, her hypnotic eyes would not blink. This was what lay hidden beneath his three-thousand-dollar tailor-made suits. She attempted to regulate her breathing and calm her heart.

She imagined going to him, blocking out the sun so he'd wake up, remove his arm from across his eyes, and see her standing before him. It would be his turn to soak up the vision of her in her shorty robe as she shed it. It would be his turn to eye her nipples pressed hungrily against the silk, straining, pleading for him to free them, taste them. His hands would sear hot all over her body while they began to explore each other in frenzied bliss. Removing clothing, touching, tasting, caressing—

Jared stirred sleepily. His head rolled away from her.

MOVE! her inner voice yelled. *He cannot catch you staring at him!*

As if being released from a vise, she finally blinked and tiptoed past him, through the dining room, into the kitchen before she dared to exhale. Her breath came in ragged bursts and she panted as if she'd run a marathon. She held on to the corner of the counter for support as her entire body pulsed with desire and need, and cursed her for not acting on her feelings. This was the Jared Jaymes her girlfriends saw. Was she blind? She took down a glass, opened the fridge, and poured grapefruit juice. She held the cold liquid to her head, then lodged it between her breasts. She gulped the tart liquid, then put it back to her temples.

Her thoughts returned to him. This time she imagined going to him and kneeling beside his magnificent form. She'd kiss him into wakefulness beginning with his chest, nipples, and navel. He'd stir and take that powerful arm from across his eyes and envelop her and say something like "Now, that's a wake-up call I can get used to." He'd place those luscious lips on hers and pull her onto him in the most delicious way and they would—

"Good morning," Jared said from behind.

She jumped at the sound of his voice without turning around. She hoped he'd put clothes on that body.

"Sorry, didn't mean to startle you."

"Good morning." Georgia turned slowly, re-lieved to find him in the baggy pants and button-ing that ugly plaid shirt. But you can't unring a bell—she'd already seen the Holy Grail in a thick gray sheath . . . and it was fierce!

He looked at her and smiled. "Freckles," was out before he realized it. He knew he shouldn't have, but she looked so cute with her clean-scrubbed face and ponytail. "Sleep well?"

"Yes. Thank you." She couldn't say that he looked cramped on her couch; then he'd know she'd seen him. "Did you?" she asked innocently. She was trying so hard not to blush. Not to look down at his male area.

"As well as can be expected."

"I was going to make some breakfast. What would you like?"

"Nothing for me, thanks." He looked out of the French doors to her backyard. "Weather looks good. I've got to get across town, shower, change clothes, and make it to work on time."

"Oh, sure." She ran her hands across her hair and thought, *I must look a fright.*

"I'll bring some things over tonight so I won't have to make this trek tomorrow."

"What?" Georgia said, following him into the hall. "You don't have to come back tonight."

He turned to face her, and stopped her abruptly.

Now it was his turn to stare at her. She watched his eyes survey her silky camisole pj top, which outlined her breasts and grazed her nipples. The espresso pair drifted to her exposed mocha skin, which peeked out from her midriff, down to her navel and the flat stomach, which gave way to the flare of her hips beneath those silky pj bottoms. She watched him redirect his eyes as quickly as he could—but not quick enough. Despite his best effort, his eyes lingered . . . and Georgia was enjoying this naughty display.

She pulled her robe close and repeated, "You don't have to come back. Really. I slept so well last night—"

"I thought we settled all of this already." He began walking again.

"What are you going to do? Take a bullet for me?" She tried to diffuse the charged situation.

"If I have to," he said seriously.

The intensity of his gaze flustered her. *Breathe,* she told herself.

He felt her nervousness about the ordeal and said, "Listen. I will be staying until Cusamano is apprehended. It won't be much longer. Truth be told, if he had the juice, neither of us would be here now. The Mob isn't going to waste their chits with the likes of him, which means he is working solo on his brother's behalf. He's not that bright, so he's about to do something stupid. I bet I'll be out of here by the end of the week . . . and life will be back to normal."

"By the end of the week," Georgia repeated absently.

"We'll make it fun . . . Scrabble, chess, watch movies and TV. Hey, you like sushi? I'll make sushi tonight." He walked to the door and she followed him. "I'll pick up nori and sushi rice on the way home."

She looked at him strangely for referring to her *home* as his. The sound of it both ticked her off and made her smile.

He opened the door and summoned one of the cops from the sidewalk. He bent, picked up, and handed her the morning paper. Her robe had fallen open again, exposing her pretty body with only one thin layer of silk covering it. "Company's coming," he said, inclining his eyes to her fine brown frame.

Georgia looked down, pulled her robe close again, and began tying the attached belt.

"Where will Courtney think you are?" *Damn!* She didn't know why she asked and hated the question the moment it left her lips.

A bemused smile crinkling his eyes, he looked at her evenly and asked, "Why should that concern you?" Was this Georgia's way of keeping a distance between them? he wondered, or did Georgia really not know about him and Courtney? The stunt his former girlfriend had pulled in the elevator nothwithstanding. Either way, it gave him a ray of hope on which to hang his dreams.

"Why do you care?" he asked.

His smile with dimples appeared and she asked, "Why are you smiling?"

"No reason." His luscious lips separated into a full grin that said, "you care."

"I don't care. I have a right to know if a jealous crazy woman is going to try to kill me too."

"Not her style." He thought, *The Academy Award goes to Georgia MacKenzie.* She was fighting her feelings for him—so hard—but he knew, one day, someday soon, she'd have to acknowledge them.

Admit that she was falling for him too and he'd be ready to accept the greatest gift since breathing.

Georgia folded her arms in defiant answer. *Why is he smiling?* she wondered. Did he think this meant she was interested in him? His rich, espresso eyes sparkled, and like espresso coffee, Georgia knew she loved the smell of it, but never indulged. She admitted loving the idea and thought of a Jared Jaymes–type in her life, but she would never date this one. He was her boss. Period.

"Mornin', sir," the policeman said.

"Good morning. Take good care of our prized ADA," he greeted, then told Georgia, "See you at work." He turned and jogged down her front steps to the rented car.

She watched him talk to the other two cops before she realized that the one with her was watching both her and Jared.

"I would have know him if he was in his Hummer," the policeman offered cordially.

Georgia was silent. She'd traded the Cusamano crisis for a Jared Jaymes crisis. *Heck*, she concluded, *I can only handle one life-threatening disaster at a time.*

"He's a good guy," the cop continued.

"Yeah. A real peach of a guy. Sent here to complicate my life," Georgia said, and closed the door.

Chapter 5

Georgia dressed and went to work with her bodyguard in tow. She was thankful that it wasn't a Monday and therefore there would be no case review meeting; however, this relief was short-lived. Jared called a special meeting and informed his office of the threat on ADA MacKenzie and the court-ordered twenty-four-hour surveillance.

"The man in her constant company is not a new suitor but a policeman doing his job," Jared said as a tense chuckle arose from the other ADAs.

Jared warned his staff to stay alert, report any suspicious activities, and be careful as they went about their normal duties going to and from the court building.

What Jared didn't share was that once the police captain realized that it was Tony Machado's fiancée who'd received the threat, the captain ordered the extra police coverage and vowed to get Cusamano for daring to threaten the life of his revered, deceased detective's "lady." An expert CIA-connected field operative was coming to the States to personally address the situation. Whether the captain was kissing up to Jared or really respected Machado's memory, Jared thought a CIA operative was overkill, but he wasn't about to look a gift horse in the mouth. If the captain wanted the National Guard and *Air Force One* to take Cusamano out to save Georgia's life, Jared was all for it. The DA and the police captain surmised that unless Cusamano'd fled to the Bahamas by now, it wouldn't take long for him to make a costly mistake that would lead to his capture. The Caprese family had already made it known that they were in no way backing or protecting either Cusamano brother. They were loose cannons. Jared deduced that the Caprese syndicate was using the judicial system to rid them of the expendable pariahs while saving face within the family. With the police force and the expert operative behind the apprehension of Cusamano and the Mob turning its back, Jared knew his time with Georgia was short and he planned to make the most of it.

"Okay. Just wanted you to know," Jared concluded to the group. "Any questions?" He looked into the eyes of each of his ADAs and his administrative assistants. "Okay. Thanks."

"You all right?" he asked Georgia.

"Yes. Fine. Thanks," Georgia said, filing out with the others.

Jared watched the bodyguard fall in behind her. Professionally or personally, he didn't like any man close to her. But he understood. *That plainclothes policeman better do his job*, he thought.

Georgia convinced Neal that she was not

moving in with him and Brenda and jeopardizing their safety, and that she was handling it all. She watched Neal go back into Jared's office. Somehow, despite the closeness of the two men, Georgia wasn't concerned that Jared would tell Neal that he was spending nights with her. She trusted Jared with that bit of information.

Thankfully the day went quickly and Georgia went to tell Jared that she was leaving, but he wasn't there. She left a note on his desk—"Gone home. Mac."

Once at home, with a policeman at the front and back doors, Georgia changed into her drawstring lounge pants and tank top and began to melt the caramel for her apples. Tomorrow was Halloween. From attic storage, she got her fiber-optic pumpkin, plugged it in at the arched window, and watched it change colors twice before returning to the kitchen to check on the caramel. Her tradition was to treat neighborhood children to her famous apples for Halloween, and Cusamano wasn't going to stop her. As she rolled the second set of six apples in the nuts, she heard Jared come through the door.

Georgia!" he called, walking to the kitchen with two bags of groceries. "Georgia!"

She smiled, hearing him call her name, and purposefully did not answer until he reached her in the kitchen. "Hi," she said.

"Why is the door unlocked?"

"And how was your day?"

He shot her an unamused look.

"I knew it was about time for you to come, so I turned off the alarm and unlocked the door.

Besides there's a policeman right there on the porch—"

"He could be shot with a poison dart from across the street and Cusamano could waltz right in—"

"A poison dart?" Georgia interrupted with a laugh.

Jared stopped and squelched a chuckle. "Would you please lock the door and turn on the alarm when you are in here—even if I am expected. I can ring the doorbell."

It was more of an order than a request and Georgia replied, "Yes, master."

Jared cut his eyes playfully and put the bags on the counter.

"Where are your shoes?" she asked.

"At the door. You don't want to track in all the dirt of the day into your home."

"Uh-huh."

"You might want to do the same."

"Uh-huh. Well, what do you have there?" Georgia asked of the groceries, like an inquisitive child whose parent had just returned from the market with bags of goodies.

"Sushi makings. Where can I wash up and change clothes?"

"Oh. Since you are determined to be a guest in this house—take the guest room upstairs on the front, and the hall bathroom is yours for the duration."

"Thanks." He smiled, glad that she was beginning to accept the idea.

Georgia hunched her shoulders, and returned his smile. It was a purely selfish motive. Only she knew that she couldn't bear to see him draped over her sofa like a gorgeously crafted human afghan in all his lean and wondrous splendor. Moving him upstairs, down the hall behind four walls and a door, seemed far less dangerous.

When Jared returned, Georgia was tying her apples in colorful cellophane and twisting ribbon around the sticks.

"That's a lot of dessert." Jared eyed the two trays of apples as his hands plunged into the bags of groceries.

Georgia glanced at how expertly the black T-shirt hugged his muscles midbiceps, leaving his arms exposed. "Halloween's tomorrow and I'm noted for my candy apples."

"No."

"No?"

"I mean, I wish you would reconsider."

"It's been my tradition for three years—"

"And it will be again next year." He watched her roll her eyes. "We want you here next year. Think about it. You cannot take the chance of being a target every time you open your door for a kid." He watched her tilt her head the way she did when she was considering something contrary to her logic. He loved that about her. But he knew how to appeal to her. "Do you want to put every child that comes to your door in jeopardy?"

"I hate this."

"I know." He also knew that Cusamano was a knife man who preferred to get up close and personal. But Jared couldn't take the chance that Cusamano wouldn't try a gun and shoot from across the street. Either way it was too risky for Georgia and the children.

"I'll take them downstairs and let my tenant give them out. May I do that?"

"I'd prefer if you let the cop—"

She shot him a look of disbelief.

"Okay. Compromise, you can take them down and the cops can direct the children tomorrow."

"I'll make a sign for them." Georgia grabbed the tray and headed out the door.

God, he loved that hardheaded, independent, stubborn woman with the ponytail and the silk drawstring pants. As she walked away from him, he admired the way the material seductively grazed her hips.

Despite the rocky start, Jared and Georgia settled into making sushi. As they assembled their dinner, they put on Sly and the Family Stone, followed by Prince, and danced until they sat at the dining room table.

"See this lopsided one?" Jared teased, holding one between his thumb and index finger. "You rolled that one."

"It still tastes good." Georgia popped it into her mouth. "What happened to our music?"

They had been talking so neither of them realized when the CDs had stopped. "Now we need music for chess."

"Chess? Tonight? It's a school night, you know. Work tomorrow," Georgia said.

"It won't take long for me to whip your butt." He pulled music from her classical section.

"Aw, that wasabi's given you heat you don't have." Georgia began clearing the table of dishes.

Jared beat Georgia to all four of Vivaldi's Seasons and Tchaikovsky.

"Good game," Jared said.

"I was distracted by the Sugar Plum Fairy." She helped by gathering her chess pieces. "Tomorrow I pick the game and the music."

"You're on." He loved the sound of it; loved being here with her like this.

"Scrabble—the game. Jazz—the music."

"If you think it will help."

"We'll see who gets the trick or treat."

They both chuckled and let it die naturally.

"Well, school night," Georgia said again. "Anything I can get you before I go up?"

"No. I'm going to read a little first, then turn in."

"Okay, then." Georgia made her way to the stairs. She stopped at the newel post and banister, turned toward him. "Thanks for everything."

"You're welcome." He smiled and shoved his hands into his pocket to fight the urge to touch her, hold her—kiss her.

"Good night."

"Night." Nothing good about it, except that he was here with her, he thought. A *good night* night would be when they could both ascend the stairs together and make delectable love.

Jared made a few calls and listened to her walk overhead, run water for a shower, and then settle down. This was just what he had in mind. The life he wanted for himself and his family. Five years ago, he had wanted to be mayor so he positioned himself to attain that goal and, in so doing, got a firsthand glimpse of all the position entailed and all you had to give up getting there and once you were there. He was lucky to have had that insightful opportunity ahead of time. That was how he knew it was an inexhaustible, sociopolitical scene of posturing, promoting, and game playing. He figured he would still give to his community without sacrificing himself and his family. He wanted his family to have what his parents had, and what they had given to him and his siblings. Love, stability, and *time.* He wanted this with her—Georgia MacKenzie.

When he climbed the steps her bedside lamp was off but the television cast shadows on her walls. *This could be my life*, he thought, and he would gladly welcome it. Only difference would be that he would turn right into that room with her, instead of left into the front guest room. "All in due time," he told himself. "All in due time."

Jared was up and gone when Georgia awoke. She'd been sleeping like a narcoleptic patient since he'd moved in, not even waking in the middle of the night. She dressed, gathered her bodyguard at the door, and proceeded to work. She had two minor trials, a suppression hearing, and was helping with jury selection. The courtroom had to be cleared whenever she was in attendance, and except when Neal was still in court, she ate with him in her office. She left early and made spaghetti for her houseguest. When Jared arrived the table was set for dinner and the Scrabble game to follow.

Jared rang the doorbell, and when she opened it, he said, "Hey." He grinned. "You do listen."

"It was a logical argument."

"Argue? Us?" He watched her eye the flowers in his hand. "Oh, do you know of a vase that would like these?"

"I think I could find one." She left him to hang up his coat and fedora in the hall closet and remove his shoes.

"Wow, this looks great and something smells good."

"My game, my dinner, my music—my win," Georgia said.

"I could get used to this."

Georgia made no comment.

"Do I have time to wash up and change?"

"Sure, but don't take too long or the spaghetti won't be al dente."

"Is there anything worse?" His eyes sparkled. "I'll be right back."

Georgia watched him sprint up the stairs like he belonged there. She took the Chianti that had been breathing and put it on the table with the salad and garlic bread.

"I could get used to this myself," she said quietly. "But it's only temporary. Like playing house."

"Did you say something?" Jared came down the steps.

"Wow—that was fast."

On this night Phyllis Hyman and Luther Vandross crooned them through dinner and Georgia replaced them with jazz as they settled in for Scrabble.

"I've been admiring your 'old school' album collection. Admirable in one so young," he teased.

"Yeah. You *lived* that era and I just *heard* about it."

"Ouch."

"Good taste in music has no age limitations. I like the classics."

"I'm going to have to reevaluate some things about you too, Georgia MacKenzie." He fed her own words back to her from the elevator. "What is your middle name?"

"You'll die knowing."

"Hey, a rose by any other name—"

"Stop stalling, Jaymes. It's your turn."

Jared could not concentrate as Georgia absently sang "Living Inside Your Love" with Earl Klug while fingering her blocked letters. Jared imagined how wonderful it would be if she were singing that about him. "Didn't George Benson make that too?"

"Um-hmm."

Georgia won with a triple word, triple letter . . . *vex.*

"What an appropriate word . . . *vex,*" Jared said with a gleam in his eye. *It's what you do to me,* he thought.

"Trying to make it real compared to what?" She did her victory dance to Les McCann and Eddie Harris's hit from the *Swiss Movement* album, *Live at the Montreux Jazz Festival* as Jared tallied the score.

He laughed at her moves. "You are so competitive."

"I play to win. Otherwise, what is the point?"

"For fun maybe?"

The doorbell chimed and it startled them

both. When was the last time Georgia had heard her doorbell ring this late?

"I'll get it." Jared went to the door.

"Probably just a lost trick-or-treater." Georgia followed him to the door.

The door whined open and Jared spoke to the cop.

"*Willow* MacKenzie?" Jared repeated after the cop. "Destroy it."

"No!" Georgia came from behind Jared. "That's from my grandma Mac."

Jared and the cop looked at her.

"Is the postmark from Evelyn, Tennessee?"

The cop looked, then answered, "Yeah."

"Give me my Halloween candy." Georgia pushed past Jared and took the box with a smile. "Thanks," she said to the policeman.

"Georgia—" Jared began to protest.

"Save it, Jaymes. It's a box from my grandmother. It's her handwriting and our tradition."

"Thanks," Jared said to the policeman, and closed the door. He watched Georgia tear into the cardboard box and lift out a note amid the colorful carnival of candy.

"What's your pleasure, Counselor?" Georgia asked, surrounded by her own personal trick-or-treat booty.

"My dentist would love you." Upon closer scrutiny he asked, "Are those Moon Pies?"

"Yep. I don't have any RC Cola, but they're just as good without. Oh, wow!" Georgia unsheathed a Sugar Daddy as she draped herself in a candy necklace.

"Now, this takes me back." Jared bit into

the graham-cracker shell through to the chewy, gooey, white marshmallow filling.

"Jawbreakers! And you almost destroyed my bounty."

"Willow?"

"You think Cusamano doesn't know my first name is Georgia?"

"Okay. What's 'Willow'?"

"The tree. When I was a child, I had to play one in Ross Preschool and my grandma Mac helped me become the willow. The name stuck and it's her pet name for me."

She smiled and Jared could imagine a four-year-old Georgia being the best willow ever.

"I knew a girl named Willow once," Jared mused absently.

"Yeah, right," Georgia said. "I need water to wash this sugar down. You'll be up all night if we eat any more of this. You'll be up all night anyway. You don't need much sleep, do you?"

He smiled at the fact that she knew he stayed up late. "I think it's habit. My schedule has always been pretty hectic before college, during college, at work, and with my mayor's office pursuits."

"My daddy didn't need a lot of sleep either, but he liked to fish. That was his downtime."

"Maybe I just need someone to teach me to relax." He looked up at her.

She handed him a glass of water. "Hmm." She glanced at the clock. "It's too late for me to call her. I'll call her tomorrow to thank her for the Halloween goodies." She took the note penned in her grandmother's familiar script as Jared got the empty box to throw away.

The note began: *Willow,*

Happy Halloween! Sorry it's a little late. I had to send it special delivery to get it there on time. I hope it gets there on time. But this year I wanted to make you some divinity. I know it's early but I thought you might like a real "treat."

Enjoy. Love, Grandma Mac.

"Aw! Jared, stop!"

"What?"

"She sent divinity!"

"What?"

"My grandmother made us divinity." She scrambled in the box and found an old Valentine's Day tin with two golden, interlocking hearts. "Oh my."

Georgia just stared at the gold hearts on the red background. *This is a little spooky,* Georgia thought, that her grandmother would break tradition and make divinity so early, and that Jared was here to receive it at the same time *and* that it was in a Valentine's Day tin.

"Maybe this is a sign, Georgia," Jared said, reading her mind. A huge grin claimed his face.

"What?" Georgia asked.

That Jared knew what she was thinking was doubly spooky. "It's a sign pointing you to the best divinity ever." She couldn't let him know she was thinking the exact same thing. Georgia wondered if she'd had that much wine at dinner. She offered him a piece of the confection. She watched his luscious brown lips wrap themselves around the white candy. He licked his mouth with his tongue.

The contrast was sensual. She licked her own lips in response, then thought, *I am feeling no pain.*

"This is delicious," Jared decreed. "It tastes just like my grandmother's."

"Oh, Negro, please."

"No. It really does."

"I can see we'll just have to wait until your grandma Hattie Mae sends hers to do a real test and maybe we'll have Neal and Brenda as tasters too."

"Fine by me. Bring it on."

"Okay. I think I better get to bed now. These late hours and the wine and candy aren't making me feel really great right now. So I'm going to say good night."

"Okay, Georgia. Night. And thanks for dinner, the game, and divinity."

"You're welcome. See you tomorrow."

By the time she reached the staircase, her head was spinning. She was tipsy, so she carefully negotiated each step. *This is so embarrassing. Yet another reason why you should not date your boss,* she thought as she fell into her bed. *But I am not dating my boss,* was her last thought. She couldn't shower this night; she'd shower in the morning.

Georgia rose an hour after her alarm clock chimed, showered, and got to work late, and Neal was beside himself with worry.

"Calm down, Neal."

"You women are going to drive me crazy. Brenda and you."

"Here." Georgia threw him a bag full of Squirrel Nuts and Mint Juleps.

His face broke into a wide grin. "Grandma Mac's Halloween goodies."

"They came last night. All forgiven?"

"I'll just be glad when my child is born and Cusamano is caught—then my life can get back to normal."

"Yours and mine both. Let me ask you this. She sent divinity too. What do you make of that?"

"Divinity for Halloween? Have you talked to her? Maybe—she's not going to be around at Christmas?"

"What an awful thing to say."

Georgia called her grandmother immediately. After thirty minutes of Grandma Mac's reassuring Georgia that she was all right, Georgia hung up. *I'll have to go home this holiday*, she thought. Or maybe the "sign" was that she—Georgia MacKenzie—wasn't going to be around for Christmas. Georgia was on edge all day. She made her plane reservation just so the universe knew she intended to be in Evelyn, Tennessee for Christmas and New Year's this year, and many years to follow.

Jared sent Georgia an e-mail indicating that he'd forgotten to tell her about the mayor's monthly dinner meeting. He'd be late tonight and she should eat without him, unless she wanted him to cancel. Jared gave her the number to the mayor's office and said he would keep his cell phone on vibrate and if she needed him for anything to call and he'd come home immediately.

Georgia smiled and reread, that he'd *come*

home immediately. She called and told him to enjoy the meeting.

At lunch Georgia had two keys made and put them in a sealed envelope with a note: *Here is my alarm code—125802. Don't abuse it. :-) See you tomorrow.* She addressed the envelope simply "J.J." and, when no one was watching, slid it on his desk on her way back from the bathroom.

Through two sets of plate-glass windows, she watched Jared pick up the note and read it. He looked up at her, smiled, and gave her a two-finger salute.

Georgia blushed and warmed all over. Her stomach flipped and she couldn't stop smiling. Instantly, she felt better. As good as she'd felt all day.

A few hours later, Neal came in with news. "Jared has a lady. He's crazy about her."

"What?"

"I would think you'd be a little more interested since he's the godfather to your godmother."

"What?" Georgia kept making entries on the file.

"Mac!"

Georgia dropped her pen. "Okay. What?"

"I saw a note from her. The envelope had 'J.J.' on it."

"And? So?"

"All he did was grin and say he was 'crazy' about her."

Georgia hid her smile with her hand. "Is that all you got? No name. No suspects?"

"Well, not right now."

"I got work to do. Keep me posted." Georgia

went back to work, then looked up and asked, "When *is* Brenda due?"

"Funny, real funny. I can take a hint. All this is hard on a man."

"Well, take a Midol and get a grip."

Georgia went home after work and the silence screamed at her. In just a few days she'd gotten so used to having Jared there. Now the house she loved so much seemed so sad without him. No food simmering, no music, no games laid out, no dancing. Her sanctuary was now chafing her mind, heart, body, and soul. She ran five miles on her treadmill, showered, ate, called a girl-friend, and she was still missing him. She cut a wedge of cake, poured a glass of milk, and took both to her room. This had been her life before Jared; this would be her life after everything re-turned to normal—boy, it was so empty. She'd miss him when he went. The thought made her ache a little. She walked to the hall bathroom and saw one renegade hair left over from his morning shave. She looked at the towels he'd used and discarded in the hamper. There was no ring in the tub, no toothpaste globs in the sink, and the toilet bowl was pristine. *He's such a neat-nik,* she thought.

She stood on the threshold of her guest room—his room while he was here. She shouldn't tres-pass but she did. She looked in the closet where his clothes were neatly filed. His shoes were in a neat row under the front window. His bed was spread. She sat, then lay on it, inhaling his scent. She rolled and fluttered out her arms like she was making a snow angel. He was a nice guy, was all

that Georgia would admit. *The truth hurts so we lie,*
she thought . . . *to ourselves, and to other people so they
can reinforce the lie we tell ourselves.* The only safe con-
fession she'd make was that she liked him.

"*He's crazy about her.* "Neal's words reverberated
in her heart, shaking it like Jell-O and making
her giddy, like a newborn baby with gas. She'd
tried not to think about it, but she laughed and
thought how her life could change with Jared in
it. She could have what they already shared and
more . . . not only two powerful attorneys fighting against the injustices of the world, but the
feel of his hands caressing her body, the touch of
him lying beside her in the middle of the night,
the taste of his lips and the scent of him filling
her senses always, not to speak of the free access
to his projectile, sheathed beneath gray boxer
briefs; all that would add such depth and dimen-
sion to their relationship. "Ooh." She grew
flushed and hot.

But he was her boss.

The sober reality intruded on her daydream.
She could not fall in love with her boss. *Wouldn't
that be the oldest professional cliché?* she thought.
When she was old and ruined, someone would
ask, "Why are you such a wreck?" And she'd sadly
answer, "I fell in love with my boss." "Oh. Enough
said," the person would answer with a shake of
the head.

She *would not* fall in love with her boss, she re-
solved. Once Cusamano was caught and Jared left
her house, all she needed was time and distance,
and whatever burgeoning feelings she'd have
would eventually pass, like a bad cold. Then they

could resume their former professional relationship built on mutual admiration and respect. She rolled over and fingered the fringe on a throw pillow and told herself that she wouldn't date him even if she changed jobs. She told herself this because the thought that he wouldn't date her was too hurtful to bear. She was no Courtney and didn't want to be, not even for him.

Jared was so wrong for Georgia on so many levels; not only was he her boss, but she could never be involved with a public figure. She had no desire to be the First Lady of Philly. She didn't want to be hounded on what she did or said, what she wore, where she went and with whom. She was too selfish to share her husband and family with the public—she wanted her, him, and their children to herself. She wanted to spend weekends at local festivals that their kids thought were corny. She wanted to travel on family road trips with them asking "are we there yet?" in her ear. She wanted holidays at home, to decorate her house for Halloween, have Easter egg hunts in the backyard, and fall into a pile of autumn leaves they'd just raked. She wanted noisy sleepovers and loud cookouts. Jared couldn't give her any of that. He'd be bored beyond compare. But, she thought of his mahogany magnificence, he could give her a night or two to remember. She smiled wickedly as she rolled over on his pillow. Sometimes it was like he could read her mind. With someone like that, lovemaking had to be a phenomenal experience. No man had ever come so close or gone so far in her psyche as Jared Jaymes. What she felt for him wasn't anything akin to love—but it might be lust and curiosity. And just one mind-blowing, blissfully gratifying time would satisfy wondering and be memorable. Revisiting such a tryst from time to time would keep her company on many lonely nights.

"Stop it," she admonished herself aloud as she rolled over and sat up. "Don't play with fire, Georgia MacKenzie, or you will surely get burned." She smoothed out the comforter and went to the window. "Fifth-degree burns from which you will never recover." *I need to go*, she thought. *He does not need to find me in here.*

She ate her cake, brushed her teeth, and put the television on snooze control—just like the old, pre-Jared days—and eventually fell asleep.

Jared came in an hour later, removed his shoes at the door, and turned off the one light that burned near the stairs. He quietly ascended the steps, turned right, and looked into Georgia's dark room. He knew the lump in the middle of the bed was her. He leaned against her doorjamb and smiled. He could hear her breathing deeply. He'd missed her tonight and could barely focus on what the mayor, the police commissioner, and the city manager were saying. He'd hoped she'd buzz him to come home, but knew she wouldn't unless Cusamano were in her face. She felt she could handle anything—except dating her boss. His was not to reason "why?" His was to recognize, acknowledge, and respect her beliefs. Beliefs he'd shared until recently. Until her. For him it was a commonsense philosophy, but for her it was a family commandment—both heritage and tradition. Now, it was a challenge, but it was all about to change without her compromising her principles one iota. He loved her that much. Needed her that much. Without even knowing it, she had reordered his priorities and put herself number one. She'd made him realize that all the success and acclaim meant nothing if he didn't have her. In all his years, he'd never felt the chemistry and compatibility with a woman that he felt with Georgia. This revelation would scare and confuse him, if the clarity of loving her didn't soothe him so.

She stirred, turned over, and stuck her foot out from under the covers. He backed down the hall to his room. She couldn't find him spying on her.

The next morning Georgia's alarm went off and she wasn't sure if Jared had come home last night. But the perfume of freshly brewed coffee tickled her nose and she glanced down the hall to see his door was open. She pulled on her robe and went to his bathroom; the room was moist and humid, meaning he'd come and gone. She smiled.

She dressed for work in a chocolate pin-striped suit she knew he liked. He never said a word, but whenever she wore it, he'd given her more attention. *Had I always known that?* she wondered as she gathered her briefcase and headed down the back stairs. There on the counter was an empty juice glass he'd set out for her and blueberry bagels he must have brought in with him last night. She smiled again. "Yeah, I could get used to this too," she said, echoing his words. Her heart rejoiced, but her mind went berserk. She checked herself as she poured tart liquid into the waiting glass. *Just allow me this little temporary interlude,* she bargained with her sober mind. *Just until the danger passes and everything returns to the status quo.* It'd be easy to do when she didn't see him in her home. She could handle him at work. She could put him off at work and he'd lose interest and move on to the many other willing women waiting in the wings to nab Jared Jaymes.

She went to the hall closet. His shoes were gone. She noticed the empty hook where he usually hung his fedora. *His vicuna coat is there, so he must be in his raincoat today,* she thought as she grabbed her coat. "Whew, I know too much about this man." She closed the closet door and opened her front door.

"Good morning," she said the policemen.

Being at work was becoming a grueling task. She hated being there because she was scrutinized, and couldn't really leave to go to lunch or run an errand without making a major production of it. It was restrictive, like being under house arrest, and she hated it. The idea that she couldn't stroll around freely or take a walk was really wearing on her. *Thank God it's Friday,* she thought. She wondered if Jared would stay with her for the entire weekend or just make sure the cops were there. He did have a life to live. He could go to the Homes for Humankind or play racquetball or get his truck washed. She was the one under protection. She was the one Cusamano wanted to kill. She really wanted to go with her girls tomorrow to celebrate the November birthdays. She hated lying to them and they were not at all pleased that she was begging off. Maybe she would send Jared in her place. She smiled. Boy, that would make them ecstatic. They wouldn't miss her at all.

"Ready?" Neal appeared in her doorway.

"I have a bodyguard to walk me to the car."

"Two bodies guarding you are better than one." Neal got her coat and held it out for her. She glanced over and saw that Jared was gone.

"He left about an hour ago. Don't have to tell him to have a nice weekend. He's in love," Neal teased. "Not that you care."

"I've got a few other things on my mind." With a start Georgia wondered if by chance Jared could be in love with someone else, or could it be Courtney? Maybe he wasn't with the mayor and the Task Force last night. Maybe he was with this new lady friend and because of his commitment to his ADA, he told his new lady that he had to see this assignment through and afterward he and his love could be together. Was that what Georgia was? A commitment? An assignment? She didn't want to be a responsibility to him.

Well, what the hell do you want? her mind shouted. *You don't want him because he's your boss, yet you don't want him to find anyone else. Not going to give him any grass, but going to tell him where to graze, Georgia MacKenzie?*

"You're quiet tonight," Neal said as he flanked her on the right and the bodyguard was on her left.

"I'm just tired . . . of all this. I want Cusamano

caught and my life back. I want to come and go as I please. I'm tired of this thug controlling my life."

"It'll be over soon, Mac."

"Not soon enough." She opened her car door as both Neal and the bodyguard looked inside.

"You sure you don't want Bren and me to come over for the weekend?"

"I'm positive."

"Well, get some rest."

"What else is there for me to do?" Georgia turned the key in her ignition and the police car behind her blinked its lights. "Thanks, Neal. Love to Brenda."

A cop removed the traffic horses and Georgia parked her car in the reserved space in front of her house. As she exchanged greetings and looks with the other policemen, she swore she smelled charcoal—like someone in the neighborhood was barbecuing. *It's dark and cold, I know it's impossible that anyone would be cooking out tonight,* she thought absently as she climbed her stairs, punched in her alarm code, and opened her door. All of her lights were on, and as she hung up her coat in the closet, she noticed Jared's hat on the hook, and a beautifully carved wooden box. She didn't see or hear him, but Will Downing sang softly. *Must be in the bathroom,* she thought, and then glanced over at the sofa and saw that the fireplace had been lit. The once roaring fire had rested into a smoldering, welcoming flicker. A perfect night for a fire, she surmised as she walked toward the flames and saw a blanket on the floor with place mats. *What has this man got up his sleeve tonight?* she wondered with delicious anticipation.

She walked past her dining room, kicking off her heels before she got to the kitchen. Home-made potato salad, steaming corn on the cob, and a pitcher of iced tea stood at the ready. "An indoor picnic," she said aloud, and smiled.

She decided to go upstairs to change and pro-ceeded to the back stairs when she saw movement outside her French doors. Automatically, her heart stopped. Cusamano was on her deck. She looked right and left for a butcher knife, then thought of the policeman at her front door. She'd go get him and then realized that there should be one at her back door as well. Had Cusamano killed him? The man wasn't trying to get inside—he was standing there—waiting. Georgia tiptoed closer toward her doors. She carefully pushed back her sheers. Panic ceased when she then recognized that, on the other side of the glass panels, it was Jared. Wrapped in a blanket of black smoke, with a long fork and spatula—grilling. That was what she had smelled as she parked her car. He was grilling for *her*. The tip of her nose burned like a thousand prickly needles, and her heart leaped with joy. Her mind had no defense against the tide of feelings that flooded her senses. This man left work early, braved the dark and cold to grill a hamburger for her. No grand gesture could ever mean as much to her as this simple one—giving her something he knew she loved. Her eyes were bright with tears watching him flip and place the meat on a tray. At this defining moment, she knew. Despite her best defenses, she knew she was falling for this man. Her heart somersaulted with an "I told you so," her stomach flipped, her knees grew weak, her pulse raced, and she grinned like a child at Christmas who'd just received the only gift she wanted. She was falling in love and in trouble, and from sheer habit, her rational mind ran the old commercial—*he is your boss; this cannot turn out well.* Her other senses conspired and told her not to be so hard on herself. When all the threat was over, she could handle this flirtation with time and distance. *Right now, just enjoy the picnic,* she thought. *You deserve this special feast.*

Pleased but paralyzed by her conflicting emotions, Georgia stood there looking at Jared. How could this happen? Why did it happen? When? Twice in one lifetime? There are women who have never loved once and yet she'd found two exceptionally good men one after the other. Can lightning strike twice? Her mother had found love again. After her father's death when Brody Mac Jr. was in high school, her mother had found Myron. They married only after her brother graduated from college. Georgia was hard-pressed to forgive her mother when she sold their family home and moved into a new house with her new husband; but her mother was happy and now Georgia finally understood. Myron wasn't her daddy, but he made her mama happy. Jared wasn't Tony but he made Georgia happy. At least for a little while. But why did she feel like she was cheating on Tony with Jared? Did she feel guilty that she and Jared had connected in just one week in a way she and Tony never had? She and Jared shared a thread of commonality that wound itself around them like a loving cocoon.

Jared opened the door. "Hi. You're home." He rubbed himself and said, "Whew. It's cold out there tonight."

Georgia didn't trust herself to say anything and blinked in an effort to dry her eyes. She looked at him, tall and handsome and engaging.

"I remembered I owed you a grilled hamburger from the night we were stuck in the elevator."

He smiled—that all-out Jared smile; the one with those luscious lips, when his eyes crinkled and his left dimple appeared.

"Fried chicken over here," he said, walking toward the kitchen. He wanted to kiss her hello but passed her, not trusting himself to stop.

He hadn't left early for somebody else; it was for *her*. Overcome with emotion, she managed to ask, "So, whose skillet is that?"

"That's my trusty cast-iron skillet. Grandma Hattie Mae seasoned it for me."

Jared looked at her. He was just a reach away. He could so easily take her in his arms and just kiss her, and it took all the restraint he could muster not to pull her to him. He could see in her eyes that she was pleased. That made him happy. That would do for now. They stood in the kitchen and the last of the chicken sizzled, like applause. Clapping that she finally knew how he felt about her. And maybe—just maybe—she could feel that way about him.

"Well." Jared broke the silence with his soft voice. "Why don't you change out of those work duds and get ready for an indoor picnic?"

"Okay," she said quietly. "What's up with the box by the door?"

"Oh. You noticed that."

"My house. New furniture. Yeah, I did."

"You like it? It's kinda nice. It's a ceremonial box I got from a trip to Belize."

"Oh, really?" Georgia said, and thought, *I don't want anything that you and Courtney picked out in my house.*

"I bought it a while back when me and my boys took a spring break jaunt during college," he said, reading her mind. "It's made of Honduran mahogany. I added the cushion so I could sit on it when I remove my shoes." His knowing eyes were full of mischief as he toyed with her.

"Oh."

"Did you see any shoes?"

"No."

"In the box."

She was smiling up at him, enjoying this as much as he.

"I'm glad something is in the box," she said, before scurrying up the back stairs, leaving him playfully perplexed. "'Cause you sure won't stay there . . . boss," she said out of earshot as she went into her room and began shedding her work clothes. "But I ain't mad at ya. Not tonight."

Jared finished setting the blanket in front of the fireplace, whistling along with the music. His feelings were undeniable. Her eyes were saying things that her lips weren't, but that was all right with Jared. He had all the time in the world; he had a lifetime. The old saying sprang to his mind, "The race is not always to the swift or the battle to the strong."

Returning downstairs she asked, "Can I help you do anything?"

He looked at her freshly scrubbed face and said, "Freckles."

She blushed. "Just a few."

"Like everything with you, quality, not quantity. The few you have are really prime."

Georgia chuckled but didn't speak.

He wondered if she had freckles any other place on that beautiful body. He wondered if he could connect the dots and make an animal or spell a word. "You can put ice in the glasses for the tea." Jared backed away. "We have lemonade in the fridge."

"No wine?"

"Not after the other night. I think you should lay off the spirits tonight."

"I can handle it."

"No, you can't."

This night was for reflective conversation. As they lay on the floor in front of the fire they swapped stories about growing up as a true minority—being black and smart and always living in a world of double-consciousness. Jared spoke of his experiences at Princeton, then U Penn, his meteoric rise to become one of the youngest DAs in the country; of possibly staying where he was, of considering being mayor or going into private practice. They began a game of Monopoly but didn't finish before they went off to bed.

On the back stairs, after they'd cleaned up, Georgia said, "Thank you, Jared. This was a perfect end to a long, tiresome week. It's just what I needed."

"I'm glad. It was fun. We'll do it again sometime. I still owe you a leg of lamb."

"You don't 'owe' me a thing."

"It's the sweetest of debts." He touched her mouth with his fingers.

She wished it was his lips gently pressed upon hers instead. She couldn't remove her eyes from his lusciously inviting pair. If he'd tried to kiss her, she would have let him. "Well, good night."

"Night."

As she ascended her stairs she heard Brenda Russell urging her on with "If Only for One Night." She paused on the upstairs landing. They could make love for just one wonderful night.

Don't be stupid, her inner voice admonished. *Go to bed. You don't have a new boss yet.* Reluctantly, Georgia completed her climb up the last three steps and thought—

But if and when she did . . . Jared Jaymes was her second stop.

Chapter 6

Rainy, cold, dreary weather ushered in Saturday morning and Georgia slept until eleven. She rolled over and looked at her silent clock. She had nothing to do and all day to do it in. The next twenty-four hours stretched out before her like a long, empty tunnel and the only thing waiting for her was chores. She smelled the coffee and knew Jared was up and out on errands—he'd told her last night about going to the cleaners, fixing his parents' garage door, and winterizing their window air conditioners. She washed up, changed into sweats, and gathered the laundry from her hamper. She hummed absently as she began to sort clothes in front of the hall washer and dryer hidden behind the louver doors between her bedroom door and the back stairs to the kitchen. She wondered if she should offer to wash some of Jared's things, but thought that too intimate and would be highly inappropriate. He wasn't really a houseguest; she'd offer him the use of her appliances but not her labor.

She went to the kitchen, which, despite the morning's early rain, was now bathed in wonderful afternoon sunshine. She opened her fridge, got a piece of cold chicken, closed the door, and saw the note:

Gone on errands. Should be back about four. You have my cell number and here's my parents'—call me if you need me or want me to pick up anything.
Jared.

Georgia spent her day in captivity cleaning, washing clothes and her hair, and setting the treadmill for five miles but doing only three. She was out-of-her-mind bored. She talked with three of her girlfriends, her mother, and her grandmother, and was painting her toenails when Jared returned.

"Hi," he said with a bright smile, noting the curve of her brown legs and the cotton that separated each of her freshly painted toes. He had wanted to invite Georgia to his parents' house. Unlike Courtney, Georgia would have come. Courtney never understood why the Jaymes' children didn't hire a handyman or convert their parents' house to central air. She never understood that having them all converge on the family home on a Saturday in late October or early November was a thinly veiled guise to get the family together. His mother liked to "eyeball" her children, their spouses, and her grands. Although Mother Jaymes spoke frequently to her children during the week, she liked to take visual stock of who was tired looking and who looked happy; she liked to carve out some alone time with any of her children who fit in the former category. Mom cooked, Dad supervised, and all the siblings and their families just enjoyed being together for no special reason. It was their annual tradition.

"Hi." Georgia smiled, glad to see him. "What you got there?" she asked of the bags.

"Dinner."

"I wanted to cook today. It's my turn."

"Turn? No turns. I like cooking for someone with such a robust appetite."

"So what's on for tonight?" she asked, walking toward him and the bags on her heels so that her toes stayed elevated and dry.

"Fried catfish, fries—cooked in the same grease—and greens."

"I can do the potatoes and greens."

He looked at her, smiled, and thought, *I love this woman*, but said, "Okay."

"And in the video bag?"

"Ah yes. Movie night. Since we can't go out— I brought them to us."

Georgia was touched. He could very easily have had other plans tonight. "How'd you know what to get?"

"Well, I tried calling but the line was busy and your cell went to voice mail, so I had to freelance."

"Hmm."

"The classics. *Butch Cassidy and the Sundance Kid* for me. And *Out of Africa* for you."

"That's pretty good, Counselor. Two of my favorites."

"I aim to please." His eyes sparkled.

Georgia smiled, then broke their gaze.

"I'll start on the greens," she said. "Neal called. He and Brenda spent last night in the hospital."

"The baby?"

"False alarm." She destemmed the greens and put them into water for the first wash. "I know he'll be glad when this episode is over."

"Just imagine. Do they know how lucky they are?" Jared stopped at the refrigerator before putting the ice cream into the freezer. "Peach," he identified to her inquiring eyes.

"I love peach ice cream."

"I know." Then he continued without missing a beat. "Lucky to be in love and expecting their first baby?"

"Yeah. They are lucky. They're good people. I'm happy for them."

"Do you want children?" he asked casually as he began to peel the potatoes.

"Of course." She washed the greens, filled a pot of water, added crushed red pepper flakes and a smoked turkey drumstick. Her back was to him.

"How many?"

"Maybe three," she mused as if thinking about it for the first time. "What about you?"

"Three is good, but four is even better. Even number."

"Just so you can afford to keep and educate them." She turned around and saw him peeling the potatoes. "I was going to do that."

"I'll peel and put them in cold water. Mustard greens don't take that long to cook. The potatoes will keep until we're ready." He gave her a quick wink.

Until we're ready, Georgia repeated in her mind. *Will* we *ever be ready for what you have in mind, Jared Jaymes?*

"I plan to stay home with my children until they reach school age," she said as she began chopping a small onion.

"That's a good plan. My mother stayed home with us and look how well my brother and I turned out."

"Don't you have a sister too?"

"Two out of three ain't bad." He chuckled.

A buzzer went off.

"What's that?"

"My dryer."

"Where is it?" He glanced around.

"Upstairs. Behind the louvered doors in the hallway. Feel free to use it if you like." She wiped her hands dry.

"Thanks. But what Rosa doesn't wash I take to the cleaners."

"Rosa?" Georgia asked on the back stairs.

"My cleaning lady."

"I bet she loves doing your house; you're such a neat freak."

"Now, how would you know that?"

Georgia rolled her eyes and proceeded up the stairs.

When Georgia returned Jared was dragging the catfish through the egg wash, then a corn-meal mixture.

"The key," he explained to Georgia, "to having crispy catfish is two parts cornmeal to one part flour. Come-sa." He shook off the excess flour and laid the catfish into Hattie Mae's sizzling skillet.

"How did you get into cooking?"

"Survival. I had good food growing up. My mother cooked from scratch every day—all four food groups. I never got into fast food. On a college campus or anywhere else that means cooking for yourself. I even took a cooking class, the summer I studied in Paris. "

"I'm happy to be the beneficiary."

"It's just chemistry and . . . love." He looked over at her. "But that's a recipe for almost anything. Don't you think?"

His deep obsidian eyes challenged and caressed her at the same time. His words and gaze were so intense that they took her breath away. The greens boiled over, simulating her feeling at this moment, and she turned the flame down. There was an intimacy to cooking that she'd never felt until Jared. Two people in close proximity, talking, almost touching in small confines, sharing, relating, and creating—something together. She went to the refrigerator to get the potatoes, hoping the cold temperature would cool her down. She drained them in the sink, blotted them with paper towels, preparing them to accept the hot grease after he finished the catfish.

"Smells delicious."

"Hope it tastes as good." He removed a few pieces of the cooked fish, laying them on a paper towel, and replaced them with those left to be cooked.

Again, she reminded herself that he was just no match for her. He was her boss, but he could outcook anyone she knew. He was extra neat, smart, studied law and cooking in Paris—cheez, what was he doing here with her? Courtney was the perfect match for him. With her smooth dark complexion, Swiss finishing school diction, Philly connections, parents' money, renowned shopping sprees to Paris, and monthly spa visits, Courtney was an Ivy Leaguer's spousal dream and mayor's wife material.

But he's not with Courtney now, is he? her heart challenged. *You are a bright, smart, intelligent, attractive, professional woman,* her mind spoke up. *Any man would be happy—no, lucky—to have you in his life.*

But not your boss! her mind yelled.

"Georgia?"

"Huh?"

"Can you hand me that platter?"

"Sure."

"Where were you?"

"Just thinking."

"I guess I'm not doing too good a job distracting you from reality. It'll all be over soon. I promise."

"No, actually I would really be going crazy if you weren't here with me. But I just can't stand being trapped in my house. Not when it was such a pretty day today and tomorrow is supposed to be gorgeous."

"Well, things have a way of working out," Jared said with a secret smile.

Georgia looked at him suspiciously.

"If you hand me the potatoes, I'll put them in and you can plate up the greens. We'll be ready to eat."

"How about a glass of wine to cut all this grease?"

Jared shot her a mock-shocked look.

"Oh, excuse me. Wine to aid in the digestion."

"Just one bottle. Not two like the last time."

"We did not have two bottles of wine the last time," Georgia shot back jokingly.

"You're right. You had one and a half bottles—I had two glasses."

"Aw!" She laughed. In a normal relationship this would be when she'd jab him playfully in the side and he would grab, then kiss her. He'd rub his body against hers, turn off the burners, they would make love, and in a couple of hours come back to a ruined, greasy dinner. They wouldn't even care; probably order in—Chinese takeout. But this wasn't a normal relationship. "Even tipsy, I still kicked your butt in Scrabble."

"Touché. Women are more verbal than men. *Vex* was the perfect word."

"I think you better cut your losses right now, Counselor. Or you'll be eating and watching those movies alone."

"Too far?" He smiled.

His gorgeous lips parted and the left dimple appeared. "Yes." She laughed with him.

They ate and talked generally about everything, yet nothing. Somehow just being in each other's company was comforting and easy. They watched the movies, putting the player on pause when her girlfriends called from the restaurant thanking her for the champagne. While she talked, he went to spruce up the potato chips by reheating them and adding spices. When he returned they began by lying at opposite ends of the couch, their knees and feet meeting in the middle of the cushions. They'd thrown in *Lady*

Sings the Blues for good measure only because neither was ready to go to bed. By the end of that movie, Georgia had fallen asleep on Jared's shoulder. He loved the feel of her there next to him. When the music stopped, she awakened.

"It's over?" she asked groggily.

"Yeah. Billie died." He stood and offered her his hand. "You want my arm to fall off?" He quoted the Billie Dee Williams line from the movie.

Georgia laughed. She took his hand and he helped her up and into him like he had done in the elevator. Georgia almost swooned like Diana Ross had. The nearness of him was intoxicating to Georgia. The feel of him tantalizing. His chest grazing her breasts ever so gently. They hadn't been this close since slow-dancing in Neal's basement. A quiver of restlessness moved between her thighs. She took a deep breath, wishing that he would bend to kiss her. She was a fearless tigress in the courtroom; however, here in the privacy of her own home, she was timid, tentative . . . it was yet another new feeling for her compliments of Jared Jaymes.

"You better get up to bed," he suggested huskily, his jaw flexing and relaxing as he fought the urge to taste her lips.

"Yeah." She broke the hold he had on her. She went to the steps and turned. "Thanks, Jared. This was the best Saturday night I've had in a long time."

"I'm glad." He smiled and shoved his hands into his pockets.

He looked like an impish boy of twelve with a

crush on an older woman, Georgia thought as she climbed the steps.

She combed her hair, brushed her teeth, and took her shower. She longed for a return to a time when nocturnal lovemaking would require a morning shower as well.

Down the hall Jared Jaymes did the same thing—only his was a cold shower, to cool the blood set to a boil by Georgia MacKenzie. When finished, he opened the bathroom door. The light was out, her room was completely dark, not even a glow from the television. He smiled, turned right, and went to his room in the front of the house. He'd have to step up his plans. This was killing him.

Georgia stretched into a stream of sunshine. She heard the faint sound of music, and the aroma of freshly brewed coffee tickled her nose.

"Darn it," she said. She had wanted to rise early and cook Jared a Sunday breakfast: French toast.

She washed up, dressed, and sauntered down the back stairs, keeping the syncopated rhythm with the spirituals from the radio.

"I like your taste in music," she said, announcing herself, causing Jared to look up from the Sunday paper.

"Good morning," Jared greeted, turning from the den's couch to face her. He took off his glasses and put the paper down. "Freckles."

Georgia smiled and gave him a quick glance, taking in his casual black ensemble, knit shirt, belt, slacks, and socks. He looked like a bittersweet Hershey's bar —good enough to eat.

"Gospel music? Who knew? I dunno, Counselor," she teased. "Once again, I'm going to have to reevaluate you." She looked over at him on her sofa with the papers strewn around him. He looked like he belonged there.

"Next best thing to being there." He let his eyes drink in her form and smiled appreciatively.

He rose and she watched him walk toward her. Her pulse quickened and her heart said a special good morning to him as her mind grew cautious at his approach. He was going to kiss her quick on the lips, she thought with anticipation. He walked past her into the kitchen, leaving her to inhale his freshly washed body and a subtle splash of aftershave.

"Hungry?" he asked with a smile. "Silly question."

"Something smells good." She had to redirect the electric energy being generated on this holiest of mornings.

"Frittata." He beamed, checking to make sure the eggs had cooked all the way through. "You're up earlier than I expected. It's supposed to be eaten at room temperature."

"What happens if we eat it hot?"

"Let's live on the wild side and see." He took it out of the warmer and touched it with his fingers. "Perfect."

Just like you, she thought, watching him reach up for juice glasses. "Don't you ever sleep in?"

He looked at her evenly and said, "When I have reason to."

His dancing ebony eyes sparkled. Georgia blushed, and her knees buckled.

He would love nothing more than to sleep until noon with Georgia wrapped in his arms. Truth was that he was too excited at the prospect of seeing her to lounge in bed. He preferred to get up and get her up so their day together could begin. "I set the table. Grab the juice and toast and we can eat."

She followed him to the dining room, where he had fried potatoes and onions keeping warm in an unlit chafing dish. Beside each place setting was a mask with fake, plastic glasses and funny noses attached. "What's this? Catch an after-Halloween sale?"

"I'll explain later. Right now . . . let's grease please." He held her chair out for her and watched her position, then place her cute little derriere in the seat.

"Thank you."

They said grace, ate, and listened to Patti LaBelle sing "When You Are Blessed, It's Like Heaven."

"That was better than the International House of Pancakes." She sighed with contentment.

"I should hope so."

Georgia looked at the brittle sunshine cascading through the arched window of her living room and said, "What a beautiful day the Lord hath made."

"Amen," Jared testified. "How would you like to enjoy it?"

"From the inside out?"

"Let's go for a good old-fashioned Sunday drive."

"Really?"

All that was missing was a snaggle-toothed smile and pigtails, Jared thought. She looked like an expectant child who was just granted her most precious wish.

"Sure. We'll wear our disguises." He smiled and held up the glasses and funny nose mask.

She laughed.

"You game?"

"Heck yeah!"

"Go get dressed."

Jared put the dishes in the dishwasher while she changed clothes, smiling at how excited she was at the prospect of going out. His heart had broken last night when he overheard her make arrangements with the manager of the restaurant to send the bottles of champagne to her friends' table. Georgia had cabin fever and it was his job to do something about it. He got clearance from the police chief and an extra detail to follow them on their drive. Little things that didn't cost a thing but time and creativity made her so happy. That was one of the things he loved about her.

"Ready!" She sprang down the stairs dressed in chocolate slacks with matching boots, a tangerine sweater, and her leather jacket.

Although a little disappointed that she wasn't showing off her legs, he smiled and said, "That was fast!"

"C'mon. Before you change your mind." She got her shoulder bag and looped her hand through his arm and dragged him to the front closet. She got his leather jacket, removed his shoes from the box, and reached for the door.

"Wait!"

"What?"

"Don't forget these." He held up the fake nose and glasses.

"You nut. Anything to get out of here."

There was a knock from the other side of the door. Jared opened it and his Hummer was waiting and running at the curb, behind it an unmarked police car with two men.

"Okay. Take her first," Jared directed as policemen flanked Georgia on either side and whisked her into the open car door, then slammed it shut. In two seconds, Jared appeared in the driver's seat.

"Wow. Impressive," Georgia said to deflect her edginess, trying to forget that someone wanted to kill her.

Jared flicked on the gospel station they had been listening to in the house and said, "Here we go. Music for a Sunday drive."

Philly disappeared behind them. Jared opened the moonroof and watched Georgia finally relax.

A lone rider on a Harley wove in and out of traffic and she thought momentarily about Tony. During Sunday drives, she'd been on the back of that bike holding on to him for dear life, her hands wrapped around his waist, her head resting on his back. Today instead, she was well protected in a tank called a Hummer, cruising leisurely down life's highway. To redirect her thoughts, she looked at the trees, naked of leaves, spiked against the clear, cloudless blue sky. She would miss the change of seasons if she did take the Los Angeles offer she'd been contemplating.

The prestigious Felton, Mayfield and Dasher Law Firm had been relentless in pursuing her even without the Cusamano win. "Your ninety-five percent conviction record is impressive enough," the headhunter had said. Georgia wasn't interested in L.A., but then she thought, *Why not?* She'd entertained a career change from time to time, but she really wasn't interested in California. Probably only her brother, Brody Mac Jr., would visit. Her mother had her own life, and Georgia couldn't get Grandma Mac to come to Philly, let alone three thousand more miles away. That firm had been after her for some time, relenting only when she became engaged to Tony, but they were hot on her trail again. So Georgia threw ridiculous contingencies at the law firm, starting with a healthy six-figure salary, and they agreed. She had her house in Philly; they said they'd rent it for her and provide her with one in any L.A. area. She asked for the Brentwood neighborhood, they countered with "what style?" She asked for a Jaguar, a vintage XJ12, and they asked, "What color?" It was deliciously frightening that they wanted her so badly, but she'd heard a lot about L.A. and its penchant for money and conspicuous consumption. They pressed her for a visit and she'd put them off until after the Cusamano case. They'd called to express their concern about the threat and ended with "only the good ones are threatened. You must be ready for a change. We want you in L.A., Ms. MacKenzie." Once she put Cusamano away and his crazy brother was no longer threatening her life, she'd have to get serious about the L.A. offer. It had more appeal than the New York firm's offer. She could stay in Philly . . . but—

As Jared made a turn, she looked over at him before his gaze swung back around. If she stayed here, he would still be her boss. If she went to L.A. he wouldn't be her boss but he would be three thousand miles away. He would never move to L.A. Jared came to Philadelphia when he was two. For all practical purposes, he was Philly born and would die here; he loved this town. Either way, she was going to lose him.

He glanced over at her. "Penny for your thoughts?"

"Just noticing the trees. They must be beautiful in their fall color. Sorry we missed them."

"We'll have to come back next fall and see." He smiled.

Her heart leaped at the prospect that they wouldn't even know each other next fall, and her mind gave an internal *Hmph*.

"Do old-fashioned Sunday drives often?" she asked.

"Actually, it's been quite a while. I've missed them. With the eighteen-hour days and the hectic weekend commitments—no time to breathe before Monday morning comes and I'm back at work." He steered off the expressway and smiled remembering. "After Sunday dinners my dad would pile my mom and the three of us in the car and we'd go for ice cream, then take a ride in the country. They're from the South and I think the

Philly asphalt Monday through Saturday would get to them."

Georgia chuckled. "I know that feeling."

"We had to stop by my house first."

"Your house?"

"Yeah. I loved this one huge, four-story, stone Victorian house with a mansard roof that sat on the corner of a neighborhood we could only drive through then. Sure couldn't afford it. And if you dawdled too long a police car would come and ask if you were lost."

"Those were some times. Ever wonder what happened to 'your' house? Who lives there now?"

"Nope." He glanced over at her. "I do."

"Well, that's quite a coup."

"Dreaming, goal-setting, and action—that's all it takes."

"So have you *ever* wanted something and not gotten it?"

"Nope, not yet." He looked at her. "The jury's still out on a couple of things."

Georgia surmised that she was one of them.

"I really don't want to break my streak," he said with a wink.

At one o'clock the radio station switched from gospel's *Sunday Morning Joy* to *Memory Lane*. The couple sang "Papa Was a Rolling Stone" with the Temptations and "I'll Take You There" with the Staple Singers.

"I think your radio is almost as good as mine," Georgia said.

"This bass is fierce."

When Jeffrey Osborne crooned that they both deserved each other's love, they grew quiet and reflective. Georgia relished the comfortable silence; a man driving a car he loved on the open road, and her being in the clean, crisp air. They could have been seen by the outside world as lovers on a Sunday afternoon, out for a drive in the countryside. The only other car on the two-lane road was the police car behind them about a quarter of a mile. Jared slowed on the fringes of a little hamlet called Harmony. Tucked off the road sat the Brookside Inn, its inviting candles flickering in the window.

"It's almost dinnertime. You hungry?" he asked. "We can get a bite to eat before heading back."

"I can always eat," Georgia said with a wide grin.

Jared made the left turn and the truck's tires crunched on the gravel as he parked and cut the ignition. He walked around, opened Georgia's door, and held out his hand. She took it. He didn't let go. Her heart raced as they walked though the inn's restaurant door, separating only when they were seated at a small table for two next to the fireplace. Their knees touched under the white linen tablecloth. Their long legs tangled, and they laughed as they rearranged them so they straddled each other's, settling in like they were going to slow-dance before going still one against the other's. Georgia was glad she had on pants, although the thin layer of lined wool did nothing to calm the warmth generated by his legs. In the glow of the embers from the fire and the dancing candle on the table, a tuxedoed man softly played old standards on a piano as an unobtrusive backdrop to more old stories from childhood to the present. They spoke in hushed tones for more than three hours. Every now and then, Jared would rock their legs together, just to take advantage of the connection. Only when they rose to leave did they notice other patrons in the restaurant.

Georgia excused herself for the ladies' room while Jared paid the bill.

The smiling woman cashier handed Jared his change and asked, "Newlyweds?"

"From your lips to God's ear." Jared grinned.

"You go for it. That girl's in love with you," she confided with a wink.

"I hope you're right."

"Right about what?" Georgia asked, approaching.

"That this is a lovely place," Jared said.

"Yes, it is," Georgia agreed.

"We have cabins with fireplaces down by the stream," the lady offered with a suggestive gleam.

"Ah, thank you," Jared said. "Good night."

"You two come back—after—you know," she said with a wide smile to Jared.

Georgia eyed them both suspiciously. "After what?" she asked as she stepped up into the Hummer.

"After the ball is over," Jared teased, closed the door, and climbed in on the other side.

"I tell you, Jared Jaymes, there is no end to your charisma and charm. I mean, you wowed a middle-aged, white woman in Harmony, Pennsylvania."

"I'm only interested in 'wowing' one woman," he said, glancing over at her. He reached over and touched her hand, caressing it in his. It felt good there. She didn't pull away. That made his heart happy.

When the policeman tooted lightly, Jared turned the ignition.

The truck purred in the darkness and the rocking was soothing to Georgia. Jared's hand wrapped about hers seemed so natural. It was warm, dry, soft, and protective as he rubbed his thumb gently over hers. He didn't let go until they reached the outskirts of Philly and had to negotiate the beltway.

We got back too fast, Georgia thought. The day ended too quickly.

As they pulled onto her street, she and Jared sat in the car while policemen swept her house. The pair waited for them to come and escort her back inside.

She looked at his concerned profile whittled against the pitch of the night. It had begun to drizzle.

"Thank you, Jared," she said, breaking the silence. "I really needed today."

"I hope you enjoyed it." He looked at her and in the reflective streetlight, his eyes sparkled. "I know I did."

As Etta James began singing "A Sunday Kind of Love," Georgia focused on his handsome face, his lips, and she fought to breathe in and out. He took her hand again, rubbed it gently with his fingertips, then brought it to his lips and kissed it. "I love this song."

"Me too," Georgia said weakly.

"I'm not surprised. We have a lot in common."

Georgia couldn't respond. The sight and feel of those luscious lips on her hand made her heart pump double time. She then heard the sound of his leather jacket on the leather upholstery and realized that Jared was moving closer to her. Her heart stopped as he tenderly took her face in his hands. She let out a soft gasp of surprise and pleasure, as his long tapered fingers caressed the sides of her cheeks. She tilted her head and he hesitated—he looked at her as if he were having some internal dialogue, weighing the pros and cons of his actions. Then he closed his eyes and pressed his lips, ever so gently, to hers. The sensation rioting through her body forced her eyes shut, as her stomach flipped and her spine quivered. When he parted her lips with his tongue and tangled it with hers, it catapulted her to a place she'd never been. A place only their kiss created. It seemed like the earth peeled away and Georgia was on the other side of the universe, dotted with quiet stars and filled with the peaceful tranquility of space. Sunday or not, she heard the rustle of cherubs' wings and the shuffle of angels' feet. As she and Jared kissed, she didn't know who she was, or where she was, but figured it must be heaven. She shuddered and her unseeing eyes fluttered open, but then her heart closed them, and she relaxed and melted into him.

Omigod, this man can kiss! He tastes as good as he looks, were her only mortal thoughts. She heard a moan and didn't care whether it was from him or her. Her cheek nestled on his shoulder, his hands expanded across her back, bringing them still closer than close. Out of this world, she rode on a single raindrop back to earth, wanting to savor and remember every detail when . . . Jared stopped.

They were forehead to forehead when he said,

"Sorry." He didn't want to take advantage of her and the wonderful afternoon they'd shared. He hadn't meant for this to happen in the car like impulsive, necking teenagers.

"Don't be," Georgia managed breathlessly, her bodily juices flowing from every pore of her being.

There was a light tap on the window. "All clear," the policeman said.

"Ready?" Jared asked.

Georgia nodded her head.

"It's raining. You want an umbrella?"

"No."

The truck door swung open and policeman flanked her and returned her to the house with Jared behind them.

Jared thanked the cops, closed and locked her door, and engaged the alarm, as Georgia checked her messages. She listened to those from her girlfriends, mother, grandmother, brother, and Neal.

"Where are you, girl?" Neal asked. "Pick up." He waited a few seconds. "Don't make me come over there. Pick up." He waited a few more seconds. "I guess you're washing your hair or something. I would tell you to call but I can hear you say 'I'll see you tomorrow.' So I guess I will. Let me know if you need anything, Mac. Bye."

"So loved," Jared said, returning from the kitchen.

"I'm lucky," she said with a smile. "And a little tired." She wasn't really but she had to get away from Jared. It was one thing to kiss in the car under the watchful eye of law enforcement, quite another to do so in the privacy of an unchaperoned house. She didn't trust her mind to rein in her totally out of control heart.

He took her hand and said, "It's early."

"For you."

"How about one last dance of the evening?"

The music at the inn was still swirling around in her head. She smiled. "We heard some great sounds tonight."

"Music is the laughter of the heart."

Georgia chuckled. "The poetic Mr. Jaymes." She realized that Jared had brought music back into her life. She played it all the time, but this week with Jared—this night, she *heard* it again. It enveloped and filled her to overflowing. She'd missed it.

"Just one dance?" he repeated as he took her hand and led her to the center of the living room. "Whatever is cued up on your old-school tape?"

He gave her that irresistible Jared smile with the dimple.

"Not 'A Sunday Kind of Love.'"

"We'll see."

"Okay." She hoped it was. "One dance." She'd like something slow.

Jared punched the machine and The Main Ingredient twirled through the room with "I Want to Make You Glad."

"Ah! You planned this!" Georgia accused playfully, but Jared didn't let go of her hand.

"It's providence." He grinned and drew her to him.

"It's a conspiracy." She let him wrap her body with his.

She felt his projected maleness, now clothed in

black, against her inverted femaleness, and her body reacted as if she were still in the car. Her heart and soul were celebrating the feel of him holding her as the lyrics spoke of her being too on guard with her feelings and a little too alert; of his just wanting to love her and make her happy to come home in the evening. With the whirl of sounds, and the feel of him, Georgia felt herself losing the struggle, succumbing to the familiar and the yearning for more than was currently offered. The floor seemed to vaporize and only Jared held her on terra firma—in this place called earth. Sensations pooled in her secret garden and radiated out to every molecule, nerve, and synapse in her body. She was responding to not only a desire but a need for him, as if she were narcotically addicted to his touch; as if she couldn't help herself. The song ended and Georgia reluctantly pulled away. He let her go.

"One record," she reminded him, breathlessly.

"One record."

Why is he such a damn gentleman? Georgia thought as she walked slowly to the steps and stopped on the second one. Jared looked up at her. She looked over and above his head, and her eyes fell on Tony's picture on the mantel. She smiled and said, "Do you remember that day when we ran into you and Courtney in the park?"

"When I first noticed your freckles?"

Georgia chuckled, surprised that he'd recall it. "Tony picked you for me. If anything happened to him, he picked you."

Jared stepped up on the first step and said, "I want you to pick me, Georgia."

She stared at him for a long time. Her heart and mind were battling again as the next song by Donny Gerard, "Stay Awhile with Me," pleaded Jared's case.

"I don't want to take his place, Georgia. I can make a place of my own. If you let me."

Georgia heard him, but couldn't respond. His words were so profound. She had no answer for him.

"Thanks again, Jared," she finally said. "I really had a great time."

"My pleasure," he acquiesced, backing away. Had he gone too far? "I'm leaving early tomorrow, so I'll see you at work."

He watched her climb the stairs and touched his lips where hers had been and smiled. He'd kissed her, but she had kissed him back. She'd given him a kiss to build a dream on.

Georgia reached her bedroom and prepared for her nightly shower. She went from drawer to drawer to get her nightclothes but couldn't concentrate. Her mind was distracted and not because of the Cusamano threat. Finally, with no reservations, she admitted that she was *in* love and yes, trouble. In love with the wrong man—her boss, and in troubled conflict with her own values and beliefs. She showered quickly and jumped into bed. All she wanted to do was sleep—fast, deep, and hard. Maybe her good sense would return tomorrow. Maybe she'd be out of love with him tomorrow.

Jared emptied the dishwasher of the clean dishes he'd washed before they took the drive—before they kissed. He kept replaying the kiss. He hadn't meant to kiss her. He'd stepped over the line, but he couldn't help himself and she didn't resist. She had tilted her head and leaned into him, returned the kiss accompanied with a pleasurable moan. He couldn't let her go. The one dance with the perfect record he hadn't planned, followed by another. He looked up to the heavens and thanked Big Brody Mac. He smiled as he wiped off the counter. That kiss and the dance were both release and filling up—with love, pride, prayers answered, and realties denied.

He had to make sure he didn't make any other advances—not now. He didn't want her mind to later rationalize that he knew she was vulnerable, frightened, not herself, and he took advantage of her. That anything that happened now was all tied up with a resolution over Tony, the Cusamano threat, and being cooped up in her house with no other friends or outlets. She'd say that it was the only reason she fell for her boss. The only reason she allowed him to kiss her.

Despite her lips' denial, her eyes spoke volumes. He felt her heart, body, and soul were on his side, but her mind was too grounded. He couldn't do anything to offend it and have it throw a red flag on the play, call "Foul!" and have her close the door on them forever. Her mind was doing a helluva job as guardian of her values and morals, even when her heart wanted otherwise. Her mind had served her well this far, telling her the difference between right and wrong—no matter how much she wanted that candy—not from a stranger. Don't ride in the car with boys, don't fool with married men, and don't date your boss. MacKenzie maxims that had been passed down from generation to generation like an heirloom grandfather clock, but her treasures were more traditional than anything tangible. Her maxims were a family's badge of honor; no one in her family had ever done drugs or gone to jail, gone hungry or been a pregnant teenager; hers were family facts, not value judgments. Traditions, good, bad, or otherwise, all have to start somewhere by somebody, and he was happy that Georgia's had been so honorable. All these tenets were at the core of her character, which set her apart from all the other women he'd known. They'd served her well as she'd made strides, achievements, and accomplishments for which she could be proud. She'd never had them challenged or compromised before. Her reward was that she'd lived her life, this far, with no regrets.

Jared didn't want to be her first regret or humiliation. So he needed to approach her when she was free and clear and knew what she was doing, and why—because she loved him. Another move could be premature and jeopardize the life he envisioned for them both. There were guys who would gladly take advantage of her vulnerability, but Jared wasn't one of them. He didn't want her for this week of playing house or even a few months—he wanted her for always and forever. Jared intended to prove to her mind that, despite being her boss, he was worthy of Georgia MacKenzie. He would either be her greatest love . . . or her greatest regret.

Chapter 7

The clap of thunder awakened Georgia from a deep fretful sleep. Instead of being satisfied by Jared's kiss, it had left her wired and wanting more. She listened to the rain beating down on the roof. The sound that used to soothe her, now made her anxious. The torrential rain fell like heavy footsteps above her head. She lay there for a few minutes, then rolled over on her side facing her balcony door. In a streak of lightning she saw something . . . a figure . . . a man dangling from her roof. She bolted upright with a scream.

From down the hall Jared heard a shrill and it took him two seconds before he realized it was Georgia. He sprang from the bed and met her running toward him in the hallway.

"It's Cusamano—on my balcony!"

Jared pushed her behind him and she pressed right up against him as he slowly began advancing toward her bedroom.

"No, Jared. No." She pulled his arm. "Oh God . . . don't go in there."

Jared held up his finger to silence her.

She was visibly shaking. She didn't want him to go into her room and be killed. She didn't want to leave his side. "Jared," she whispered.

He pushed her to the side wall, positioned her against the louver door, and with his eyes motioned for her to stay.

Jared eased into her bedroom. He quickly turned to find her balcony door closed and a rope swinging from the roof. Jared breathed a sigh of relief and Georgia rushed into his arms.

The police filed up the steps and filled her room. As Jared and Georgia were locked in an embrace, they heard the police report into their walkie-talkies that "Cusamano tried from the roof." They heard the order to seal both sides of the row of brownstones.

"Are you all right?" Jared asked, her body shaking uncontrollably against his.

All Georgia could do was nod her head.

She was terrified knowing that Cusamano was so close to carrying out his threat against her. She could have been murdered in her sleep and Cusamano could have killed Jared as a bonus. With Jared there she had been lulled into a false sense of security. Her heart beat rapidly and she shuddered at the thought.

"Georgia, it's okay."

"No, it's not! Stop saying that! We could have been killed!"

"Shhhh," Jared soothed. Despite her resistance, he pulled her tighter to him and rocked her like a frightened child. "You're trembling."

He held her even tighter. "Trust and believe, I wouldn't let anything happen to you."

There was a flurry of activity swirling about them. She felt as lost as a Gypsy in the twilight zone, but Jared never broke his embrace as he gave information and remained nonplussed. Somehow, Georgia felt as long as he was there, holding her tightly, she didn't have to worry about anything.

As Jared held her he saw something—a man— ease from her backyard through the fence and into the alley. "I'm going out front," Jared said, startling Georgia.

"Wha? No!"

"It's all right. I'm just gonna take a look-see."

"No! That's what the cops are for."

"Listen." He held her by both arms like a recalcitrant child begging for a time-out. "I'll be right back. Officer," he called to one of the cops in the room. "Watch her for me. I'll be just minute."

A stunned and numb Georgia stared at Jared tumbling down the back stairs; then she saw him run down her deck stairs through the gate to the back alley. "Oh God, oh God, oh God," she prayed as the darkness ate him up.

Jared followed his hunch. He wasn't sure, it might be nothing. He speculated that as the cops sealed off both ends of the town houses and checked the rooftops, Cusamano had waited a few minutes hidden in the foliage of her garden before going into the alley. Jared just couldn't stand there and let the cops churn about him and not do something, anything that required action. By the time he explained his theory to the cops and was told to let them handle everything, Cusamano could be out of the vicinity. Free to try to kill Georgia another day. This was all too close. Too bold. Jared advanced down the alleyway, stealthily, scrutinizing shadows. A cat meowed and ran past him and Jared pulled out the gun tucked inside a leg holster. A dog barked a few blocks over, and, as Jared approached a streetlight, he listened for other movement. He heard nothing. Then out of the pitch, a figure stepped out and pointed a gun straight at his head.

Cusamano laughed uproariously and said, "I get a two-for. You now and that lawyer bitch later!"

In one swift movement, Jared raised his gun, but he was too slow.

A single shot rang out, piercing the quiet night.

Stunned, Jared waited to feel the bullet rip his flesh.

Cusamano dropped to the ground with a thud, like a sack of potatoes.

Jared looked at him, then his gun. He hadn't fired a shot.

He turned and behind him a lone man stood tall, defiantly, a smoking gun by his side. His face was in the shadow with the streetlight behind him, and Jared didn't know if the man was friend or foe. Didn't know if he was a hit man for the Mob hired to eliminate Cusamano and about to do the DA as well. The man put away his gun in a back holster.

Jared went to check Cusamano to make sure he was no longer a threat.

"He's dead," the gunman announced confidently from where he stood and began walking toward them both.

Jared rose.

The gunman stopped advancing. The dimness of the streetlight shone on the right side of the man's face.

Jared thought him vaguely familiar but was not sure. His wild facial hair concealed most of his features, but his eyes. Something about the eyes. Jared knew them. Kind, playful eyes that did not compute with his recent, casual act of violence.

"Tony Machado," Jared identified, not knowing how or why, the way one might speak the name of an old high school classmate he hadn't seen or thought about in years.

"In the flesh."

"I thought you were dead."

"To everybody I love and care about, I am." He began chewing the gum in his mouth.

"For how long?"

"Forever. It's safer that way for them and me."

Jared wiped his mouth thoughtfully once and said, "I have to tell her."

"Why? By the time you do I'll be back under-cover in another country. No one can find me. I find them."

"You've taken a big risk revealing yourself to me."

"I don't think so. I know you don't give a damn about me. But you love Georgia. You'll keep the secret to avoid her pain."

Jared didn't speak. He felt no need to discuss his feelings for Georgia with anyone.

"Putting her and my family through the ordeal

of a funeral and the mourning afterward is the only thing I have guilt about. Not my decision to join the forces."

Jared stood there looking at the man who hurt Georgia by dying but then, just saved her life.

"Down the road, I would have ended up hurting her anyway. I think of this as my penance for all the pain.

"I was right about you, Jaymes," he chuckled. "You're the best choice for her. You take good care of her or I'll be comin' for you next."

"You don't have to worry about that."

"I know. You better get goin' before the cops discover that what they thought was a car's backfire was a homicide. You don't want to be around here."

Jared looked back at Cusamano lying there, dead. It had begun to rain again, falling like silver needles, and soaking the slump of humanity. Jared turned back around—and Machado was gone.

As Jared walked back to Georgia's house, he wasn't sure whether to detest or respect Tony Machado. He supposed there was a breed of man who suffocated under the yoke of routine; adrenaline-driven men whose brains were hardwired for continual thrills, men who could not handle the transition from carefree passion into mundane martial reality; men who'd rather die than live a predictable, ordinary life. Jared revered and longed to live a predictable, ordinary life with Georgia MacKenzie—that was his goal. *One man's riches is another man's treasure*, he recalled an old saying; Machado had proven how much he'd loved Georgia—first by letting her go.

When Jared arrived at the house, he took the steps by twos and when he entered her bedroom, Georgia ran to him and held him tightly. He returned the bone-crushing embrace as the policeman left down the steps and through the front door. As he held her, Jared supposed if he had to define a feeling for Machado right now, it would be gratitude. Cusamano was dead and Georgia was safe, alive and well in his arms.

Finally, it was quiet and just the two of them.

"You okay?" he asked, still trying to process what had just happened. "Do you want a cup of tea?"

"No. Where'd you go? Are you all right?" She looked into his eyes and felt his face. "I want this over."

It was almost an hour later when Jared broke their embrace by sitting her on the bed. She wouldn't let go of his hand. He knelt in front of her. "It's almost three and you have to get some sleep. Believe me, he won't be coming back tonight. They've got police on the roof now."

"Suppose you hadn't been here?"

"But I was."

"I can't sleep now." She glanced at his handsome face. "You must think I'm an idiot."

"Don't be so hard on yourself." As if suddenly aware that she was half-dressed, he took the robe from the foot of her bed. "Here, put this on."

"Thanks."

"C'mon." He led her down the hall to his room. He pulled off his still-wet shirt, and she averted her eyes as he stepped into a pair of dry slacks and slid his gun into the bureau drawer. He pulled out two pairs of clean sweat socks. "You know I still have your sock from tennis. When you twisted your ankle," he said with a chuckle, realizing how far they had come since then.

"Keep it." She put on his big fluffy socks.

"Since you're not going to sleep, hot chocolate for two."

She followed him down the back stairs to the kitchen and noticed the policeman's silhouette beyond her French doors. Not willing to let Jared out of her sight, she watched him pour the milk into a saucepan, heat it, break up chocolate pieces, and simmer them together. She got down two mugs and cookies from the cupboard. She stood there.

"Almost over." He touched her cheek tenderly and wiped wet from under her eyes.

He poured the brown liquid into the waiting mugs, sprinkled the tops with cardamom, grabbed them both, and said to her, "Lead the way."

Georgia grabbed the cookies and napkins and sat at her dining room table. Jared sat across from her.

She sipped the hot liquid. "Good," she said, still livid at her lack of control and embarrassed by her predicament. "Where did you go?"

"I had a hunch. A bad hunch. I'm here and everything's going to be all right." He smiled quickly, then asked, "Tell me about the first time you had hot chocolate."

"What?" Now she added annoyed to her list of feelings.

"Tell me when?"

She looked at him like he was crazy. "Why the hell would you want—"

His warm soulful eyes calmed her.

"Okay," he began. "You were at your grandma Mac's."

"No. I was with my daddy at a church fair. There was a stand. I must have been only two or three maybe—"

Jared put his chin in his hands, his knuckles pressed to his mouth, as Georgia recounted all things chocolate she, her daddy, her mother, and Evelyn, Tennessee, had. She talked and drank and talked and talked, as Jared continued to process the shock of Machado's return and reinforce his decision not to tell her. To what end? Although he never wanted to keep anything from her, he couldn't prove Machado was here and once the former cop vanished, the information would only serve to hurt her, that Machado chose the excitement of his job over a serene life with her.

As a young prosecutor, ADA, and DA, Jared had been privy to many scandalous, heinous, and outrageous revelations before. He had a lifetime of professional experience keeping secrets under the attorney/client privilege proviso, but none had been as personal as the fact that Tony Machado lived. If he told Georgia, nothing would change for her—more grief and pain and whys? The Tony Machado Georgia knew and loved no longer existed. The Tony Machado she knew and loved would not have left her for a thrill-seeking job. Jared now saw this macho Machado as a coward who sought adrenaline rushes and adventure—like an adolescent who never grows up; for

Machado, leaving was the easy choice. The test of loving somebody was to be with them day in and day out, year after year through the good, bad, and ugly, through happy times but also the tragedy; through babies, bottles, boredom, bodies falling out of shape, bills, bad breath, baldness, mood swings, and the flu. "Sickness and health" wasn't a cliché, because the hard part of sincere commitment was building a rock-solid foundation and facing whatever life hurled your way—together. That was the true test of a man, and Jared's father, grandfather, and great-grand had paved the way for him to be "nothing but." Based on the men in his family before him, Jared's judgmental matrix did not allow him to mock, question, or trivialize Georgia's values, a position left to the small-minded and arrogant. It had been his experience that criticizing a loved one's beliefs only bred eventual resentment.

His daddy used to say there are only three things you can do about a problem: fix it, get rid of it, or live with it. Jared would live with it. Jared would trust that Machado, if he ever loved Georgia, would not reveal himself, and he believed that if Machado did, Jared and Georgia would be able to handle his reappearance together. Clearly, Jared couldn't do anything about the situation but worry himself to death, and he had never given up his life worrying about something over which he had no control, and he wasn't going to start now.

Jared respected Georgia's love for Tony Machado and her right to feel as she did. The same way he respected her creeds. He would do nothing to challenge either, but for her sake, Machado needed to stay gone.

Some old lovers make better memories than resurrected men, Jared thought.

Hours later Georgia interrupted herself with "Omigod." She looked beyond Jared to the closed drapes where bright lights lit the perimeter of the arched window. "All the police cars are back." She jumped up to peek out of her window. She disappeared behind the drapes and then laughed and laughed. She stepped back and opened the drapes. The flood of sunlight assaulted their eyes.

"We've talked all night, Counselor."

Jared smiled.

"Jared Jaymes, you are some kind of man."

"So I've been told," he said without conceit.

"Modest too. Well, time for work."

"Oh no. Not today. Not for you."

"I prefer to work than to sit around here all day."

The phone rang like a referee's bell. Jared answered, listened, and then hung up. He looked at her and said, "Cusamano was killed. Resisting arrest. It's over."

"It's over?" Sheer relief lit her face.

He heard Georgia scream for the second time in his life. He hoped it wasn't his last.

"Thank you, Jared. Thank you, thank you, thanks for everything. I just couldn't have made it through this ordeal without you!" Excitedly, she headed for the steps.

"Where do we go from here?" He blurted it out. Unscripted.

"I'm going to work and back to normalcy."

"What about us? You and me." His coal-black

eyes caught hers. He could see her inner struggle, an optical resolution, then a complete glazed-over look.

"This time we spent here together was special, Jared. And I respect you even more now—"

"Don't insult me with that sophomoric crap. I'm supposed to be the politician." He had almost died. They were almost lost to each other. He turned toward her. "You love me."

"What?"

"I know you probably haven't even admitted it to yourself but you do." He walked forward. "I love you."

He said it with such strong conviction that Georgia almost keeled over. Under any other circumstances she would have given her eyeteeth to have heard Jared Jaymes say this to her. But not here. Not now. The audacity—

"Did you hear me? I love you, Georgia."

"No. No. No. No. No, you don't. It may *appear* that—"

"Cut the snow job."

"Okay. Are you speaking now as my *boss*? Because that is who you are. My *boss*."

And there it was. Jared had known this would happen. Like an automatic weapon, her defenses sprang up and walled her off from him. He knew he shouldn't have pressed her now. It was too soon. But he had just stared point-blank into the barrel of the gun pointed to his head . . . and lived. Life was too short and too precious and they shouldn't waste one millisecond. "Wow," he said. "The hunter gets captured by the game."

"Excuse me."

In for a penny; in for a pound, he thought, and against his better judgment, he forged on. "I think we have a chance at something really special. No one can afford to push love away regardless of where it comes from. We should play this out. See where it leads."

"So what do you suggest? Sneaking around? Being discreet?"

"I'm all for an open, honest relationship."

"I'm not. Never have been. Never will be. And this is low because you know that."

"That's too bad for both of us."

"We will just return to the status quo—"

"If you think you can."

"I *know* I can." She hadn't meant to snap at him, but she had. He'd been nothing but good to her. "We can be friends—"

"No. We can't."

"Let's not do this now."

"When? When do you think will be a good time, Georgia?"

"When you are no longer my boss." She held his gaze and then said, "I'm going to get dressed for work. That place where we both go and *you* supervise *me.*"

He watched her ascend her stairs probably for the last time. She could not accept that, despite her credo, she loved him and he her. He was inspired and vexed by the current situation, but he knew something she didn't. This was not over by a long shot. He needed all of his plans to fall into place before he could share them with her. He had found a way for him to have the woman he loved and for her to love him *and* keep her self-respect. He needed his plans to work out sooner rather than later. He had to come to her correct and the plans had to be ironclad, logical, and flawless. Until then he knew she would retreat to that safe distant place away from him. He had to make sure he could lure her back when everything fell into place. He hoped he wouldn't be too late. Admitting that you love someone shouldn't be painful. Until then, he'd accept her as the Mistress of Denial.

Georgia would not allow herself to believe that Jared loved her. The idea was ludicrous. Like a rock star who was enchanted by something different, that was all she was to Jared Jaymes: someone different. The women who lined up to just date the brother were an impressive bunch. Even if it were true, he'd get over her in no time. She'd never admit it to anyone else, but he was right— she loved him, but she'd get over that in time too, and life would go on for them both. Meanwhile, she'd keep with her five-year plan and be distantly friendly. Besides, now she was just happy to be here, threat free, and revel in all the job prospects, although she'd pretty much decided on L.A.

Georgia was giddy with the freedom to come and go and "be" again. She sent Jared a huge floral arrangement of spring flowers with a note:

Thanks for everything, Willow.

It was a genuine gesture of gratitude but also a

signal to her mind that this was the period at the end of a great, weeklong interlude. It was over.

She immersed herself in the Cusamano case and, by the end of the week, listened to the judge pass sentence. "Four counts of first-degree murder, conspiracy to threaten an officer of the court, to wit ADA MacKenzie, and holding her and this city hostage for two weeks notwithstanding, sentenced to life with *no* possibility of parole."

Georgia looked at Cusamano and they shared a dull, blank look. She'd expected an outburst from him, a vengeful promise to get her at all costs as he lunged for her throat and was held at bay by guards. Instead of a menacing, dagger-glare sneer at her, he looked tired, beaten, dazed like he didn't care and was glad it was all over. Georgia supposed with his brother dead and the Mob turning their backs on him, he had no clout, no reason to live. It was all anticlimactic and she couldn't believe that it had all happened in just two weeks—the length of a good vacation; one week she'd kept the threat to herself and the second week she and Jared had shared her house.

Closure and relief settled upon her as she accepted congratulations from everyone in the courtroom. Her life had changed so dramatically in such a short time. But defining moments make life-impacting changes—in just seconds, someone wins the lottery, or a mother gives birth to a child—life-changing flashes that occur in a split second. She knew after the week with Jared—her life was irrevocably impacted in the sweetest way. He had touched her on so many different levels and left her so indescribably nurtured. She would never be the same. On one hand she thought their association seemed longer than just seven days, yet on another, it was like the snap of a finger—a blink of the eye in eternity. But it was over—wasn't it?

When Georgia walked into the hallway the media descended upon her and she handled them with her classic grace and aplomb as she continued walking to her office. She'd expected Jared, her boss, to be there. He wasn't. She'd expected him in the courtroom—she hadn't seen him. Neal and the others invited her out for a celebration. She declined. Truth was there was only one person with whom she wanted to share this victory; it might be their last shared win. Her sixth sense told her that Jared was at her house preparing a private celebration, an act of contrition for his absurd proclamation as much as congratulations. That he was sorry he'd overstepped and of course, she was right, they couldn't be more than boss and subordinate. They could be friends—Georgia could live with that. *He's cooked something for me,* she thought. Maybe grilled hamburgers again. No, he wouldn't repeat. The leg of lamb dinner—that was it. She was buoyed by the prospect of something scrumptious. She hadn't seen much of him over the past week. He'd thanked her for the lavish bouquet of spring flowers in November, but they'd both been too busy to share a personal good-bye between them.

Despite herself, she drove home with a wide smile that had anticipation painted all over her face. She couldn't stop giggling. *Okay, just allow me this one last hurrah,* she bargained with her mind. *Then it will be truly over.* She checked her hair and makeup at a stoplight, spritzed perfume from her purse atomizer. She parked and ran to her front door, stifling her enthusiasm just before she inserted her key. Not wanting to ruin his surprise, she slowly entered the dark house and clicked on the vestibule light. She hung her coat up. His hat was not on the hook. The richly carved mahogany box from Belize that held his shoes was gone.

He thinks he's so slick, Georgia thought, and stepped into the dark room. The light clicked on. She smiled.

Quiet.

The light had come on by timer.

"Hello," she sang out. "Anybody home?" She walked into her living room. "It's ADA MacKenzie home from the 'big win of a lifetime.'"

She put her hands on her hips and stood akimbo. "Come out, come out wherever you are."

When only silence answered her, she noticed that there was no soft music or food aroma. Just darkness and stillness mocked her presumption. She went to the French doors and looked at the deck beyond. The grill was as cold as the feeling in her heart. She flicked on the light and went up the back stairs across to the front bedroom that had been his. By the time she came down the front stairs, tears were her only company. Her house was as empty as Monday morning church.

"You fool," she self-chastised. *What did you expect?* she thought.

Again, this *was why you don't date your boss,* her mind yelled as she fought tears.

"Well, Georgia MacKenzie. I guess the surprise is on you."

How had a man come into her *home*, turned it upside down, inside out, and left it a *house*—four walls, a roof, and doors. The past week she hadn't had time to notice the lack of Jared, but now his absence screamed at her. She was insulted and offended. "Stupid, stupid little girl. Daddy was right."

She sat on her steps, looking up at the ceiling so the tears would go back to their origin. *You foolish woman. Fell in love with your boss and didn't even get a ninety-day affair. All of this pain and none of the passion, like getting a divorce and never being married. We never made love, what a gyp*, she thought.

She let her forehead drop into the heel of her hand. In the echo of her empty house she could hear Bobby Blue Bland singing "Members Only" to her—a party for the brokenhearted, "don't need no ticket." She turned sideways and through the banister she saw Tony's picture looking at her from the mantel. He seemed a lifetime ago. They would have been married by now and she wouldn't have gone through this Jared trauma. She and Tony would probably have been pregnant with their first child by now. Their children would have been bright, beautiful, and bilingual. He was teaching her Spanish, the tango, and the samba. Tony was an adventure and they would have had a good life with big arguments and even bigger make-up sex. She was his "Black Magic Woman" and he'd blast Santana's song and they'd dance around the house until they were old and gray or until he just didn't come home one night—the latter came first.

Her love for Tony had been heart-to-heart, but Jared—Jared had been soul-to-soul. The feelings she had for Jared were deeper, richer, wider, and higher and it was only based on one toe-curling kiss and a few slow dances, but when he held her—it was like she was his. Not only did their hearts beat in syncopated rhythms, but their very souls touched.

Georgia felt such guilt over Tony—not like she was cheating *on* him but like she had cheated him. She thought she'd given Tony her all until Jared. Jared had taken intimacy to a level she never knew existed. With Jared, there was an ease and comfort she'd never known with any man before. With Jared it was natural, organic, muscular, and reassuring like sinking your tired aching body into a soothing warm bath and just saying, "Ahhh."

With Jared there was a sameness, no need to explain because he understood being black in America. Instinctively, he could give her comfort or space based on the look in her eye, the slump in her shoulder without being patronizing. Jared brought laughter and music back into her life. They sang the same oldies, from jazz to gospel. He could dance. Could do the D.C. bop. *You can't teach anybody to do the D.C. bop*, she thought, chuckling. He even had a grandma Hattie Mae who made divinity. That thread of commonality wound around them.

She was thankful that she'd never openly dated him. Thankful that she'd been spared the embarrassment of a breakup. Her girlfriends would rally around her, sad-eyed and sadistic about the cold-hearted dog and, after a respectable length of

time, one of them would ask Georgia, "Would you
be offended if I gave him a go?" At least Georgia
only had to deal with her private hurt and humiliation, not anyone else's especially from coworkers
and staff.

Georgia thought, *This is the place in the movie
where the girlfriend would say, "Just sleep with him.
You're moving to L.A. Might as well make a memory."*
Georgia was famous for making memories of her
loved ones. On hard or cold rainy days she'd dust
off their images and attach a memory that would
put a smile on her face. Her daddy was Old Spice
and apples; her granddaddy was bay rum and
pipe tobacco. She'd do that with Jared. He'd be
dead to her when she went to L.A., but she could
use a memory of him. But she wanted a surefire,
for-real tactile remembrance. She wanted to make
love to him before she left and started over. She
wanted imagery she could haul out on a bad day
and hold on to for years to come, until she found
his replacement in the flesh. She could make love
to him for weeks until she left town. No harm, no
foul, but plenty of lovin'. That would be her closure. There would be no unfinished business, it
would be full circle. She'd give herself permission
to do it like the guys do when they "hit it and
quit." Before she could make that happen she had
to take the job in L.A. first—then he would not be
her boss. He wouldn't know that, but she would,
and that would secure her MacKenzie maxim.
That would be good enough for her, provided
that he was willing to operate in secret as they
had successfully done during the threat. No one
could find out about them—she hadn't left yet.

If Jared was unwilling to meet her conditions, then she would forgo the memory-making with him. Even he was not as important, or lasting, as her career. Maybe she'd whip it on him so fiercely that he'd gladly follow her to L.A. for conjugal visits. That would be a win/win situation if they played their cards right.

"Sounds like a plan," she said aloud, and blew her nose. "Maybe he'll be a horrible lover." She went to the refrigerator and took out the last piece of cold chicken. "Yeah. Right."

There were remnants from his cooking: a half-used jar of wasabi, barbecue sauce he'd made, spices he'd mixed for his potato chips, dark chocolate he'd shaved into hot milk, veggies from the frittata. She closed the door and Grandma Hattie Mae's black cast-iron skillet laughed at her from the stove's burner.

Georgia felt in control again, which appealed to her mind. She was going to give herself until after the holidays to call Felton, Mayfield and Dasher, but the prospect of making love with Jared prompted her to do so now. The quicker she finalized that deal, the quicker she could get on with, then get over Jared Jaymes. She yanked up the telephone and called the L.A. firm. They were happy to make arrangements for her visit.

Georgia hung up and looked around her quiet house. Now it was time to pay the piper for that week of heaven. It was just as well that she was leaving. Her Jared-less house would never be the same again. L.A. was both her saving grace and her ultimate tragedy. But now her mind was on sheer bliss. For the remaining weeks she had left here, she intended to enjoy Philly's DA and possibly string a cord from his boxer briefs to her L.A. house. First things first, accepting the job in L.A., then having Jared Jaymes as her own personal good-bye genie.

When Georgia went to work the next day she marched into Jared's office.

"Well, hello, Counselor," he said with a wide grin. "Congratulations."

"Thanks. I'd like to take a couple of days."

"Understandable. You got it."

"Thanks."

"Want some company?"

"No. Thank you." *Some nerve,* she thought. *But if you want to play, I've got plans for you this weekend.*

"Where to?"

"Someplace warm. I'll take the first three days of next week."

"Why not take the whole week?"

"I'll let you know."

"If you don't mind, I need to pick up some of my things."

"You got a key," Georgia sassed.

He watched her walk away from him unable to gage her flippant, quasi-hostile mood. "How was the celebration last night?" He hoped she'd missed him among her friends.

"What celebration?"

"Neal—all of your colleagues. From the big win."

"I went home. *Alone.*" She winked, turned on her heel, and proceeded through the door.

Jared contained himself until she cleared his threshold. *Damn,* he thought. After witnessing her victory in the courtroom he'd left without being seen. He couldn't bear to share her with Neal and everyone else. To be close to her and not be able to touch or hold her would have been agonizing, so he'd left early. If he'd been around in the throes of the jubilation, it would have been suspicious if the DA had declined the high-profile victory celebration of one of his ADAs. He knew there was a chance that his colleagues could see the pride and love he had in his eyes for Georgia MacKenzie—neither of them wanted that. So he'd gone home. He'd put on Ray Charles's "Georgia on my Mind," which kept him company while he whipped up an omelet. Watching CNN as he ate, he imagined her happiness as she celebrated, wishing he were by her side and wondered if she even missed his being there. He quieted his own jealousy that their colleagues could enjoy her judicial coup when he could not. If all went according to his plans, he would be by her side for the next win and all those to follow. He'd finally turned off Ray and gone upstairs willing morning to come so he could see her.

Now, knowing that on the most prestigious triumph of her career, she'd gone home alone stabbed at his heart. He would have loved to go with her, cook her something special, and share a victory dance or two. He'd make it up to her in the most delicious way.

Georgia bided her time and later that afternoon when most ADAs were still occupied in court, she gathered a file and made her move. She knocked on Jared's door and entered.

"There's a *Lady Sings the Blues* and *Mahogany* showing at the Fox in Delaware. Interested?"

Pen poised midair, Jared looked up at her. His eyebrows knitted together as if he hadn't really heard her right. "Come again?"

"You heard me."

He dropped his pen on the desk. "Delaware?"

"Just far enough away so no one will see us."

He eyed her sideways. "Does this mean what I think it means?" He smiled unabashedly.

"See, Jaymes. Already giving it away with that cheesy grin. Please look professional." She stood directly in front of him so passersby could not see his expression. "I thought you'd be good at this . . . but if you're not up to it—"

"Ooohh, MacKenzie. I am up for it. No doubt." He looked down at his desk as if pursuing something there. "But I can't sit through *Mahogany*. There's a film festival at the AFI Theater in Silver Spring, Maryland: *Made For Each Other*—"

"Jimmy Stewart as a young lawyer."

"And *Reckless Moment*."

"You're not suggesting an overnight stay are you, Counselor?"

"Only if you're willing—"

"I am not. We are taking this slow. Snail slow, all the way back to first-date slow or no deal."

"Oh, so no sleepovers until the third date?" he teased.

"Is that how you operate?"

"When they can hold out." He reared back in his chair. "I have standards."

"Speaking of which." She looked in her file for show. "I have conditions of my own. This . . . date and any others, if you choose to accept them, is contingent on us . . . you and me . . . operating surreptitiously. To wit . . . no one, and I do mean 'No Neal One,' must know or find out about us. If they do . . . this deal is off. No questions asked. "

"Sounds fair. I accept," he said too quickly.

Georgia looked into his eyes and said with all seriousness, "I mean it, Jared. I cannot compromise my career for one reckless moment."

"I understand and appreciate that. I promise nothing will happen that you do not want and I will do everything in my power to maintain our privacy. If our cover is blown . . . the deal is off."

Georgia sighed in relief.

He knew what it took for her to come this far and he was beside himself with glee. "So, we'll drive two hours down, see the films, have dinner . . . there are plenty of restaurants on Colesville Road or at City Place or we can go to Bethesda, then drive the two hours back."

Relief washed her face again as she agreed. "I'll leave the details to you. Just so we have the basic understanding."

"We do. One thing. Can I get a kiss good night?" he teased. "Can we neck in the car?"

I love this man, Georgia thought, but said, "We'll see." She smile-smirked, swooped her hair around her ear, and left. By the time she arrived at her office and sat in her chair, swiveling it away from Jared to the Philly skyline, she was as blissful as she'd ever been. She drove her thumbnail between her bottom teeth and asked herself, "Lordy, what have I done?"

The remaining days of the week crawled by with only professional contacts at work, no e-mails, some aboveboard "thinking about you" texting, but there were long evening phone calls. On Friday, the evening went as planned; better than anticipated. They laughed and joked and touched like a normal couple on a Friday night date. At four in the morning when Jared took her home, she did not ask him in and he did not press. But there was a replay of the original kiss that had unleashed all of her feelings weeks ago. He cut his engine and they sat in the car saying their long good-byes. She heard the sound of leather on leather and knew he was sliding toward her. "What are you doing, Counselor?" she teased.

"I'm going to kiss you long and hard."

"Promise?"

Again as their bodies meshed, Georgia's mind catapulted away from earth into the stars with Jared as the rocket launcher. The searing of his hot hands on her body, his fingers exploring and delving beneath matching panties and bra unnerved sensations she could not deny. She was glad she was in front of her house, for there was no telling what she would have done if they had parked elsewhere.

"Okay, okay, stop," she said breathlessly. There was no way she could make three dates, if this was just the first one.

"As you wish." He did as he was told and backed away, a playful, taunting grin complete with dimples graced his handsome face.

She rearranged her clothing and fixed her hair, tucking it behind her ear.

"What time tomorrow?" he asked. "Or rather, later on today."

"Two days in a row? Aren't we a little anxious?"

"I'm not the only one." He grinned.

She blushed in the moonlight.

"Trying to get to that third date," he said with a smile. "I'll make reservations at the Brookside Inn . . . and, with your permission, reserve a cabin, just in case. We can always cancel the reservation if we don't need it. Easy enough to cancel one than to want one."

Yippee! Georgia's inner voice yelled. "Do what you like. You always do."

"No, I don't. If that were the case we'd be in your house or mine dead asleep about now."

"Good night, Counselor."

"Good morning, Georgia," he said seriously. "I really had a great time."

"Me too." She watched him kiss her hand.

"I'll watch you in. Flick the lights so I'll know you're all right."

As Georgia went though her nocturnal paces preparing for bed, she thought how wonderful this was. She and Jared. After tomorrow they would have the life he described—in his or her bed. Wednesday when she returned from California, they'd be inseparable, at least for the few weeks before she left to work in L.A. Maybe she'd stay and they could just continue like this . . . secret lovers. That was just hormones and her heart talking. She'd made a deal with her logical mind that she'd have this fling before she moved to L.A. If it worked out between her and Jared, they'd have so many frequent flyer miles between them they could start their own airline. With the way they were going . . . it looked like this had the potential for a lasting, long-distance relationship, and that suited Georgia just fine.

On Saturday night they returned to the Brookside Inn and Georgia had taken time to dress for seduction and easy access. The same lady cashier remembered them or, rather, him, and they garnered the same table for two by the fireplace. The musicians played the same love songs and the candle glow splashed in the couple's expectant faces as they ate leisurely, partly foreplay and partly nourishment for the anticipated night ahead. Their long legs tangled beneath the linen tablecloth. This time she was in a dress and her bare legs were exposed to his discreet, intermittent touches, skin on skin. He fed her a slice of his butter-soft veal and she allowed him to taste strands of her linguine wrapped around a lobster sauce. They devoured dessert almost without tasting it, but lingered over coffee, then after-dinner cognacs. Holding hands across the table, they were caught in a world of their own making and had all the time to enjoy it . . . until three o'clock checkout tomorrow. There was no rush, for this was to be an event of gargantuan portions . . . the start of a brand-new life . . . together.

Jared settled the bill, chatting amiably with the woman, when suddenly—

"Jared Jaymes!" a booming voice said.

Jared turned to face Burt Snyder, an obnoxious attorney from a downtown law firm.

"Hey, Burt," he said as evenly as possible, hoping that Georgia would spot him before he spotted her. "How goes it?"

"Can't complain. You come here often? Nice out-of-the way place, if you catch my drift," he said, winking, not introducing the woman he was with.

"Great food. Music. Ambience," Jared said just as an excited Georgia bounded around the corner, pulling her shawl up over her silky shoulders.

"Hey, thought that was you, MacKenzie," Burt bellowed, then let out a long wolf whistle. "Who knew you had all that hidden under those strait-laced suits?"

Georgia's body froze, as did the plastic smile on her face. "Burt."

"So you going or coming?" Jared asked to redirect the attention from Georgia.

"Going. We've been here all night. Saw you two over there. Tried to get your attention but you were . . . eating." He looked between the two of them. "Let me let you continue your evening."

"Yes. We'll be heading back now," Jared said so Burt wouldn't suspect they'd reserved a cabin.

"Sure. Sure. Good seeing you both," Burt said as he and his woman friend stood in the lobby of the inn.

Georgia pulled on the coat Jared held up for her and walked calmly toward his truck. She felt sick to her stomach like she was about to throw up all that wonderful food she'd just consumed along with her hopes and dreams for her and Jared . . . and most importantly, her reputation.

Jared sat in the truck and reached for Georgia.

"Don't. Just drive, please."

As they drove away, Burt waved to them and took his friend's hand as they walked toward the cabins.

"Georgia—" Jared began tentatively.

"It's over. That's it."

"Georgia, we don't have anything to worry about."

"How can you say that? Of all people, Burt 'the mouth' Snyder? Cheez." She held her head and rubbed her temples.

"He won't say anything."

Georgia shot him a glare.

"That woman is not his wife," Jared said with a chuckle.

"I don't give a flying fig if she's his daughter. He saw us, Jared. You and me!"

"Georgia. It's all right. So what if we had dinner—"

"Oh no. No! Do *not* do this to me, Jared. We had a deal. A pact. You promised. . . . You cannot be that kind of man. Not you. Anybody but you."

They rode in silence.

"Georgia—"

"Jared, I am asking you to make good on your promise. I don't think that's too much to ask. If you care about me *at all*—you will do this for me. Don't make it harder. I am on damage control now."

"This is not over."

"As long as we are here, in this time and space, it is."

Chapter 8

Georgia sat in the first-class lounge waiting for her flight to be called. She was relieved that she had to face neither Jared nor her colleagues for this Monday morning's case review. She didn't know how fast Burt's mouth shot off, but she was thankful for the reprieve of a few days: her vacation had been scheduled and previously approved. *Timing is everything,* she thought over and over again. If she had just held off until she accepted the L.A. position, moved to California to work, and then come back and dated Jared, then this would have been moot. *Horny Georgia just had to jump before she was ready,* she self-chastised. Georgia relished the distraction of this job conference and decided not to think about the catastrophe that awaited her until she returned.

She was flown first class and met at LAX by Wally, her designated partner from Felton, Mayfield and Dasher. The limo took her to the Beverly Hills Hotel, where she settled in before Wally took her to the law firm and made introductions.

They escorted her to the corner office that would
be hers, and Georgia noted that it was plush
and cushy with two windows overlooking the
L.A. skyline—basically the same view, but a different city. Between the meet and greets with all the
essential players, Georgia noted that the twenty-
five women of the administrative pool, who probably made in excess of fifty thousand a year, had
not one black face among them. That seemed
odd for a "culturally progressive" law firm that
had one black male, two Hispanics—male and
female—one Asian, and a pair of Jews—male
and female—all the rest lily WASP-y white. Obviously, Georgia was to be the black female of the
corps and they were willing to give her anything
she wanted for that privilege.

Wally took her around to the preselected
condos in Brentwood, down the street from the
infamous O. J. Simpson house, and to a Jag dealer.
He squired her around town to sell L.A. and the
L.A. lifestyle, and all Georgia could think of was
how fabulously fake it was; there was a reason it
was the cosmetic surgery capital of the free world.
Once left on her own, she strolled down Rodeo
Drive and bought Baby Preston her first gift from
Prada. She saw a soft-as-butter, black leather jacket
in Versace's window made for Jared's broad shoulders and tapered waist. She shook her head at herself and said, "You po' child. You do have it bad."

She thought of her conversation with Neal.
She'd called to check on Brenda, and Neal
seemed to relish telling her about the surprise
birthday party some of Jared's female admirers

had thrown for him in a private room at Garrick's, a posh downtown restaurant.

"I would have thought you would be invited," Neal had teased.

"Why?"

"Oh, dunno. I thought there may have been some sparks igniting between the two of you at the baby shower."

"See what happens when you think?"

"Well, apparently all the Philly Fillies know it's 'fini' between him and Courtney." He chuckled at his own rhyme. "They gave him some kind of civic award, but it was a thinly veiled 'take any of us, we're willin' kinda tribute."

"Poor Brenda. I just don't know how she stands you."

"It's love. You ought to try it sometime."

"Bye. I'll be back Friday."

"Where are you?"

"That's for me to know and you to find out."

Georgia stopped at a trendy-looking outdoor café, ordered, then sipped a cappuccino as she watched the Rolls-Royces and Bentleys try to outgleam one another in the perpetual L.A. sunshine. Her eyes fell on a wedding dress in the window across the street. Amid all the faddish, barely there, garish clothes, this traditional white gown stood out like a soothing tribute to her principles, an outward sign that her stance, no matter how unpopular, was the right thing for herself and her career.

Maybe Burt was her father's emissary sent to prevent her from making the mistake that could tarnish her sterling reputation and career.

"Sleeps with her boss.'" The label made her ill. The seedy wink and nod and liberties Burt took with the short conversation were enough to turn her stomach all over again. She hadn't done anything yet . . . she could look in everyone's eyes with that conviction, although she hated being put in that situation. Hated being the brunt of half-truths, speculations, and outlandish innuendo. "I knew she couldn't be that good; he had the hots for her all along and tossed her the good cases. He probably coached her every step of the way." Years afterward, the folks with the long memories and shallow minds would always suspect that she'd dated him.

Her career and Jared: two things that meant so much to her were at odds with each other. She had to choose. She was used to having most things she wanted. She took the chance with Jared because she thought she could pull it off. Her mind ruled the day, but once Jared moved back to his house, her heart had begun telegraphing different dreams, projecting images of him—of them. The first one at the swimming hole in Evelyn, Tennessee, had evolved into scenes of her in a wedding dress walking toward Jared, as he stood tall and handsome waiting for her at the end of a long aisle. Images of them living in his four-story Victorian house . . . with a dog? Dressing a Christmas tree in his bay window. Sitting down to a food-laden table at Thanksgiving surrounded by a bevy of jubilant black faces. Of her giving him a massage—of him rubbing her feet. Of them luxuriating at the beach or, skiing down a mountain-top. Of the two of them dancing in front of a fire, then suddenly being interrupted by two boys and a cute little girl. She should have just waited as she'd planned and she could have had them both, but it was too late now. It was an expensive lesson to learn. She was coming to L.A.

She dipped her chocolate biscotti into her cappuccino as more of a distraction than a desire for the taste. She swirled it around the cup a few times and thought of the color—of the Reese's peanut cups he had on his desk. Of how the color mimicked his hands on her bare ankle at the tennis courts. In the deepest, unspoken recesses of her mind, pure and simple—she hoped he'd follow her to L.A. Jared in L.A.? That would be as bizarre as a blizzard in August. He had the smarts, charisma, and style to make it anywhere in the world, but L.A. would eventually chafe him around the neck and grate on his sense of integrity, of values and fair play. L.A. would never be home for him. Philly was. *Jared in L.A.*, she thought, chuckling wryly, placing it in the never-gonna-happen bin, like his ever being on Grandma Mac's porch or the swimming hole in Evelyn, Tennessee, despite her initial dreams.

She paid her check and strolled in a column of sizzling L.A. sunshine. Hot here and snow in Philly, all just a plane ride away. He said he loved her, she mused. She believed him. She loved him but it was just a hopeless situation. They'd tried to make a go of it as he'd cavalierly suggested and missed their connection by just one click— and like an old western, she had to get out of Philly. She'd worked too hard and too long to get where she was. This was no movie where she was guaranteed a happy ending—where DA and ADA lived happily ever after.

Despite her nagging feelings to the contrary, she knew taking the plum L.A. position was the right thing for her. There were thousands of lawyers who would kill for this chance. In three to five years when her relationship with Jared tumbled to its eventual end, she didn't want to look back and wish she'd had the guts to "just say no" and take this job. Despite how good it might be with him for a few years, in the larger scheme of things called "her life," she'd regret a decision made while in love and not based on what was best for her in the long run. She could suffer now or suffer later. At least now she could still look at herself in the mirror with her self-respect intact.

She ran across the street against the traffic light like a California native. The little girl in her wanted to run to Jared, jump in his arms, bury her face in his neck, and never let go. The adolescent in her wanted him—his touch, his kisses, his hard body in all her soft places as he professed that he loved her and would never leave her.

But the professional woman, the law school graduate who'd passed the bar on the first try and built a flawless name for herself, knew it for the no-win situation it was. Her values were not porous, like those of the kind of women who pay lip service to values but, when challenged by a handsome man with a great body, don't hold water. Georgia MacKenzie's values weren't for sale even to exceptional men. *Women need to think with their heads and not their hearts,* Georgia thought. After being away from work, she knew she could return and repair any damaged part of her reputation that needed addressing. She could look folks in the eye, knowing in the end, she had not compromised her ideals. She wanted to, but she didn't. Damage control in Philly and reestablishment in L.A. were her career prescription. Burt's mouth or no, Georgia would not become the type of woman she despised. She would not give up on or gamble her values, sanity, gut feelings, and good sense for a man. Not even Jared Jaymes. Especially not Jared Jaymes.

As Georgia strolled back to the hotel, she knew she'd still think about Jared from time to time. She supposed letting go altogether would be easier if she just had more time with him; time to demystify and perhaps tire of him. She'd wanted more time with him, but it just didn't look like it was in the cards for them in this lifetime. So she'd put on her "big girl panties" and deal with it. She and Jared were going to be separated. Period. Maybe somewhere down the line, when she visited girlfriends, she'd look him up. There'd be no frequent flying to L.A. Too hard . . . relationships should be easy, and with his access to women in his own backyard, he wasn't coming all this way for long. But she'd remember, gather her week of heaven with Jared Jaymes, and dust it off on an "as-needed" basis. When she needed to be reminded that there were wonderful men out here in this world—when she had a curious granddaughter who wanted to know about her grandma Georgia's life before she met and married Granddad—Georgia would tell her about an extraordinary man who was mayor or could be governor, maybe even president by the time her granddaughter asked. Jared wasn't her first love and he wasn't going to be her last. Somewhere between the perfect life and the bottom line, Georgia would find her life mate, her future husband who'd be honest, handsome, and loved her and she him. They would have a wonderful, enviable life, but it wouldn't be the life she'd have had with Jared. Jared would have been the best for her. Jared, the one who got away. Georgia chuckled; she finally had a "one who got away."

The L.A. trip had been good for her personally and professionally. It had shown her a life without Jared and she forgave herself for her momentary lapse in good judgment and she'd recommitted herself to her career and its protection. Georgia accepted the offer from Felton, Mayfield and Dasher with the proviso that she would not report until February. She wouldn't ruin Jared's or her friends' Christmas holidays with the news, but would give her four-week notice the first of the year, so Jared could find a replacement. She'd report to L.A. February 1.

She didn't know big girl panties could be so painfully constricting . . . but life goes on.

Georgia returned to Philly and caught up with her girlfriends. They had an old-fashioned pajama party, watched movies, and acted like fools when Billy Dee Williams extended his hand to Diana Ross in *Lady Sings the Blues*. She tried not to think of Jared and with a bittersweet regret, she hoped her girls would come to visit her in

L.A. often. She had two guest room suites and a pull-out couch in the den just for them.

Jared strolled into Garrick's, the posh downtown restaurant, scene of his birthday party. The coat-check girl took his vicuna coat and hat as the maitre d' said, "Your party is here, Mr. Jaymes. Please follow me."

"Thank you," Jared said, but thought, *Party?* He didn't see dinner with the mayor, the commissioner, and the police chief as a "party." Being with Georgia would be a party. He wondered if she was back in Philly yet. He hadn't had any contact with her since the scene at the Brookside Inn.

Just as he passed a table, Jared glanced at the woman seated there. "Georgia?"

A shocked Georgia looked up at him. ""Jared? Hello."

Jared looked quickly at the man—not him—sitting next to *his* woman.

"When'd you get back?" he asked, pulling at his monogrammed cuffs. "I see them," he said, dismissing the maitre d' and waving perfunctorily to the mayor.

"Friday night," Georgia said. "I'll be at work tomorrow."

Jared couldn't decide whether to drink in the sight of Georgia looking too good in that creamy velvet suit or to look at the man she was with. She obviously wasn't going to introduce them, so Jared thrust his hand out to be shaken by the man and said, "Jared Jaymes."

"Yes, of course," the man said, half standing.

"My *boss*," Georgia clarified quickly.

"Wally—" the man began introducing himself, and winced under the pressure of Jared's firm grip.

"A friend in town from L.A.," Georgia interrupted before Wally offered his last name.

"Be here long, *Wally*?" Jared asked him tightly.

Jared is jealous, Georgia thought. The supremely confident, fundamentally cool Jared Jaymes was jealous. This was a new side of him and she was enjoying this.

"I'll be leaving tomorrow morning," Wally said.

"Ah. And where are you staying tonight?"

"Jared!" Georgia admonished.

"We want 'Wally' to be in the best hotel Philly has to offer," Jared said without apology. "We want to be good ambassadors for our L.A. visitors."

"I'm trying to do just that," Georgia said, attempting to hide her amusement as the mayor called Jared over. "Public life beckons. You better run along. Have a great dinner, Jared," she said, dismissing him.

"Your *boss*?" Wally identified as Jared walked away.

"My boss."

"I can see why you want to leave. Ever bring him up on sexual harassment charges?"

"No. Nothing like that. He's just a little intense."

"Is that what you call it here in Philly?"

Georgia never looked back at Jared, but she could feel his eyes boring into her back. She could scarcely concentrate on what Wally was saying about renting her Philly house, moving arrangements, and the closing and settlement on her new L.A. home. Why was she reveling in Jared's discomfort? That was so bad of her when he'd been nothing but cooperative all this time. At her request, he'd maintained his distance. She didn't have to go to the bathroom but went anyway, savoring the look on Jared's face when she reentered the dining room. She moved slow and easy, sensually, and Jared couldn't take his eyes from her. She flipped her hair when Wally half stood as the waiter held out her chair. She slid her cute derriere onto the upholstered seat as the waiter replaced the napkin in her lap.

Following Jared's attention, the mayor asked, "Isn't that ADA MacKenzie?"

"Yes, it is."

"She's a stunner." The mayor grinned broadly.

"Yes, she is," Jared said, and added, "Very competent." He then shot the mayor a look that squelched any further observations on ADA MacKenzie from him. Jared looked back at her. She was gorgeous, but with all he felt about her now, her outer beauty didn't compare to her inner beauty—her good heart, her intelligence, her standards and principles, all the things that would last when the outer beauty began to fade. *Outer beauty attracts, but the inner beauty keeps you,* his father used to say. Georgia was not a wannabe or a dying-to-be—Georgia MacKenzie just was. She knew who she was and liked it. She was the living, breathing epitome of that old saying—"it's not who you knew or what you did—it's how you lived."

"Yes, she is," Jared repeated absently, still trying to figure out a way back into her life. His cell phone rang.

Moments later Jared appeared at Georgia's table. "We have to go. Wally, can you get to wherever you're staying?"

"I beg your pardon!" Georgia protested.

"I just got a call from Neal. Brenda's giving birth."

"Oh!" she said to Jared, then to Wally, "This really is an emergency. I'm about to be a godmother."

"Congratulations," Wally said. "I'll proceed with everything we discussed and call you next week."

Out front, Jared had Georgia's coat at the ready and they scurried out to the curb.

"We'll take my car," Jared said.

"No. I have my car and I'll take it. See you at the hospital."

"Why don't you just let me—"

"Jared. I have my car and I'm driving myself. Nothing's changed. I'll see you there."

"Drive carefully." He tipped the valet and climbed into his Hummer.

When Georgia arrived at the hospital, Jared was waiting for her.

"You didn't have to wait," Georgia said, refusing to be touched by the gesture.

He punched the elevator button, glanced at her, and said, "We're in this together."

She did not respond at first and then said, "Nothing has changed between us, Jared."

Jared and Georgia waited in the room designated for maternity, absented by the fathers who were in the delivery rooms with their wives.

"Want something to drink?" Jared asked.

"No. I just ate."

"I hope Wally gets back okay."

"He's a big boy," she said with a wicked smile-smirk.

"What does that mean?"

"What?"

Neal came bounding from the hallway. "It's a girl," he announced.

"We know that." Georgia kissed her excited friend.

Jared slapped him on the back and they exchanged one quick, manly embrace.

"She's beautiful." Neal beamed. "She's got ten fingers and ten toes and—aw, man—the entire experience is mind-blowing. I got to go back. How can anybody ever abuse or leave his child? You all can see her in about twenty minutes."

Jared and Georgia laughed at the black tornado that was their friend. They walked down to the gift shop and bought balloons and flowers, returning to the maternity window just as Baby Preston was brought in.

"Ooh. Look at her," Georgia sighed. "She *is* beautiful."

"She sure is." Jared tapped on the nursery's glass lightly.

The nurse responded by bringing Baby Preston to the window before putting her down in the crib.

Neal came out and stared at his baby daughter. "I've got to make some calls, my mom, Brenda's parents and sisters. They've been through two false alarms."

In a half hour the foursome was in the room dodging balloons and arranging the flowers that had begun to arrive. The baby entered, demanding all their attention. Brenda took her daughter, Sydney Renee, to her chest and cradled her gently. Neal was on one side of the bed with Georgia and Jared on the other. Neal was keyed up but not so much that he didn't notice how Jared stood behind Georgia with one hand protectively on her shoulder. It was natural and very unbosslike. He was about to say something just as Brenda's parents and sisters bounded into the room.

A few minutes later, Neal caught Jared giving Georgia a "let's go" sign and she agreed. *Who are these two people?* Neal wondered.

"We're going to leave now and let her grandparents and aunts have some time," Georgia said. "Anything we can get you or do before we go?"

"Don't leave me here with them," Neal teased.

"She's gorgeous, Neal. If you need *anything* let me know."

"Ditto," Jared said. "You do good work, man," Jared teased.

"Oh, good grief, like Brenda didn't have anything to do with it," Georgia said, kissing the new mom on the cheek. "Bye, Bren."

Jared walked Georgia to her car.

"Wow, that is pretty awesome," she said.

"I'm always blown away by birth. It's such a miracle that a new life can come into the world like that," Jared said. "Born from love, brought to love, forever loved."

"Parent and child. That is *truly* unconditional love, isn't it?"

"From the cradle to the grave." Jared opened her car door for her. "You want to go and get a nightcap or something?" He didn't want to let her go.

"No. We just ate."

"Not together. And that was hours ago."

"We've got work tomorrow." She was tired of hearing herself say "nothing's changed."

"Guess who won't be there."

"Are you kidding? He'll be there with cigars . . . just to get away from his in-laws."

"You might be right."

"I am about most things." She fired up her ignition.

"We aren't talking about Neal anymore, are we?"

"See you at work in a few hours." Georgia tried keeping it light.

"I miss coming home to you." His obsidian eyes sparkled like morning dew.

Georgia's heart tripped, fell, and melted— gooey and sticky, filling every pore of her entire body. Her breath stuck in her throat. He couldn't say things like that to her anymore. It wasn't fair. It wasn't right, but it sounded *so* good. It made her soul take notice.

"Night, Jared." She drove away.

Jared watched her car disappear into the pitch-dark just as he had that night at Neal's. He never meant to say those things, but they just came out. Sometimes his heart bypassed his calculating brain and his lips said what he felt. That's how it was when you love somebody. But he really didn't love Georgia. What he felt for her was beyond love; deeper than love, the word *love* seemed so inadequate to express what he really felt for her. Love seemed trite and overused by every man who wanted to bed a woman. What he felt for Georgia he had never felt before—nothing near it. He *cherished* Georgia. He cherished her spirit, her mind, body, and soul. He wanted to be with her, around her always. He wanted her as sure of him as he was of her. He wanted to make her feel that if she were in a football stadium filled with women, she knew there would be no other woman in all those bleachers who was more loved, honored, and respected by her man than she was. That's what he wanted for her.

He knew she loved him. Her eyes said so. He could feel the love, the chemistry, the unspoken emotion, and it pained him that she was so unwilling to let their feelings flow when it could be so free and easy. As she'd demanded, he'd maintain a purely professional relationship with her, but he feared that if she didn't admit her love for him soon, they could lose everything they had and everything they deserved to be, and that would be a tragedy. He had one more piece of his plan to complete that would give them both what they wanted and not compromise her principles one iota. The thought of its finality made him smile. "Hold on, Georgia MacKenzie. Forever is on the way."

I miss coming home to you rang in her ears and tore at her heartstrings. She didn't know how she made it home. Didn't know when she opened her door or stepped into the shower.

"Damn!" she said aloud. *It is unprofessional of him to say things like that*, she thought, wishing it was this time next year, she was settled in L.A., and she could just remember Jared Jaymes with a smile and a "I wonder if he ever thinks of me."

She went downstairs to the kitchen, poured juice, and checked the front door, and on her way back she noticed something shiny from the mantel. She looked at the object in the glow of the streetlight. It was keys—Jared's keys to her house, the ones he'd used for that week. He'd placed them right next to Tony's picture and her engagement ring as if saying, "I am next in the evolution of your life." It signified that Jared had his own place on her mantel . . . in her life—whenever she was ready.

The phone rang and Georgia answered, "Hello?"

"Mac," she heard Neal's voice and not Jared's. She had to stop this destructive thinking. Jared was respecting her and doing exactly what she'd asked him to.

"You alone?" Neal asked.

"Yes, I am. What is that supposed to mean? What do you want?"

"Whoa. It's me, the new daddy with the new baby."

"Where are you?"

"They kicked us out, but I get to bring Bren and Syd home tomorrow afternoon. I'm calling to make sure you're coming for Thanksgiving dinner."

"You don't expect Brenda to cook Thanksgiving—"

"Naw. Her moms, my moms, and the family. And since you're family and have been here for the last four years, I expect you here this Thursday too."

Georgia smiled and remembered that Jared always took his ski trips on the long holiday weekend, so she wouldn't run into him. "Why break tradition? I accept. What do you want me to bring?"

"Nothing but your appetite and the willingness to change a diaper or two."

"You got it. Thanks, Neal."

"Well, I'm too wound up to sleep, so I guess I'll count my cigars to pass out tomorrow."

"You did good."

"I did, didn't I? Night, Mac."

Georgia hung up the phone and glanced around her quiet house. Her Jared-less house. It just didn't seem fair to have all this pain and none of the pleasure. "You'll be all right, girl. You got no choice."

Chapter 9

Before, during, and after the Monday case briefing Jared maintained an impeccable professional demeanor with Georgia. Besides, everyone was preoccupied with finishing in time for an early split on Wednesday in anticipation of Thanksgiving. As was Jared's tradition over the last five years, he disappeared on Wednesday afternoon. She felt strangely that he did not say good-bye. *He owes you nothing,* her mind reminded her.

She and her girlfriends had had their Thanksgiving gathering on Tuesday before two of the three went to their respective out-of-town family celebrations. On this Wednesday evening, she prepared a sweet potato pie and a peach cobbler as she talked with her family in Tennessee, promising Grandma Mac that she was coming home for Christmas and yes, she consented to meeting Pernell. Why the heck not? It would make her grandmother happy and she was leaving Philly and Pernell for L.A. in a matter of weeks.

She slept late on Thanksgiving Day and at two

dressed for dinner, taking the pie, cobbler, and Prada jumpsuit from Rodeo Drive for Sydney.

The Preston house was brimming with family and friends. Men watched the game, women talked of clothes, hair, and Hollywood gossip as they devoured hors d' oeuvres and put the finishing touches on dinner taking time to "ooh" and "aah" over little Sydney Preston.

Georgia was in the kitchen putting the greens into a serving bowl when she heard Neal's very impressed sister-in-law ask, "Who is *that?*"

Georgia looked up to see Jared moving easily through the living room toward the family room, introducing himself to folks he didn't know. The unexpected sight of him made her heart lurch and beat double time. *Jeez*, she thought as she watched him exude his fundamental cool: the way he walked, talked, and dominated a room just by entering it. His signature black-on-black-in-black attire punctuated his innate grace, charm, and presence, which made him a hit wherever he went—he was a man's man, but made for the comfort of a woman. She knew; she'd had the pleasure of a kiss or two.

"That's my boss," Neal answered, then shot, "Right, Mac?"

Georgia tore her gaze from Jared's commanding image and went back to lifting out the smoked turkey bone that seasoned the greens without answering her friend.

"He is fine. Where is his woman?" the sister-in-law continued, her eyes riveted to Jared's body.

"Right there," Neal said.

Georgia's head automatically snapped to look

LIVING INSIDE YOUR LOVE   223

for Courtney dogging Jared's steps. Was he back with her? She didn't see any woman in the living room who wasn't accounted for. What was Neal talking about? Georgia wondered, and looked quizzically over at him; both Neal and the sister-in-law were looking dead at her.

"You crazy nut," Georgia dismissed Neal with a roll of her eyes, and carried the greens to the table.

After a few moments she heard the greeting, "Happy Thanksgiving," from a voice she'd know anywhere.

"Happy Thanksgiving," she said, looking up into his warm, liquid eyes. "I'm surprised to see you here. Isn't this the time you take your usual ski trip?"

"Change of plans. It's nice to mix it up every now and then." He smiled over at her as she busied herself, rearranging hot dishes on the table. "I had no one I wanted to take skiing. No one else I wanted to snuggle in front of the blazing fire with. No place else I wanted to be than here with—everybody."

"Your parents must be disappointed that you are here instead of with them." She tried to control the blood raging through her veins at the unexpected sight of him.

"Not really. They expect me to be skiing too." He watched her fiddling with the dishes needlessly. He liked that she was uncomfortable by his presence. "You look great. How are you?"

"Fine," she said tightly, giving him a quick insincere smile. His nonchalant, relentlessness charm was disturbing her equilibrium.

Responding to Neal's call, the other guests

entered the dining room crowding in on Jared and Georgia.

"Everyone grab hands. Let us pray," Neal announced.

Jared took Georgia's hand in the most natural way. To jerk it away would have caused a scene.

His fingers were as warm, dry, and soft as she remembered when he had first touched her ankle after the tennis match. Just as warm, soft, and dry as when he took her hand in the truck on that old-fashioned Sunday drive. Just as strong and caressable now, as when he had held her hand a few weeks ago as she drank hot chocolate and talked until the sun came up, or when he took her face in them and kissed her tenderly. Jared stroked her hand gently with his thumb. The nail she knew had the little mole embedded in it. Georgia couldn't concentrate on Neal's prayer. All she felt were sparks from Jared's hand jumpstart her bodily juices. *The only person from work here is Neal,* she thought. *And he is preoccupied with his wife and new daughter, so play it cool.*

During dinner, they didn't sit near each other. The sister-in-law sat between them, but they did manage to awkwardly glance in each other's direction from time to time. When the tryptophan from the turkey set in and folks quieted down, the desserts were brought out. Jared was in the family room where the game was winding down with a sample of both peach cobbler and the sweet potato pie. He tasted her homemade goodies, smiled, and motioned a thumbs-up—the thumb with the mole embedded in the nail. Neal must have told him that the desserts were hers. She returned his smile.

After the kitchen was cleaned, Georgia slipped upstairs to see Sydney. "Hey, precious baby," she said, leaning over the basinet. "You up here all alone? I bet you are happy to be left alone for a change, huh?" Sydney wasn't fussy, but she was awake, aware, and chewing on her knuckles. Georgia picked her up and sat in the rocker near the lamp's soft glow. "You are just an amazing little girl already. You know that? I'm your auntie Georgia. You and I are going to be fabulous friends."

Georgia rocked quietly, soaking in the sight of this six-pound, seven-ounce miracle. *I want one of these*, she thought. No time soon, but sometime. Not knowing any lullabies, she hummed "My Girl" absently. She looked up and Jared was leaning against the doorjamb, hands in his pockets, taking the scene in.

"How long have you been there?" she asked him.

"Long enough."

"Long enough for what?"

"To know all I need to know."

Behind them both, Neal stopped Brenda on the stairs. They were going up to check on their baby and saw Jared against the door and, between his legs, a view of Georgia sitting in the rocking chair holding their newborn. Neal and Brenda backed down the steps to the landing without being noticed.

"There's something going on between them," Neal said like a proud father pleased with his daughter's choice of suitors.

"And it started with us setting them up for tennis." Brenda leaned on her husband's shoulder. "They'd be so perfect for each other."

"Let's give them a few minutes," Neal suggested, and they returned downstairs.

"You're a natural," Jared said to Georgia.

"You sound surprised. I do everything well."

"You put your foot in that cobbler and sweet potato pie. Which reminds me, I owe you a dinner."

"You don't owe me anything," Georgia said, rising to tenderly place the now sleeping Sydney back in the basinet.

"Leg of lamb, asparagus, au gratin potatoes."

"How can you talk about food after the meal we just had?" she teased, walking past him toward the steps. She couldn't stay up here with him.

Her hand touched the newel post and he placed his over hers. She looked back up at him. He took her hand in his. "Let me do this. Before you go home for the holidays. Saturday after next before you take off. Nobody will know but you and me."

Georgia stared at him. She had never been so emotionally intimate with *any* man before. No man had ever seen her cry, break down, or freak out. No man had ever seen her so vulnerable or felt her tremble by the nearness of him. "Has anyone at work said anything?"

"Not to me."

"Of course they wouldn't say anything to you or Neal."

"That doesn't mean things haven't been said."

"I know."

"Mac? Dinner before you go?"

"Go where?" *Does he know abut L.A.?* she thought.

"Home for the holidays," he repeated.

"Okay. I have to return your grandma Hattie Mae's skillet."

"Gee, so enthusiastic." He smiled.

"I've promised to go and see a girlfriend," she said, reclaiming her hand from under his on the newel post. Even in the darkness of the hallway, she could see his dimples.

"I made a similar promise to my brother. But I'm glad I came by."

"Me too," she was surprised to hear herself say.

Georgia left her girlfriend's at midnight and went home pondering her dinner with Jared. As she poured her juice nightcap, she rationalized that *holidays are for the heart.* She decided that there was one gift she'd been denied at the Brookside Inn. She'd received the pain without the pleasure. There might be stories about them flung around City Hall, so she was getting the punishment for a crime she hadn't committed. If she was doing the time, she might as well enjoy the benefits of the crime. Of course, this might be another test from Big Brody Mac or it might be some celestial latitude and her one opportunity for a Last Supper with Jared before she moved to L.A. Technically, she now had a new firm and a new boss . . . and the only unaccomplished goal for her was to make love to Jared Jaymes. She'd been hard-wired by her parents to be self-protective and make smart choices, and knew it was personally irresponsible and professional suicide to sleep with her boss, but she'd waited long enough, wanted him bad enough, and it would *feel* oh soooo good. She was sure of it. Instantly, Georgia felt better.

Like she knew the sun would come up tomorrow, she knew Jared Jaymes was a lover with a slow hand and a hard body built for southern comfort and infinite pleasure. She would sleep with him once—just once—and this dinner was the perfect time. She'd dine with him, have one toe-curling, unforgettable night of passion, leave for Tennessee, and when she came back, she'd give her notice. She could deal with Jared being upset, momentarily. She could deal with his wrath. What she couldn't handle would be his indifference. With her plan she wouldn't have to deal with any of it.

She showered, put on her pj's and cami, and jumped into bed, mentally making a "things to do" list; she'd have the sleepover with Jared and then meet Pernell for her grandmother, and that would tie up all the Philly-related loose ends—then she'd be ready to make a clean start in L.A. "Never make someone your priority when you are just their option," she heard her mother say.

She set her clock and nestled down between the sheets, revisiting her exit strategy. She couldn't stop smiling. Finally, she'd make her memory. Then it would be over. They say you never remember your last kiss, or the last time you made love, because often you don't know it was the last time. But Georgia would know. She planned a spectacular night. When she was done, there would be no unfinished business. She would orchestrate the end of this great love affair—at least for her.

* * *

With all the anticipation of the upcoming Yuletide holidays on everyone's minds, the next two weeks sped by. Georgia appreciated Jared's professional distance and control. She caught herself glancing through two sets of plate glass in his direction from time to time, but she never saw him reciprocating.

On Friday night when everyone was leaving her intercom buzzed.

"MacKenzie."

"See you tomorrow night at eight." Jared's soothing voice caressed her ear.

Georgia looked over at his office, and his back was to her. She watched him swivel around, wink, and hang up.

With just that one look, he stirred emotions in her and Georgia blushed like a schoolgirl.

On Saturday morning she did her usual chores and that afternoon she prepared for her last dinner with Jared Jaymes. She dressed for success. Dressed for him to remember her. She shimmied into a hot-pink thong, no bra, no stockings. She let a chocolate halter top silk number slide over her soft, lotioned body. In the full-length mirror, she admired how the dress skimmed her curves, showcased her breasts, and dropped open to midthigh when she sat and crossed her legs. She tousled her hair and sprayed cologne on all her pulse points. She donned earrings, no necklace, and stepped into five-inch heels that arched her feet and exposed her calves in the most beguiling way. She leaned in and touched up her lipstick and wondered what parts of his body her painted pair would color tonight. She smiled approvingly, wondering on what part of her anatomy his luscious lips would similarly be placed. "You don't have a chance, Jared Jaymes. You're going down tonight."

At precisely eight, Georgia sauntered up the stone stairs of the four-story Victorian house with the slate mansard roof and rang the doorbell. One side of the double doors swung open and Jared smiled widely. "Right on time." His eyes glimpsed a stunning dress that glimmered against her skin. "Please come in."

Said the spider to the fly, Georgia thought, eyeing how his totally black ensemble made him look like a sleek, virile panther, making her feel like she was entering into the charged danger of a wild jungle.

He took her coat and she let her eyes scan the house, beginning with the richly carved chest from Belize that had lived at her house for a week, back in its rightful place. She'd only been here once before, with Tony, but she was just as impressed with Jared's home this time. It was solid, well built, understated, and elegant just like her host.

"I forgot the skillet," Georgia offered blithely.

"Some other time," he teased her playfully. "It's in good hands."

"Well, Counselor, let's see. No skiing trip this Thanksgiving. No Yuletide wreaths on the door. No traditional Christmas party for the work folks—"

"I took them all to dinner at Garrick's. You were on vacation."

"No decorated Christmas tree in your living room's bay window behind your baby grand," she continued. "What's up with you?"

"Times change. Things change. The only constant *is* change."

"Hmm. Confucius? How profound."

"You look nice."

"Translation. I have on a dress." She smirked playfully. "You match your truck."

He chuckled, enjoying their banter. She was so different from all the eager-to-please women who seemed to populate his life. Those who gave up everything and anything too easily just to have a man in their bed no matter how briefly or how otherwise attached he was.

"This is for you." She offered the bottle of wine.

"You're brave to bring your own poison. I'll make sure you don't get inebriated," he teased.

She visually surveyed the room bathed in the glow from the fireplace; the only other light was provided by the amber glow of candles strategically strewn about the room.

Wow, Seduction City, she thought.

In front of the dancing flames, the Asian-influenced cocktail table was set with two big pillows on the floor. It was beautifully staged. She only wondered what he'd done to the master bedroom upstairs. She couldn't wait to see it.

"Interesting decor. Done this a time or two, huh?"

"Just the Two of Us" was playing as he asked, "Would you like something to drink? I invented a drink just for you . . . even if it doesn't go with leg of lamb."

"Ooh. I'm intrigued. An offer I can't refuse." She referenced *The Godfather* and followed him down the two steps into the living room, through two pocket doors into the dining room and a small corner bar. "So we couldn't eat in here with a table and chairs?"

"I'm going for something a little different this time." He smiled and handed her a flute. "It's a Georgia peach."

"With a capital *G*?"

He clinked his glass to hers and said, "To the first of many memorable evenings."

To our Last Supper, she countered quietly, *a memorable sensual feast.*

"Hmm." She sipped the concoction. "This is delicious, Counselor."

He beamed like a kid who'd just won the spelling bee. "Champagne, peach schnapps, and peach juice. I recall how you like peaches."

"Nothing gets by you." She took another sip.

She liked this house; she liked him in it. She liked her in it, but even if he knew enough to ask her to stay, she couldn't—wouldn't. She was L.A.-bound with a bullet. *Keep focused Georgia*, she warned herself, and said, "Something smells good. I hope it tastes as good as it smells."

"You disappoint me. I would have thought I'd proven myself to you by now."

The kitchen timer dinged.

"We can eat now or later."

"You know the answer to that." She tilted her head playfully.

"Now?" His parenthetical smile made its first appearance.

"Absolutely. Can I do anything to help?"

"You are a guest. This time. Just grab a seat."

She sat in front of the glowing fire letting the

Georgia Peach relax her. She swayed to the soft sounds of Will Downing crooning "I Go Crazy," and Jared brought in two plates laden with food. She couldn't help but notice his form as it moved away from her toward the kitchen for the bread and pitcher of Georgia Peach.

"This looks fantastic."

Jared said grace, and they commenced to eating and talking. After they'd finished he moved the table out of the way and they sat side by side, facing the fire with their backs leaning against the sofa for support. Her shoes were off and her legs crossed at the ankle just as they had been when they were trapped in the elevator. So much had happened between them since that time, yet they were here together with their eyes fixed on the dancing flames allowing their minds to speak freely about anything.

"Okay, Jaymes," Georgia finally said. "I'll ask the question again. What is up with you? You're like the cat who swallowed the canary."

"What?"

"Don't try that wide-eyed, innocent little boy stuff with me. I can keep a secret, you know."

"In due time."

"It's later than you think."

"Yeah. I know."

Uh-oh, Georgia thought. The light mood just changed from flirty-fun to sober-somber. Could he know about her move to L.A.? No. Not even Neal knew. But Jared was nationally connected.

"So, what's for dessert?" She tried to restore the fun mood, heading toward the night of passion.

"A surprise." He stood up and disappeared into the kitchen and returned with a covered plate.

"Grandma Hattie Mae's divinity," he announced, and unveiled the sweet candy.

"No!" Georgia laughed. "Okay. Now's the taste test." She sprang to her feet and took a bite. She played with it against her palate as if she were tasting wine. She crunched and sucked at it playfully. "It tastes like Grandma Mac's."

"You think?"

"No. Grandma Mac's taste better."

"Personally, I think divinity is divinity regardless of who makes it."

He popped a piece into his mouth, and just like before, some of the white remained on his lip. Despite wanting to lick it off, she reached over to wipe it off.

The moment her finger touched his lip, a shiver went up her spine. It was the first touch of the evening. She hadn't meant to be the one to initiate it. But she had. Despite her full stomach, her body was hungry—starving for this lean, mean loving machine of a man.

"You know what we haven't done?" She volleyed into a lighter mood. "Sing Christmas carols."

"What?"

"The last time I was here you sat at that baby grand and played while we sang."

"There is no 'we,' Georgia. This time it's just you and me." He leveled his soulful eyes on her.

"But you play so well and I love to see your fingers tickle the ivories."

"I'm sure that's exactly what you thought the last time you were here." He called her bluff. She'd been with Tony the last time, and he was sure that her boss and his piano prowess were the very last things on her mind.

Donny Hathaway was singing "You Were Meant for Me," and Jared asked, "Shall we dance?" He extended his hand and Georgia felt all the play drain from her body, replaced by jelly.

She felt his hand slide around her waist and draw her near to his rock-hard body. She let out one long breath as he held her tightly but gently, and she felt the power shift; he seemed to be in charge now. Or was it just that whenever he took her in his arms, she lost all sense of time and place? Only in this moment, she decided not to fight it. This time she decided to go with the flow. Her bodily fluids had already begun their descent, her head swirled, and her spirit rejoiced. This was going to be her first and last intimate time with him; the first and last time they'd be naked together, exploring and enjoying and climaxing and relaxing. She was going to savor it. Georgia laid her head on his shoulder. She felt her breasts crush against his strong chest as her nipples saluted beneath the sheer fabric. She felt his love muscle, the one she'd seen sheathed in the gray boxers when he lay on her couch, seductively form and morph into its tight magnificence against her thigh. His hands caressed her bare back—skin to skin—and she felt herself melting into him. Like Joanne Woodward into Paul Newman in the *The Long Hot Summer* kiss. Bone-deep pleasure reduced every joint in her body into a gelatinous goo and a low soft sound of pleasure eased from her lips.

As Donny Gerard began to croon "Stay Awhile

with Me," it was obvious to Jared that this was a different Georgia. It was the woman he loved, and wanted more than anything, seemingly giving in to everything he wanted from her. She rubbed her body against his in the most lusciously seductive way as she had in all his dreams. All of this was too good to be true. He wanted her more than his next breath, but there was something unnatural about her offering. Something calculating. All of a sudden she'd abandoned her principles? He was still her boss, so why this sudden change of heart? She was like a prize you want, but not at the expense of everything you love about it in the first place. He could easily make love to her tonight, but she would probably hate him in the morning for taking advantage of her. Was it a question of his having her tonight, and not getting her all the rest of his days? Or did he play the bigger man for the greater good and not make love with her tonight so they could have all of their tomorrows? Her hands had worked their way under his shirt and the feel of her hands on his bare back was almost too much for him to bear. He struggled with his body wanting her, needing her so badly, and his mind yelling for his restraint—*Your plans are almost in place, man—don't blow this!*

"Georgia," he whispered hoarsely. "We've got to stop." He was panting like a sixteen-year-old in the backseat of a car. He removed her arms from around his back.

"A change of venue? You want to go upstairs?" she murmured.

"Oh yeah . . . no!"

She laughed. "Can't make it upstairs, huh?"

She moved in and stroked his swollen manhood with her pelvis. "Hmmm."

"Georgia, stop!" Perhaps too abruptly he grabbed hold of her two arms with his hands and kept her at arms' length. Drastic measures call for drastic actions because he was losing his resolve fast.

"What?"

As he held her hands from him, for the first time she seemed to get the message.

"What are you doing?" she asked.

"I'm your boss. Whatever happened to your not dating me because I'm your boss?"

Georgia stared at him unbelievingly. She looked at him as if he were speaking a foreign language. "What?"

"So now all of a sudden you're willing to sleep with me? You don't care what other colleagues think?"

"It's just you and me here, Jared."

"So. What are we going to do? You're willing to compromise your values and start sneaking around again?"

Did I have more Georgia Peach than I remember? Georgia thought. *Am I hearing him right?* Instead of untying her halter top, and gazing hungrily at her breasts, he was pushing her away. Couldn't he hear her body calling for him? "Let me get this straight. Because I want to be crystal clear about this. Are you saying you don't want to sleep with me? Here. Now. Tonight. After all that other crap, are you saying that you don't want me after all?"

"Lord knows I do. Just not tonight. Not like this."

"Tonight is perfect."

"It will be perfection when we do. Not yet."

She stared at him. His eyes were dull, not dancing; cold, intelligent, and distant as if he were talking to a client at work. She couldn't speak. She was . . . humiliated. She was ready, willing, and able and he didn't want to . . . "not tonight." What the hell did that mean? Confusion was quickly replaced with fury.

"What are you, on your period?" she snapped. "You're acting like a woman."

Instead of getting insulted as she had intended, he chuckled.

"You think this is funny?"

"No, it's just that I have plans that are about to come to fruition, and if we can just wait a few more—"

"*You* have plans? You think you're the only one with plans? I have plans and you have ruined them."

"Ruined what?"

"Nothing. It doesn't matter. It won't matter. It can't matter—not anymore."

Her head reeled with the failure that this evening wasn't ending as she had anticipated. From a CD, Phyllis Hyman's voice was telling him that "no one was wanted more than I want you."

"Who the hell do you think you are?" she assaulted as she readjusted her dress and headed for the door. "Where is my coat?"

"Georgia, wait—"

"You are indeed the most despicable, arrogant man I have ever met." She yanked her coat from the closet hanger. "This is the biggest mess!"

"Trust and believe this will all work out." He followed her to the door, but his third leg prevented him from going further.

"Oh, Negro, puleeze." Georgia tried to put her arm into her coat and it was the wrong hole. "And we're supposed to work together now?" she shouted. "This is why you shouldn't date your boss!"

"Let me—"

"Don't touch me. I am so out of here." She threw her coat over her arm and walked out into the cold. "We are so history." She tumbled down the steps to the sidewalk.

"Georgia, put on your coat or you'll catch cold," he called after her.

"What do you care?" she yelled back, got into her car, and burned rubber away from the curb.

She beat her steering wheel and cried out of frustration. In her thirty-two years, no man had ever rejected her. In all of her years, her plans had never "not worked out." And now—now she didn't even have a got-damned memory. She had just thrown herself at her boss and he had rebuffed her. Now she had unfinished business with Jared Jaymes. Besides orchestrating a memory, her only other aim was not to have unfinished business. What just happened? What did she do? She knew what she didn't do—make love with him as planned. Maybe he had some kind of condition or disease flare-up. He and his plans had just ruined her plans. What was that old saying, "a person without a plan becomes the tool by which others accomplish theirs"? He still had his plans intact but she didn't get hers. His plans didn't interest or include her, so why should she care? Sayanora, Philly.

"I can't wait to get to L.A. To get away from him," she said, taking a curve too fast. "God, I *hate* him. I *hate* Jared Jaymes!" she yelled inside her car, and pounded her steering wheel. "Hate him. Hate him. Hate him!"

Chapter 10

Georgia's mind rallied, attempting to convince her again that once she was in L.A. she'd be fine . . . a new position, new location, new people, and a new life. A clean slate. With the way she left that awful Saturday night, surely Jared wouldn't make a scene when she gave her notice. He had too much polish and professionalism for that. Maybe he knew something was up. Maybe he knew she was leaving and wanted to make a power play, but that was no reason to reject her. Maybe rejecting her was his way of punishing her for her decision to go, and now he would accept her resignation with a reluctant "good luck" and the classic "if you're ever back in Philly . . ."

Georgia knew herself well. She heated up and cooled down. While most of her friends called her the Queen of Compartmentalization, Georgia knew that she was the Queen of Rationalization. She reasoned that, with her about to violate the family code of dating her boss, her father had interceded, yet again, on her behalf. She was bound and determined to make love two nights ago, so her daddy, knowing how headstrong she could be, stopped Jared. She kept failing her daddy's tests when it came to Jared Jaymes. It was the first time she could remember that she didn't get exactly what she wanted. It was the first time she breached a MacKenzie maxim . . . it would be the last time she did either.

I'll be okay, she reasoned. Jared, who was probably mentally shuffling through his e-mail contact file of available women, would be snapped up in a matter of months with a wedding next year. He'd be forty in a few years and ready to settle down and get married. That was the "change" he spoke of with all that career camouflage talk. A wife and family were just a natural progression for a man of his status and age. She just hoped it wouldn't be one of her girlfriends. How awfully awkward would it be for her to be a bridesmaid and not the bride of Jared Jaymes? She and Jared were already linked for life through Sydney Preston, but his being married to one of her friends would be too much for her to bear. Whoever she was, wherever she was . . . despite his seasoned arrogance, she was a lucky woman. Georgia hoped the future Mrs. Jared Jaymes would know just how lucky.

In the two days since she'd hit Evelyn, Tennessee, Georgia had managed to see all of her old friends and have a family dinner that would already rival the one scheduled for Christmas Day. Grandma Mac said that Pernell was anxious to meet her and wanted to come to the family dinner, but Georgia said definitely not. He was not family and meeting him for Sunday dinner after church would be soon enough. The persistent Pernell was already getting on Georgia's nerves and she hadn't even met him yet.

Being here at home surrounded by family and friends was a good indicator of how she would manage in L.A. without Jared. Intellectually, the distance helped, but emotionally Jared came to mind during any lull in her thought processes. He was there in the spaces of the reverend's sermon. In the hymns that the choir sang that reminded her how the two of them sang on the Sunday ride in the Pennsylvania country. Jared was there when her friends asked about a man in her life and she said she was too busy to date. They looked at her sorrowfully and sad-eyed that she'd traded a stellar career for a man and said, "Can't have it all." He was there when someone said something about fried chicken or hot chocolate or potato chips or movies or old songs. There in Grandma Mac's kitchen. When Georgia spotted the seasoned cast-iron skillet she thought of him and his grandma Hattie Mae.

All Georgia needed was time accompanied by distance. Being in a strange place where there were no memories or imprints of them together would speed her recovery. Here at home there were things she'd have liked to show him, people she would want him to meet, places of her childhood she wanted to share, but in L.A. it would all be fresh, new, and easy, her mind told her. Her heart . . . well, right now, the absence of Jared only hurt when she breathed.

After the service on Sunday, Georgia accepted the "welcome homes" and engaged in small talk while the reverend thanked her for bringing the unseasonably warm weather and sunshine. While other family members scattered after church, vowing to be on time for dinner at four, Georgia returned home with Grandma Mac. Her grandmother was so excited at the prospect of Georgia's reuniting with Pernell that she dug out the old picture of him holding her. Georgia looked at it.

"Look at you sitting there so nicely on his lap," Grandma Mac said, grinning.

"I can't believe you let me sit on a boy's lap," Georgia teased, handing the picture back to her grandmother.

"Hush. You weren't but two." Grandma Mac smiled at the picture. "He wasn't but 'bout six or so."

"Probably thinks I'm a loose woman."

"This was meant to be. He is the one, Georgia." Grandma Mac pushed her glasses back up on the ridge of her nose.

Her grandmother hadn't stopped talking about "the Lord's intervention," "destiny," and "in the stars" since she arrived. Georgia knew her grandmother meant well and wanted Georgia happily married, but nothing she said about Pernell appealed to her. She hadn't met him and he already sounded too anxious and needy, just not the kind of man Georgia could stand "until death do us part," unless maybe she'd be the one to do the parting. He still sounded like a man with thick glasses, a part down the middle of his head, and a law office in the basement of a grocery store,

who played the harmonica and lottery for fun.
Being a Philly lawyer, he must have read about her
in the papers, which might be why he was so eager
to meet her. Maybe he wanted to hitch his ne'er-
do-well wagon to her rising star. Wouldn't he be
surprised that her wagon was heading for L.A.?

Georgia changed clothes and came down to
the kitchen. "Can I help?"

Grandma Mac wasn't the type who liked to
share her kitchen. "Good Lord, Georgia. Dressed
like that on the Lord's day?"

"What?" She looked down at her St. Thomas
T-shirt, cutoff shorts, and bare feet. "Don't you like
my red toenail polish? Painted for the holidays."

Grandma Mac laughed at her granddaughter.
"It's too cold for that gitup."

"It's eighty degrees. The reverend already
thanked me for the unseasonably hot weather."

"I'd say it's that global warming. Red toes?"

Georgia went over and kissed her grandmother.
"Relax. I'll change before 'Purnell' comes. I've got
four hours. Are you sure I can't help with anything?"

"Why you say his name like that?"

"Like what?"

"Pur-nell. And screw your nose up like he
smells bad."

"I promise I won't embarrass you in front of
your friend's kid, Grandma Mac." Georgia hugged
her. "I'll be polite and friendly and scintillating. I
make no promises beyond the meeting," she reminded her.

"I know, I know." The glint in her eyes betrayed her true wish for more. "Hmmph. Get

yourself some of that iced tea and leave my kitchen so I can operate."

"Yes'm."

Georgia obeyed and took the iced tea, the Sunday paper, and a pair of socks onto the side porch. Her body set the porch swing in motion. The sun felt good on her face and body, its rays preparing her for L.A. She glanced out over the property that her great-granddaddy bought and then built this big white house on for his family. This house and the people in it had been her anchor, her strength, and her pride. She was lucky to have been raised here in this community, proud to be one of them, and hoped they were proud of her. Home was the only place on earth that could claim you as its own. She carried Evelyn, Tennessee with her everywhere; lessons learned here had been her best companion. She'd carry them to L.A. with her as well.

Georgia heard a car approach and a door close. Footsteps fell on the porch and the doorbell rang. *Someone for Grandma Mac,* Georgia thought as she flipped the page and took the last sip of tea. Georgia couldn't make out the words, but apparently her grandmother was happy to see this visitor.

One more for dinner, Georgia thought as her eyes returned to the article on prison reform in the state before a flying insect summoned her back to the calming yard.

She looked at the tire swing of her childhood still suspended from the big oak tree and then at the hammock strung between two towering pines older than she was. *Jared would like it here,* she thought, and pictured them both lounging in the hammock, reading the Sunday paper, talking in hushed tones, and laughing at private jokes.

Hmm, she sighed wistfully, and turned her body to more closely survey the land where she was born, bred, and all her yesterdays were held; her sanctuary where she came after school, when her father was sick, and when her mother sold their house and married Myron. Her room upstairs was just as she'd left it to go off to college. Grandma Mac's land had been whittled down to about one hundred acres now; the sons, her uncles, and their families had twenty acres each. Since their father had been a "city folk" man, Georgia and her brother had thirty acres each of Tennessee prime waiting for them.

The entire property had begun as two hundred acres that Great-granddaddy Mac amassed and farmed, but by the 1920s the next generation of MacKenzie men, which included her grandfather, turned to the trades, like brick masonry or working in the textile plants—her daddy had become a supervisor at the mill. Knowing that the sons were all well placed with good-paying jobs, Great-granddaddy Mac set his sights on the women of the family. He wanted to give his daughters a boost in the right direction away from becoming sharecropper's wives with lots of babies, or being trapped at the mill with no place to go except into a boss's bed with no guarantee of advancement; not for his daughters and certainly not his granddaughter, Georgia. So Granddaddy Mac sent all of his girls to college, selling off his land for their tuition on an as-needed basis. All of Georgia's aunts had been educated at Fisk University and other teachers' colleges—that was how her daddy met her mother. Her auntie had brought her mother home for a visit and she met Big Brody Mac and it was all over for her mother. Mama was even engaged to another man back at Meharry Medical College, but Big Brody Mac took care of that inside of one week's vacation. *One week's time, just like Jared's stay*, she thought.

Georgia hadn't understood love like that until Jared. Tony Machado was handsome, fun, funny, and treated her like a princess; Georgia loved him because he never gave her any reason not to. But Jared—Georgia loved him because he gave her no choice. She could no more explain the deep, soul-stirring connection to Jared any more than her mother could explain her daddy to her former Meharry fiancé. *It just is. First Brody Mac and now Jared Jaymes. It was all tradition*, Georgia thought.

Looking out in the yard, Georgia superimposed imagines over the green grass and under the shadowy trees. She envisioned a congregation of jubilant black faces; the little boys in short sleeves and ties, the girls in frilly dresses, and all of the adults in their Sunday best. Round tables with white linen tablecloths dotted the verdant grass. She was in a long white gown and the breeze caught her veil and rode upward toward the cloudless blue sky. Jared was by her side, resplendent in a tux, holding her hand as they meandered from table to table. It was their wedding day in the backyard of Grandma Mac's—in the garden of her youth, the playground of her adolescence and the spirit of her womanhood. In the presence of the Almighty, the house, and the people whose love, values, and support made her the woman she was—she was marrying the man she loved and deserved. Georgia smiled longingly at her dream. They danced to Jerry Butler's "Moon River."

Absently, she wondered what Jared was doing right this very minute.

"Georgia," Grandma Mac said from behind. "Look who's here early."

Georgia froze. She could hear the lilt and smile in her grandmother's voice pleading with her granddaughter not to misbehave.

Pur-nell, Georgia answered silently. Not only was she ticked at the interruption of her Sunday daydreaming, but that doofus Pernell was two hours early. She was so angry she didn't even want to turn around to look at him.

"Georgia?" Grandma Mac's voice sounded worried, like she wasn't sure why her granddaughter was acting so ornery.

Georgia looked straight ahead at the swing tire and hammock, and thought, *Here I sit with no makeup, hair in a ponytail, in cutoff shorts because this yokel decides to come early. Great first impression— but I don't really care.*

"Georgia, this is Pernell," her grandmother offered to her granddaughter's back, vocally imploring her to at least turn around. She now knew why the girl wasn't married if she treated all the boys this way.

"Pleased to meet you," he said.

In preparation to face the music, Georgia sighed deeply . . . but then . . . she tilted her head to the side. Did that voice sound familiar?

On her right side, an open-palmed hand stretched into Georgia's view.

"You want my arm to fall off?" he said.

In the split second, she simultaneously heard the Billy Dee Williams's line from *Lady Sings the Blues*, and saw that the hand extended toward her—had a little mole embedded in the thumbnail.

Her head swiveled around and she looked into the sparkling, dancing eyes of Jared Jaymes! His wide, parenthetical grin, crinkly eyes, and left dimple summoned her to him.

"Jared!" Georgia shrieked, and flew into his arms. "Oh, Jared!" She hugged and clung to him.

He laughingly accepted her embrace.

"Oh my word!" a horrified Grandma Mac exclaimed. "Georgia MacKenzie, have you taken leave of your senses? This is no way to greet a strange man."

"What are you doing here?" Georgia asked him, touching him to make sure that her pining for him hadn't conjured up his apparition.

"I came to meet you. As a favor to my grandma Hattie Mae. Seems our grandmothers are old friends."

Grandma Mac, beside herself with embarrassment, said, "Georgia, may I speak to you for a moment?" Her stoic grandmother fumed. Her granddaughter was acting like one of those city-slicking hussies.

"What?" Georgia only heard Jared.

"Your grandma Mac and my grandma Hattie Mae."

"No!"

"Yes!" He lifted and spun her around.

"You're Pernell? I can't believe—"

"First name. It didn't stick once we moved to Philly."

"I cannot believe this!"

"I am calling your mother, young lady." The ignored Grandma Mac, appalled by her granddaughter's display, went into the house. "Got those citified ways."

"Wait a minute. This is too much to comprehend—Pernell?"

"You never noticed the *P.* Jared Jaymes on my degrees? They're all over my office."

"Who looks at those things? I would have thought the *P* stood for Pompous, Prideful, Persnickety." She looked at his lips and added, "Perfect." She kissed him.

"And now they are kissing on my side porch!" Grandma Mac said tightly into the telephone to her daughter-in-law. "What has happened to that girl?"

"Sounds like love," Georgia's mother told Grandma Mac.

"Are you coming over here?" Grandma Mac asked firmly.

Georgia broke the kiss, wanting to just stare at Jared again. He held and rocked her playfully while she just absorbed his being there.

"Freckles."

"In all the places in the world, I never expected you on my grandma's porch."

"You never expected me in your house or your heart either." He kissed her nose. "I hope I never stop surprising you. In a good way."

"I've got thousands of questions."

"I figured that. Ask away."

She led him to the porch swing and they sat. She faced him.

He touched her face and smiled. Happy to be with her there or anywhere.

"What are you doing *here*? How did all this happen?" Georgia asked.

"My grandmother Hattie Mae had this friend who was desperate for her granddaughter, an old maid lawyer in the DA's office in Philly, to meet a handsome, up-and-coming mover and shaker," he teased.

"Oh? Where is he?" Georgia looked around playfully.

"Funny."

"As funny as you are."

"It's all destiny, Georgia MacKenzie. That our grandmothers are old friends and remained so even after my family moved to Philadelphia. That the divinity tastes the same. That there is a picture of you and me when we were kids. We, you and me, were meant to be."

"That picture is of us?"

"Yep."

"What took you so long?" She gazed laughingly into his eyes.

"Better late than never. I've come to get you and take you back to Philly, after the holidays of course."

"Yeah?"

"Yeah."

"But still. How did you piece all this together? How long have you known?"

"Well, it started when your grandmother sent you the package for Halloween addressed to Willow. I told you I once knew a girl named Willow. I didn't know you *were* Willow all grown up."

Georgia blushed.

"I thought that was just a coincidence. Then when I was having you for dinner I wanted to surprise you with my grandma's divinity and I called Grandma Hattie Mae for the recipe. She said she hadn't made it in a few years and would have to call her friend for the exact measurements. Then my grandma Hattie Mae said, 'You know, she has a lawyer-granddaughter up there in Philly too. I took you back there to Tennessee to visit her once when you were just a little boy.' So I say, 'Yeah? What's her name? Maybe I know her.' And she says, 'What's Willow's real name?' And I say, 'Willow? Where is she from again?' And Grandma Hattie Mae says, 'Tennessee.' And I say, 'Evelyn, Tennessee?' And she says, 'You remember me taking you back there?' And I say, 'Is her name Georgia?' And Grandma says, 'That's it. How'd you know that?'"

Georgia giggled and fell into his arms, resting her head next to his heart and playing with his beautiful hands and tapered fingers.

"I was so excited I couldn't sleep," Jared continued. "It was so hard containing myself and not giving it away. So, knowing you'd be here for Christmas, I arranged this visit."

Georgia laughed, then said, "So you knew the night of our Last Supper?"

"Already had my plane ticket."

"Ergo that cynical, cat-who-swallowed-the-canary, know-it-all smile. On the night you rejected me."

"Postponed is a better word. The hardest thing I ever had to do."

"It was hard all right."

"Georgia!" He hugged her and dragged his lips across hers. "We'd come too far and I wasn't gonna let you use me as a boy toy."

"I'll remember that for future reference."

"Let me rephrase that—"

"So that was your big 'plan'? Humiliate me, then show up as Pernell?"

"All these were signs, Georgia. All roads were leading to you."

She looked lovingly up into his eyes. She didn't want to think about him being her boss for a few weeks more, or the move to L.A., or his being mayor now; she just wanted to be held by him. He loved "coming home" to her, and his arms wrapped around her felt like *home.* She just wanted to avoid any reality for as long as she could. Now maybe he would come to L.A. to see her. Or maybe she would reconsider the New York City offer if her weekends could be spent with Jared.

"So these 'signs' are signs of what exactly?" Georgia tested.

"That you and I are meant to be together. All the stars in the heavens point to us." He kissed her soft lips. "You can't go to L.A."

Georgia sat straight up, her eyes questioning.

"I have contacts all over these United States."

"But—"

"But I only needed one right in Philly."

"Who?"

"Neal."

"Neal didn't know. I did not tell anyone about L.A. Not even my girlfriends."

"But Grandma Mac did," Jared confessed. "She called Neal to thank him for the Christmas gift and the picture of Sydney."

"So?"

"She mentioned that even though you were moving to L.A., she wanted Neal to keep in touch with her."

"Ah."

"Neal didn't want to believe that his best friend, Mac, hadn't confided in him. But instead of getting into an argument with you—he called me. Then I made a few confirmation calls to the coast."

"And what were you supposed to do about it, Counselor?"

"Make you an offer you couldn't refuse."

"I'll be the judge of that."

"Let me try."

Georgia looked at him curiously. She'd listen and then tell him how they wanted different things and it would never work. She couldn't be in the public eye no matter how much she loved him, nor ask him to give up his dreams for her privacy—but they could enjoy a helluva relationship for a few great years.

"I'm ready to leave the DA's office."

"What?" she asked, wide-eyed, wondering if this meant he'd be mayor inside of a year. *Oh Lord, please give us at least one year together before I have to give him up,* she prayed, and said, "But you love being DA."

"I love doing whatever I'm doing when I do it or I wouldn't be doing it."

"Mayor."

"Last couple of years I've been restless, searching for something. And no, being mayor is not it. If I wanted that I would be mayor now."

"That's what the political pundits have said. So what have you been 'searching' for?"

"You."

"Me?"

"And everything you have to offer—the familiarity, the intimacy, the shared values, the life I could live with you. 'Cause there's no living without you, Georgia Mac. Not now that I've found you."

His words pierced her heart and brightened her eyes with tears. "Do we have Crazy Cusamano to thank for this?"

"No children will be named after him, but yeah. I think he was one of the catalysts for us getting close. I think your dad was the other one."

A single tear fell from Georgia's eye. "My dad would have liked you." He reached over and wiped it away tenderly with his thumb. "So what's the 'offer I can't refuse'? What's the plan, man?"

"That's my girl. Always on point."

"I learned from the best."

"It seems we're both at a crossroads regarding our professional lives. We both want a change. To that end I am prepared to offer you a partnership."

"Okay, but before you go on—"

"May I finish?" Jared asked, raising an eyebrow.

"Proceed."

"In November of this year I purchased a three-story brownstone on Chestnut."

"Why? You *love* your house—"

He simply looked at her.

"Sorry. Continue."

"I purchased this house for the purpose of setting up my law office."

"*Your* law office?" Georgia asked with a gleam in her eye.

"I plan to surpass Willie Gary and the Johnnie Cochran firms in revenue on the East Coast. With my reputation I shouldn't have any problem getting clients, some corporate, medical malpractice, and once we get just one tobacco, HMO, asbestos, or lead class-action suit—"

Georgia's eyes filled with tears.

"What?"

"You would no longer be my boss."

"That's the idea." He smiled widely, his eyes crinkled, and the dimple bowed. He beamed with pride.

"Oh, Jared!" She clung to him, buried her face in his neck, inhaling the very essence of him. This wonderful man had figured out a way to give them both what they wanted, respecting and not compromising her values. She was moved to tears. It seemed that everything came down to this defining moment. Even more than the grilled hamburgers in November. Of putting his life on the line for her. Of arranging a Sunday ride in the countryside for her. Of keeping her awake and safe all night long. Or backing off to preserve her reputation when he wanted her. *This* was the singular most unselfishly gallant act of all time. He was like a prince, abdicating his throne, his seat of power as DA, as mayor—for the woman he loved.

Georgia adored this man. Jared was the visible soul of her life.

"That is a wonderful plan. But, Jared." She reared back to look at him with her salty wet eyes. "It's all so final. I don't want you to give up *your* dreams. Mayor, governor, president—"

"Woman, you are not listening."

"Okay."

"I love that you care about that. But I've thought on it long and hard. It's called personal growth and development. What once seem glamorous morphed into a psychological drain so I reassessed what I wanted and changed directions because what I wanted more than anything was a life with you."

She grinned at him.

"If I change my mind again, I can get to the mayor's office from private practice. But that would be a decision for us to make together. And that's not gonna happen. We'll be having too much fun personally and professionally to want to give it up for public service. We can still serve our community by being good citizens, having happy kids, doing the Habitat for Humankind, PTAs—"

Georgia's heart soared, her mind threw in the towel, and her soul rejoiced. "Aren't we getting a little ahead of ourselves?" she said out of habit. But her smile and body gave her away.

"You're right." He played along. "I was offering you a partnership. A *work* partnership. Jaymes and MacKenzie. It would take you years, decades, to get a partnership at Felton, Mayfield and Dasher."

Georgia smiled at the completeness of his

research. "MacKenzie and Jaymes. Has a nice ring to it."

"Hmm. Now, let's see. My money, my client list, my alma mater who, on sheer rumor alone, is already pelting me with law clerk hopefuls who want a chance to clerk with Jared Jaymes, former DA."

"Okay, okay, I see your point."

He squeezed her tightly. "Nice try. But who knows? In due time, if you play your cards right, it could be Jaymes and Jaymes and who will know which is which?"

Georgia looked into his shimmering gaze and quietly admitted to him, "I love you, Jared Jaymes."

It was his turn to be filled so completely that it overflowed in his eyes. He finally heard her say what he knew was in her heart all along. It was like heaven to hear, and paradise to feel.

"To that end, we have to go public by Valentine's Day. Will Downing will be in town for a concert, after which I've reserved a cabin for two at the Brookside Inn."

"Pretty sure of yourself, aren't you? I knew you and that woman were in cahoots."

"So this is how we can play it—with your approval of course. I'll announce in January that I am not seeking reelection and plan to go into private practice."

"Free publicity."

"Exactly. I'll throw my support behind Neal, if he wants it."

"I don't think Brenda will—"

"That's a discussion between the two of them."

"True."

"What do you say about our part?"

"Hmm. Let me get back to you," she teased, and he devoured her in playful kisses.

Never were there two more perfect people for each other on the face of this earth. Jared knew that, and now she knew that too. If they both wanted it, they could have the greatest love affair of all time. He knew that in his bones.

"Trust and believe that I love you, Georgia MacKenzie—like I have never loved before and never will again."

At Grandma Mac's insistence, Grandma Hattie Mae consented to join them for Christmas and was flying in this evening. At Grandma Mac's invitation, Jared accepted one of her remaining five guest rooms. After dinner, Georgia accompanied Jared to Nashville's posh hotel, the Hermitage, to collect his things.

"I have driven past this hotel a zillion times but have never been inside," she said as she perused the plush room, noting the sumptuous carpeting, matching drapes, fresh flowers, and gleaming windows. "Leave it to you to give me yet another experience. In my hometown no less."

Jared kissed her lips before disappearing through the bedroom's double doors to get his suitcase and remove his clothes from the armoire.

Georgia pushed open the door. There before her was the big bed with a tufted headboard almost reaching the ceiling. The night lamps had been switched on by the maid, and bathed the room in a soft golden glow. The sheets were turned down, folded into an inviting V with chocolates on each pillow. She looked at the bed and smiled.

Jared picked up a shirt from the chaise longue, and, noticing Georgia had stopped talking, looked over at her. His eyes followed hers. To the bed. He put the shirt down, placed his hands in both pockets, and smiled at her.

Georgia looked at him and smiled.

"Are you thinking what I'm thinking?"

"Uh-huh. I believe we are in sync." She stepped out of her shoes. "Well, I always heard you are a man of action. Enough thinking, Counselor."

"I couldn't agree more." In two giant steps he was in front of her.

He smiled at her. His dark bedroom eyes sparkled in the muted light. Tenderly, he took her face between his hands and kissed her once, twice. Her amber eyes smiled up at him.

"Freckles," he said.

Georgia slid her hands around his lean waist and let her body cover his. There was no break-away dress, no hot-pink thong, no mood music, no strategic, pulse-point placement of perfume, no perfectly painted lips. But it was going to happen. They were going to make love. *Finally*, she thought. In her mind's ear, she heard the strings from Etta James's "At Last" cue up and swirl around them. This time it wasn't "good-bye, love," but hello and welcome to the rest of her life.

He bent to kiss her ever so gently, as if they had all the time in the world. She didn't close her eyes as she wanted to savor the bend of his jawline, the placement of his nose to the left of hers, the way the light from the Nashville skyline painted the tips of his long eyelashes just as the golden glow from the elevator's light had. But the feel of his tongue tasting and teasing her own forced her eyes closed. The sensation of his body enveloping every inch of hers and the promise of what was to come caused her to dissolve into him.

He then let his lips descend fully upon hers. He loved the feel, the taste, the texture of her hungry tongue tangling with his. At last, this woman he'd loved from a distance. This woman worth revisiting his plans for. This woman who refused to accept that she loved him . . . at last he felt her melding into him. He felt her sweet surrender to all that he wanted . . . all that they wanted from each other. His hands left her face and drew her body farther into his. The passionate kiss fired their hands to explore and probe and test; hers across his expansive back, and his cupping her cute derriere.

"Hmmmm. We've got to stop."

"Not again," Georgia said, delighting in the feel of his hard maleness saluting her soft thigh in all its magnificence.

"We've got to pick up Grandma Hattie Mae and I don't want us rushing through this."

"Haven't you ever heard of a 'quickie'? Perfectly acceptable mode of sexual expression."

"Not you and me. Well, not for our first time. We're only going to have one first time, Georgia. I want it to be special like us. Leisurely. I want a real marathon. I've waited too long for us to just rush through it. We're not in a race."

Georgia smiled at him. More than the grilled hamburgers, the leg of lamb, or finding a way for them to be together forever—she loved the romance of this man. "It's a logical argument."

"We've got a lifetime."

"Yes, we do."

He kissed the human personification of his dream standing before him. It wasn't all just want and desire, but he needed Georgia, like oxygen. He had never needed a woman before. Everything he wanted was here with him now. His body, soul, and heart's desire. Who could ask for more?

"I love you, Georgia MacKenzie."

"I trust and believe you do, Jared Jaymes." She let her hands roam across his back and rest on his taut, athletic butt. "Let's go get Grandma Hattie Mae."

Her cell phone rang. "Hello." She listened as Jared came up behind her and began rubbing her back. "All right. Don't wait up." At the conversation's end she snapped her phone closed. She turned into him, resuming her former stance. "Seems the weather at Grandma Hattie Mae's end is treacherous."

"How treacherous?" His eyes gleamed.

"Canceled-flight treacherous. We pick her up tomorrow at three."

"Really?"

"What will we do with all this time?"

They giggled forehead to forehead. "Besides thank the gods? And Big Brody Mac?"

"Let's leave my daddy out of this one."

"I'm sorry I'll never get to thank him for you."

Georgia smiled up at Jared. She saw her future in his eyes.

"You're the one, Georgia MacKenzie. The only one for me."

"I love you."

"Don't ever stop."

They kissed, long and deep and slowly, treasuring the taste and feel of each other, knowing that their time stretched out endlessly before them. As they kissed, they explored each other with their hands; touches that had been forbidden to them now came freely and more ardently. The pleasure he was feeling rose in appreciative moans as he began unbuttoning her blouse. She pulled his shirt over his head and the T-shirt he always wore came off with it, revealing his massive bare chest. She sank to his nipples as he held her head, caressing her hair. She reared back so her blouse could drop to the floor, followed by her bra. His eyes filled with the vision of her breasts, her ringed chocolate nipples, the color of a Snickers bar, demanding that he sample their excellence. As their breathing grew ragged, he swooped her up and carried her to the bed with the inviting V. He laid her gently upon the fresh sheets. She watched him unbuckle his belt and she eased his pants over the sizable love muscle that had first appeared beneath thin gray cloth as he was sprawled over her couch. This time, the object of her desire was sheathed in exotic black, and unlike her first visual of it when she had to leave the room, this time Georgia smiled with wicked anticipation. On this night, she would experience the projectile in all its splendid glory.

Jared reciprocated by laying her back so she was poised on her elbows, offering her taut breasts to him again. He gingerly eased her pants, then panties over her tempting hips. He eyed her hairy triangle with keen interest and appreciation, like unwrapping the Christmas gift of a lifetime. He smiled in genuine admiration. He had never allowed himself to get this far in his fantasy of her— lest he never reached this point. Lest that once he imagined all they could do and be, he could never come back from the despair of the reality of not having her. But here she lay—all she was, all she did, and how she lived had gotten her this far, on the altar of his primal desire and he savored her vision. He no longer had to wonder, as he was about to find out the taste of her, the sounds she made, the look in her eyes when he stroked her just right, the smell of the inside scent she emitted at the height of her pleasure that she'd shared with only a few deserving men before him. Now it was his turn—their turn.

He bent and kissed her throbbing lips, suckled her taut breasts, first one nipple and then the other, carved a trail to the well of her navel, then relished the open enticement to her swollen, secret garden. He moaned as he loved the feel of her curvaceous woman's body complete with a tactile thickness, and soft padding. He never understood the appeal of some men for the model-thin female form with jutting hipbones, little-boy breasts, and waxes, which left the women clean-shaven and bald, making him feel like he was sleeping with a prepubescent, underage girl. He loved the well-groomed, hairy allure of a woman—concealing, visually toying with that last barrier before nirvana, signifying that she knew how to move, how to savor and enjoy the full spectrum of lovemaking. He liked loving a grown, fully adorned, natural woman and the way the slick emission, sticky-sweet nectar entangled in her womanliness—messy, wild, and free.

They kissed again feverishly, she wanting him to plunge deeply, immediately, wanting to save the slow and easy for their third or fourth time. But when he rose and removed that last defense of black cloth, and presented the naked, male protrusion of his desire, Georgia thought she'd swoon at the sight of his engorged passion. His mahogany column was a beautifully crafted work of art—flawless, everything she thought it would be. He slid the latex covering upon his majestic need, preparing it for the penultimate of experiences. They kissed again, as their nude bodies rolled across the bed, changing positions, trying to prolong the inevitable, but finally, Jared melted into her garden paradise and they exploded together in symbiotic unison.

As the crescendo slowed and the film of sweat cooled, Georgia could see the city's skyline below over Jared's shoulder. Her cheek resting against his, they moved to the ultimate cessation of rhythm. She was utterly and completely satisfied by this man: physically, emotionally, and spiritually.

"It's unanimous." Jared spoke first. "You do everything well."

Georgia couldn't respond. She didn't want anything to ruin the undulating, pulsating of his body in hers. She stroked his high athletic buttocks, and moaned her agreement. She felt like a born-again virgin, deflowered for the very first time.

"MacKenzie? Speechless?"

She shook her head and grinned. She was floating on a cloud. "Be Ever Wonderful."

He laughed into her ear, remembering that old song by Rocky Robin. "I aim to please."

"And please you did." She held him tightly and there they remained and fell asleep. They awoke in the middle of the night and began round two.

As dawn began to brighten up the southern sky, Georgia awoke. She lay in Jared's arms, his heartbeat in her ear, his hand draped over her nude hips. She smiled. She was happier than she thought she'd ever be again. In fact, she was happier than she had ever been. She and her dragon slayer were an ideal combination. He'd proven to be a phenomenal man who'd had the courage and the character to honor her commitment to her credo. In this kaleidoscope of life, he'd turned the world for her so that the stones fell in sync and gave them what they both wanted and needed. He was her black knight in shining armor. Her mountain mover. Her man. She hadn't known love could feel so right. She snuggled deeper into him and found his morning maleness had risen before him. Unknowingly setting a precedent for their future lovemaking trysts, she began relieving him of his accumulated passion and they engaged in early morning love.

They'd fallen back asleep, awakened, ordered room service, and napped again, rising in just enough time to shower and get to the airport. Jared grabbed his luggage and Georgia's hand. They walked hand in hand, soul to soul, heart to heart, body to body, accompanied by happy giggles like two teens on their first date. He made her so happy. "Good-bye, Hermitage!" Georgia said as they pulled away and she blew kisses.

"Would you have come to see me in L.A.?"

"I wasn't going to let you get away to L.A."

"Just suppose it hadn't all worked out. Would you have come?"

"Oh yeah. I would have come to visit my buddies and looked you up to see how you were."

"Yeah?"

"I presume when you left that you would have said 'come up and see me if you're ever in L.A.' You know, in that flippant, casual Georgia Mac style."

"Oh, you think you know me, huh?"

"After last night and this morning—three times. Hell yeah, I know you. And once I got a taste of you? What you whipped on me? I would have moved to L.A.'"

"Good answer, Counselor."

"We have to stop by the drugstore."

"Do we have time?" she asked.

"We have to make time. We're out."

"Of what?"

He yo-yoed his eyebrows and grinned until his dimple appeared.

"We used them all?"

"Do you recall the collection of foil on my nightstand?"

"That's not what I'm recalling." She snuggled nearer to him and ran her hand up his muscled thigh.

"Hey, hey," he cautioned playfully. "I'm driving."

"Maybe Grandma Hattie Mae has a few to spare."

"Don't talk about my grandma."

"It's a compliment. That's a wonderful thing if she's getting and practicing safe sex at her age. I hope we'll still be making love in our eighties."

"I'll make that my personal responsibility."

"I'll help."

He kissed her hand. "We do make a great team."

"Yes, we do."

"Can't wait until we dispense with condoms altogether and I can run into you like a river wild."

"Oooh. I like the sound of that, so the feel of it must be mind-blowing." She held his hand and stroked his thumb with the mole embedded in it. "One of the first things on our agenda when we get back to Philly, update our HIV testing."

"You know, I can get a testing kit at the drugstore when I get the condoms."

"I have my yearly gyno exam in January. Like to start out the year with a clean bill of health."

"I'm not waiting that long," Jared protested playfully. "We'll have my brother give us a blood test—fast and free."

"Can he be trusted with such a delicate matter?" Georgia teased.

"Like us, it's his job." He kissed her hand. "You better be glad I think you're worth all these rules and regulations," he teased.

"You better be glad I have them," she counter-teased.

He smiled. "Yes, I am. Hard to get, easy to hold."

"It's been years for me, but I don't know what that Courtney was into."

"Me mostly."

"Aw—you are so modest. Well, there's a new sheriff in town."

"There's a whole new town," he laughed pridefully. "And I am ecstatic to be its only occupant."

"Amen to that! Now and forever."

They picked up Grandma Hattie Mac and she talked all the way from the airport until she reached Grandma Mac's. Georgia and Jared hardly heard a word she said.

As the reunion between the two old widowed best friends began full tilt, the two young lovers left them to openly discover Georgia's hometown.

Georgia squired Jared around Evelyn, Tennessee, to Ross Preschool where she became the infamous Willow, down Main Street where she first learned to drive, to the movie theater where she spent countless hours, the house she grew up in, Roosevelt High School and the bleacher under which she received her first kiss after cheerleading practice, and the church where her soprano voice graced both the junior and senior choirs. She took him to the swimming hole and told him about her dream.

"Jerry Butler's 'Moon River,' huh?'

"Yep."

"That is wild. When we come back this summer, we'll have to reenact that."

"You're on."

"You know," he said, thinking of the lyrics, "we are after the same rainbow's end."

"Yes, we are." She looked up into his eyes. "You

get me." She smiled and kissed him quickly. "I don't have to be anyone but me when I am with you."

"That's the Georgia I love. You. Just the way you are."

Georgia relished holding hands and walking arm in arm with Jared, showing him the sights of her youth, wishing he'd been there with her. Over the next two days, he pushed her in the tire swing and they swayed in the hammock just as she had envisioned. Having gone to midnight Mass on Christmas Eve, they rose late on Christmas morning to the smell of coffee and a breakfast of ham, eggs, pancakes, and potatoes before Grandmas Mac and Hattie Mae shooed them out of the kitchen so they could begin the holiday banquet. As was the tradition, the entire MacKenzie family descended on Grandma Mac's, where they feasted, swapped stories, and met Georgia's new beau. In the refracted light of the Christmas tree's glow, Jared sat at the piano and played Christmas carols with the family joining in. Georgia watched his fingers dance up and down the piano keys just as they had played her body so exquisitely the night before. Georgia's heart was so full of love for this man who fit so flawlessly into her family. He was the best thing to ever come into her life.

The house quieted down as folks went home and to their respective rooms.

"I'm sorry I didn't get you anything," Jared said quietly before they said good night.

"Yes, you did." She looked up at him. "The most priceless, precious gift of all."

"What? The same thing you gave me?"

"Precisely." She kissed him before she continued. "It's nice to know you're not perfect."

"I'm perfect for you."

"No argument there, Counselor."

The New Year's Eve party was at her mother and Myron's house, and as streamers whizzed by them, Jared whispered in Georgia's ear, "This is our year, Georgia MacKenzie."

"I love you, Jared Jaymes."

"I am so crazy about you, Georgia, I can't sleep at night."

"I have the remedy for that."

Once back home, Georgia gathered a big comforter from her bed and they went out and lay in the hammock and slept contently in each other's arms until a new dawn bloomed. Another day of loving Jared Jaymes.

Chapter 11

It was hard to give up the idyllic life with Jared in Evelyn, Tennessee, and return to work. *But here I am*, Georgia thought. She waited on hold and watched the parade of well-wishers stream into Jared's office. It had been that way since he announced leaving the DA's office for private practice. The media, being what they were, speculated that this was a well-calculated plan to get to the mayor's office. They were so clueless. Jared had recommended and thrown his support to Neal. Georgia would have loved to be privy to the conversation between Neal and Brenda regarding the hectic and demanding position. She knew her best friend would love the challenge, limelight, and notoriety, but Brenda had to have been hard-sold on it. She wondered what promises Neal made to his wife.

"Georgia MacKenzie," the strong male voice on the other end of the phone identified.

"Happy New Year, Wally. How's the weather?"

"Always the same. Gorgeous."

"Did you have a good holiday?"

"Yes. Went to Aspen. The wife and kids wanted snow. Yours?"

"Perfect. Just perfect." She'd been given the best of gifts—the man she loved, loved her back.

"You're not coming, are you?" Wally asked.

"No."

"I knew it the moment I saw you and your boss."

"What?" Georgia chuckled.

"I came back and told Felton, Mayfield and Dasher, unless they hired Jared Jaymes, Georgia MacKenzie wasn't coming."

"You should be on the psychic network." Georgia laughed.

"Just reading the signs and the chemistry that was bouncing all around you two." He laughed. "But thank you."

"For what?"

"I won a thousand dollars in the pool. I was the only one who said you wouldn't come."

"Glad to be of service."

"Just invite me to the wedding."

"Let's not get ahead of ourselves."

"I'm not. Don't drag your feet on this one, MacKenzie. He's the real deal."

Georgia chuckled again.

"If things don't work out, know that you will always have a place at Felton, Mayfield and Dasher."

"Thanks, Wally."

"See you in court or at the wedding—whichever comes first."

"Bye."

She quickly revisited her plans with Jared.

Everything would work out. She had never been so sure of anything in her life. Her "go to" guy and the guy she was in love with were one and the same. What more could a girl ask for?

She thought of her crazy girlfriend's joke, "Five Important Tips for a Woman: It's important that you have a man that helps around the house and has a job. It's important that a man makes you laugh. It's important that you have a man you can count on and doesn't lie to you. It's important that a man loves and spoils you. It's important that these four men never meet."

She chuckled and glanced through the two sets of plate glass, watching Jared holding court with about ten people; he was all the man she needed. That was *her man*, helmsman of her future, her everything, and the thought made her heart flip.

She'd watched womenfolk flounce into his office, flutter eyelashes, twist hair, cross legs, showing too much thigh, smile too much, laugh too loudly, all thinking that now that he was going into private practice, they all had a shot at him. But he was her man, and she was proud of it. He knew it, she knew it, and soon the world would know it. She thought of that Billie Holiday lyric, "whatever my man is—I'm his."

There seemed to have been no obvious fallout from their being seen by Burt at the inn, or maybe it was moot and irrelevant at this point. The couple planned to remain careful until Jared's final departure. Right now, no one knew that after work they spent their time between his house and hers, where they cooked, danced, watched old movies, played games, and on Sundays, drove to the Brookside Inn, but now they added discussions on the folks who visited him—what they said or did. She and Jared enjoyed the same life they had led during the Cusamano quarantine but now with the full knowledge and consent that they loved each other. That there was a future and they would go through life together shoulder to shoulder. His only strange request was that every night at her house, after they cut off the lights and set the alarm, Georgia had to wait for Jared at the front steps, and they would climb them together, her slightly ahead of him with his hand in hers or on her shoulder or around her waist, and when she reached the top she had to stop. They'd kiss and, with her, he'd turn right into her bedroom. That one gesture made him giddy. Georgia didn't understand or know why and she didn't have to know why. She was happy to make him happy.

As they lay in bed, Jared had told her that his only short-term dream was to come into the office and take her to lunch, announcing to everyone who saw them that she was his woman; that they were a couple. He wanted to hold hands and kiss her quick on the lips in public if he so desired; he wanted an open and honest exchange of feelings and free rein to express his love for her so the world could see.

"Kinda *Officer and a Gentleman,* ain't' it?" she had quipped. He'd tackled her with kisses.

Despite their initial plans, an excited Jared wanted to go public right after handing in his resignation. A cautious Georgia countered his change of plans with her own—wanting to wait until she was on board at Jaymes and MacKenzie. The compromise was the original plan; they'd go public by Valentine's Day and Georgia was to follow him to the firm in the spring; Jaymes and MacKenzie in gold stenciled letters was already on order for the plate-glass door.

Neal and Brenda knew. Neal figured it out when he went to see Jared's new office and asked why the Jaymes stenciled on the door was so far off center . . . "unless you plan on adding another name some time soon." When they went public, Georgia's girlfriends would surely have a fit thinking that she and Jared had been dating all along. When the time came, Georgia would placate them with bridesmaids' duties and the promise of more eligible, upwardly mobile black men at their disposal since they left college. Of course, Grandmas Mac and Hattie Mae were taking full credit for Jared and Georgia and suggested that their first child should be named Jordan whether a girl or a boy. Jordan Jaymes. Georgia and Jared had already decided that the two grandmothers should walk down the aisle together as part of the procession, and at the reception the newlyweds would sit under a blowup picture of Jared holding Georgia, the caption reading, THIS IS WHERE THE HAPPY ENDING BEGAN—

Despite Jared's persistence, Georgia didn't discuss a wedding beyond these thinking-out-loud musings usually brought up by him before the night's end. Georgia wanted to take it slow, date at least a year to find out if Jared really was The One. She knew he was The One and Only One for her;

the way she knew that he'd propose to her before the year was out.

Through two sets of plate-glass windows, Jared glanced over at her and winked. Her heart fluttered. *We're going all the way*, she thought, heading for forever—love, marriage, then a baby carriage. She loved this man who nourished her heart, mind, spirit, and soul. Her "old" boss. The love of her life was here all along. Who knew?

With Christmas dinner devoured and the kitchen cleaned, Georgia MacKenize Jaymes leaned her body against the doorjamb and smoothed her hand over her stomach. Her solid gold wedding band caught the refracted light from the decorated tree and bounced back spotlighting her husband, seated at the piano surrounded by all the important people in her life. After more than three years, Jared Jaymes still took her breath away and made her smile. Grandma Mac, her mother, brother, uncles, aunts, and cousins all sang to Jared's jazzy Yuletide carols. He flashed her his classic grin complete with dimple and winked as his hands flicked the eighty-eights the way they delighted her body. Last year she had spent the holidays with the Jaymes clan in Philly. This year, his parents had joined them in Evelyn, Tennessee, as did his sister, his brother, and their families, filling Grandma Mac's home with as much love as it could hold. His parents even spoke of leaving the cold Philly winters and the polluted summers and building a house on a plot of land they owned in Lenore, North

Carolina; they thought they'd "keep better" and live longer down South with the slower pace, clean air, and freshly harvested vegetables.

Absently, Georgia spun her wedding ring around her finger remembering how everything had worked according to plan. On that first Valentine's Day, she and Jared had attended the Will Downing concert and gone to the Brookside Inn. Knowing her politics on diamonds, Jared bypassed the traditional gem and gave her an eighteen-karat solid gold necklace that spelled out LOVED. He wanted her to know no matter where she was or what she was doing she was loved. Whether the word lay flat against her mocha skin, sparkling for all to see, or was hidden beneath a turtleneck sweater . . . no matter, all she had to do was reach up and, like reading Braille, feel the love in more ways than one. He had always dreamed of giving his fiancée a diamond, but Georgia could neither trust nor believe that any diamonds were conflict free. She'd stipulated that over the years, white men had felt acceptably justified in lying to folks in general, and to and about black folks specifically, and this was not the time to trust them at their word. For purposes of commerce and power, whatever it took to maintain the status quo, white folks had manipulated the truth: "we have happy nigras. We treat 'em like family." "Read my lips. No more taxes." "I did not have sexual relations with that woman." "Weapons of mass destruction . . . invading Iraq." "Heck of a job, Brownie," regarding treatment of the Katrina victims. "Madoff makes billions lying to his friends." Georgia chose not to believe a less than powerful and influential jeweler who decreed that there was "no blood on his diamonds." Safe diamonds were like safe sex . . . the only safe sex was no sex. The only conflict-free, guilt-free diamond was the one you did not buy. Georgia needed sex, but she could do without diamonds for pleasure and esteem—self or otherwise—she could and did get both from other sources. Georgia had sold her engagement ring from Tony and donated the thousands of dollars in its entirety to the Sierra Leone Children Defense Fund. *When you know better, you do better.* There were no diamonds in her future. If she ever felt the need for sparkle, cubic zirconium would serve the purpose.

For that first Valentine's Day, Georgia had gifted Jared with an original recording of Art Blakely and the Jazz Messengers' *A Night in Tunisia,* challenging to find but worth the joy expressed on Jared's face. The search was already on for Miles Davis's 1/21/49 recording *Birth of Cool.* She wanted to replicate the look in his eyes. When they'd returned from their Valentine's Day weekend jaunt, no one seemed to notice. She'd left the DA's office and joined him in May.

Jaymes and MacKenzie,
Attorneys at Law.

They had more work than they could handle and had hired an administrative assistant and a paralegal. Jared had proposed to her that Christmas Eve, hiding her solid gold, cigar-band ring with their initials carved through the precious metal in a gift wrapped Fabergé egg ornament that hung on his tree; the inscription read TRUST AND BELIEVE—FOREVER.

They were married the following spring in Grandma Mac's backyard with everyone they wanted in attendance. She had teased that she didn't want to walk down the aisle to that tired old wedding march and thought Young MC's "Busta A Move" to be a better choice. He countered that their first dance should be to Tone Loc's "Funky Cold Medina." They'd made laughing love. As it turned out, their first official dance as Mr. and Mrs. Jared Jaymes was to "Living Inside Your Love," followed by Etta James's "At Last," then Jerry Butler's "Moon River," just like in Georgia's dreams that had started it all. No time for a real honeymoon, they spent the bridal weekend in the same suite at the Hermitage where they first consummated their love.

The Jaymeses were forced to hire another paralegal and one associate, an energetic U Penn grad who'd patterned his life after the impressive DA who spoke at one of the associate's high school Career Days. Georgia and Jared increased their law practice personnel so they could maintain the rhythm they had set for themselves in their private lives. Once a month, they worked at Habitat for Humankind and once a month they attended church. They tried to schedule them both on the same weekend so the other three weekends of the month would be all theirs. They hadn't made it to Europe yet, but they took long Friday-to-Monday weekends. Besides visiting their house in the Hamptons, they were partial to Carmel and Napa. He took her skiing and she took him fishing. They were both taking flying lessons because if business kept up as it was, it would be more cost-and time effective for them to own their own plane to fly to their out-of-town business meetings and court hearings.

Despite it all, what they really relished doing was letting the answering service take all the calls, and staying in from Friday to Monday—just the two of them, cooking, eating, and dancing. Reading the Sunday paper in the hammock, which hung in their backyard gazebo amid Georgia's flowering garden, and listening to gospel music from the radio, was how they enjoyed spending the Lord's day. Georgia thought that after their first year they would become more sociable, but they'd completed their second year of marriage and were venturing into their third and still preferred each other's company to any other.

Georgia now smiled as the family group went into a rousing chorus of "Deck the Halls" and mused how most folks would think their lives humdrum and boring, but it suited her and Jared so well. Occasionally, they went out to friends' or had friends over when Jared fired up the grill, but there never seemed to be enough alone time together. They entertained three times a year: for their May anniversary, a summer barbecue in the Hamptons, and in the tradition of the premarital Jared Jaymes, a dinner party after Thanksgiving to kick off the Christmas season. They had their pet charities and attended those balls—United Negro College Fund, cancer, heart disease, Multiple Sclerosis Society, and sickle cell. They babysat Sydney Preston to give Neal and Brenda some alone time.

It worked. Brenda was pregnant again. This time, she wasn't alone.

At home Jared often rose first and brought Georgia juice and a wake-up kiss before he left for the office. Since their workdays were so hectic, it was important that they shared their evening meal together. Whoever got home first started dinner, the other joining in upon arrival, and they sat and ate and talked before cleaning the kitchen and catching the news often falling asleep on the couch. The rule was that no work could be brought to or done in bed—a novel, crossword puzzle, or Suduko—but no legal work, not even in the sitting area on the other side of their bedroom near the fireplace. While waiting for Georgia to get out of the shower, Jared often fell asleep. She didn't have the heart to wake him. But after a few hours of sleep, when dawn lit up the sky just before running across the horizon, Georgia would snuggle against Jared and seek a fully awake "Pernell," free him from his clothed confines, and, in a number of ways, begin to stimulate his sweet release. Half asleep but all aroused, they'd make delicious early morning love and fall back to sleep for a nap until the alarm went off announcing the beginning of their frantic day; it had been an established tradition.

She wondered how their lives would change with a baby. Georgia stroked her tummy again. She wondered if they'd have to give up their dawn trysts, which would be ironic as they were probably what got her in this predicament. They hadn't been trying to get pregnant, but she'd been more horny than careful a couple of times.

She'd found out just before they left for the holidays. She imagined how she'd tell Jared. A few more weeks and he'd figure it out for himself when he realized that Mother Nature hadn't made her monthly visit. She fantasized about telling him while they were running errands. He always asked, "Any place else while we're out?" And she'd answer, "Nope. Home, Jaymes." Only when Jared asked the next time she'd thought of telling him, "Yeah. We need to get two security gates for the front and back stairs." He probably would've asked why and she would've said, "We have to childproof our steps. What kind of parents would we be if we let our kid take a tumble?" He would've pulled over, laugh-cried, and smothered her with happy kisses. She'd finally decided to tell him at her mother's New Year's Eve party. Start the year off with a bang. It was the first thing she'd ever kept from him.

When a couple becomes a family, things change; they knew that from babysitting Sydney. Right after he'd moved into his house, Jared had taken the bedroom next to the master bedroom and expanded the master bath into a marble masterpiece—double vanity, sunken tub, separate shower, commode room, sauna, and walk-in linen closet. That would have made a great nursery right next door to their bedroom, but the bachelor Jared wasn't thinking about any babies when he converted that guest room to an extended bath. Next to the master bath was the upstairs parlor with the fireplace, flanked by long windows on either side. It was a large open room set off by four columns across from the back stairs to the kitchen—not suitable for a nursery. So either the guest room down the hall, which now housed all the bedroom furniture from her house, or the other room joined by a bathroom, which held all her office furniture, would be the nursery. The bachelor Jared had dug out the cellar, which had been for storing coal when the house was built in the 1920s, and made it into a rec room complete with a poker table, a flat-screen TV, and a wet bar, which housed a humidor for his Cohibas. Because of his allergies, he only allowed smoking in the well-ventilated basement. She and Jared hadn't done anything to the two rooms on the top floor yet, but their child wasn't going to be a floor away. "Mac" could stay in their room until he or she was about six months old; it was certainly large enough. Mac. She smiled. She knew the grandmothers were vying for Jordan, but she'd told Jared that she wanted their first child to be named MacKenzie—girl or boy. He'd smiled and said, "Okay by me."

Baby, she thought. I'm going to—*we're* going to have a baby. Me? She just started giggling. *Is it humanly possible to be any happier than we are right now?* she wondered. It scared her to think that she'd almost missed this heaven. That she almost moved to L.A. She now had everything she wanted and more. This *is what love is supposed to feel like*, she thought. She looked at Jared, who was now wowing the crowd with a lively rendition of "Joy to the World." *And that's what my love looks like. He is so perfect for me*, she thought.

Admit it or not, every woman wants a hero. No matter how accomplished she is in her own right,

from Eleanor Roosevelt to Condoleezza Rice to
Oprah Winfrey, a woman wants a good man—
a man who makes her feel safe, loved, and special.
An honest man she can trust—a man on whom
she can fall back and he'll be there to catch her
even before she knows she's falling. That man for
Georgia was Jared. And now they had a little bless-
ing coming. Their circle of love was expanding.
She wondered how many more times that would
happen in their lives—how many more little
people would be living inside their love. She
didn't know but she wanted them for Jared—he
would make such a wonderful father.

She thought of that old saying that "nothing
becomes apparent until you become a parent."
She supposed that one day soon she'd know exactly how her father felt, saddled with the awesome
responsibility of trying to protect his daughter
from the pitfalls of men—more so than a woman
could. Most of his maxims played out perfectly, but
now Georgia realized that "don't sleep where you
earn your meat" was more about economics and
options than anything else—a lesson on power
and choice. He used to say "if you ain't the lead
dog, your view never changes." Her daddy never
thought that she, a woman, would *be* the boss. That
she would be in control and have the power and
not be subjected to the appetites and whims of a
man. It was not the way it was in his world, or his
father's world or his grandfather's. All the men in
her family worked with what they had and passed
on their wisdom based on their life experiences.
But in Georgia's world, women ruled; her daughter's world should be even more phenomenal.

Each generation should improve. Technically, Georgia never slept with her boss; she'd taken another job, had another place to live, and another car to drive though she had not left for L.A. yet. Theoretically, for a while she had two bosses. Officially, yeah, she had slept with her boss with stipulations in place. Still, she thought her dad would be proud of her . . . and her progress. The bottom line and end results were unparalleled. She did have options and choices and chose to love Jared while still employed with him. The gamble led her to happiness, marriage, and now a child . . . maybe a woman-child whom Georgia would tell about her granddaddy Big Brody Mac. He'd be happy and relieved with the way it all turned out— that his daughter had a primo job *and* an incomparable man to boot.

When Mac or any of their other children asked about their daddy Jared, asked if it was love at first sight, Georgia would tell them that she knew their daddy for five years before they dated, that she was engaged to another man who died, and that their daddy came to her rescue on a black stallion to keep her safe from a bad man. He was her dragon slayer. She would tell them that he left an important, powerful job, and she was so in love with him that she followed him. They fell in love, got married, and had wonderful children. "Know why?" she'd ask them. They'd ask, "Why?" and Georgia would say, "Because your daddy made a way out of no way. Because I trusted and believed that *true* love will always find a way. And I am just where I want to be . . . living inside his love. . . . We're all lucky to be us."

Epilogue

From his cushioned perch, the man watched as the Jaymes family raked leaves in the yard of their four-story Victorian house. He hadn't visited Stateside in over five years, since he viewed his mother's funeral from a similar long-distance roost. Prior to that, usually when he'd whizzed past the Jaymes home, he'd never seen the inhabitants, only the house, decorated for various holidays, and a pair of hybrid cars; the Hummer in the garage was probably taken out like a 1920s classic relic for special occasions. Now he watched Jared rake as his daughter of about six ran and jumped in the pile and laughed uproariously as leaves scattered everywhere. Her daddy grabbed her up, spun her around, and flipped her back into the bed of freshly mounded leaves.

Georgia was on the porch steps blowing bubbles with a boy of about three. The house was ornamented for Halloween with cobwebs in the trees, carved pumpkins on the stone stairs, and a big haystack with a scarecrow donning a loud red-and-black-plaid shirt and an Elmer Fudd hat. Bored with the bubbles, the little boy ran to his father and threw up his hands for his daddy to take. Jared hiked him u   his head to the boy's obvious glee as he landed on his father's shoulders, delighted that he was now taller than everyone.

"C'mon over here, Mommy," Jared invited. "Let's give Mommy a big hug."

As the little girl grabbed her mother's hand, then Daddy's leg, Georgia rose from the steps, her belly swollen with another Jaymes child.

They all huddled in a group kiss together.

Georgia said something that the man could not make out from across the street, but the children yelled, "Pizza!" in answer.

Again the man was reminded of that day in Intensive Care over a decade ago. He'd been told that the bullet had missed all his vital organs and he'd survive. He'd been given a second chance and they had a proposition for him. . . .

The man fired up his motorcycle and sped away. As the chilled wind whipped through his beard he knew by heart the reasons he was alone. Seemingly a lifetime ago, he'd made a choice for them all. He knew Georgia would be all right. A woman like Georgia Mackenzie would always be all right. Months before he was shot, there was that day in the park when her boss noticed her freckles. Tony recognized the flicker in DA Jaymes's eye and what it signified before either he or Georgia did. At the time, Tony had no intention of getting out of the way so nature could take its course, but then fate stepped in with an opportunity.

Sometimes, love just isn't enough, he thought of himself and Georgia. Then he recalled the Jaymes family he'd left in the yard behind, and thought, *Sometimes it is.*

Tony zigzagged in and out of traffic, again confident that he had made the right decision despite the initial pain it caused . . . now everyone was happy.

Love is a beautiful thing, he thought, gunning ahead, zipping through the caution light without stopping.

He'd made a better memory than he would have her man.

Acknowledgments

In additional to my "usual suspects," for their continued support and encouragement, I'd like to also thank Isabel W. Powell, Nadine Robinson, Ernest and Edith Gee Jones, Andrea Bray, Tai Saunders, Betty Johnson, Dr. Judine Johnson, Sandra Y. Johnson, Juanita Jones, Judith Bremner, Bernice Wyche, Ruby Gourdine, Fran Moore, Nia Damali, Monique Powers-Welford, Sandra Dolphin, Sheila Harley-Washington, Sharon Harley-Lewis, Renette D. Hall, Janice Manuel, Lambert Boissiere, Jr., Cheryl Gray, Carla Wynn, Deborah Carpenter-Brittan, Cecile Thalley, Stephanie Randall, the Oasis Book Club, Oracle Set, Ladies Loving Literature, the S.A.G.E. Book Club, and everyone who read and enjoyed *Living Inside Your Love*.

GiGi Gunn invites readers to visit her Website at www.gigigunn.net.

READING GROUP QUESTIONS AND TOPICS OF DISCUSSION

1. Everyone has "bottom lines" and "deal breakers" and one of Georgia McKenzie's was not to date her boss.

   (a) How do you feel about a woman dating her boss?
   (b) How do you feel about dating a colleague/coworker?
   (c) What are a few of your "bottom lines" and "deal breakers"?

2. Do you think that Georgia had feelings for Jared before the Cusamano threat? If so, why and for how long?

3. Do you think Jared had feelings for Georgia all along?

4. Do you think the concepts "glass ceiling," "equal work for equal pay," and "double standards" on dating in the workplace are still viable concerns for today's professional woman? Why or why not?

5. Georgia Mackenzie and Neal Preston were best friends. Do you think it is possible for women and men to enjoy healthy platonic relationships with no sexual overtones? Why? Why not?

6. If it were not for the Crazy Cusamano threat and Jared's moving in with Georgia, would the couple have eventually gotten together?

7. Is "I got this" a more profound and romantic statement than "I love you"?

8. Given their close relationship, did Neal betray Georgia by constantly throwing Jared into social situations? Did Neal ignore and/or disregard Georgia's personal ethics? Was he a true friend?

9. In the long run, did Tony Machado make the right decision for himself and for Georgia? Why? Why not? How do you feel about his decision?

10. Do you believe that most families have shared traditions, tenets, maxims—spoken and unspoken?

11. Are our lives more interconnected than we realize?